THE AX SMASHED THROUGH THE DOOR...

Moments later there was a clatter of feet and half a dozen deputies were charging up the stairs after him. Slocum grabbed the Chinese doorman, swooped him up in the air, and while the man squealed in terror, he hurled him down the stairs at the phalanx of deputies.

"You son of a bitch," one shouted from the mass of tangled bodies.

Slocum pulled out his gun. He'd shoot first and explain later.

JAKE LOGAN
SLOCUM'S GRAVE

PLAYBOY PRESS
PAPERBACKS

1

John Slocum was down and out in Chinatown. He scooped the last bits of rice from the battered wooden bowl before returning it to the sidewalk vendor, who dipped it briefly in a bowl of tepid water and refilled it for his next customer—an ancient Chinaman who grinned at Slocum like they were two of a kind. They were.

Spring, 1884. On top of San Francisco's Nob Hill, the first spring flowers were pushing through the carefully tended grounds of the Bohemian Club where Slocum had played many a game of high stakes poker in the past. Well, tonight would be another high stakes game, in the back rooms of the gambling club just off Grant Street, the teeming main street of Chinatown. Slocum rattled the four silver dollars in his pocket. Tonight he'd wager them all. Any game is high stakes when you wager all you have.

He wished he could spare another dime for a second bowl of pork-flavored rice. It was hard to concentrate on the cards when your stomach was growling all the time.

He'd crossed the Sierras in February. Just one jump ahead of a posse of angry Mormons from Provo who hadn't shared his "share the wealth" philosophy. Not when it concerned the National Bank of Provo, Utah. He'd never seen the like. They'd chased him so hard his Appaloosa had died—just foundered of exhaustion. And when he abandoned his saddlebags, they kept right on after him, even though they had every dime of their damn money back.

They finally quit, thinking he was dead when the blizzard covered his tracks at ten thousand feet. They were almost right. By the time he stumbled out of the barranca on the western slopes of the mountains, he'd lost twenty pounds, the skin on his fingers was flaking from frostbite, and his breathing was rattling like somebody'd filled his lungs with loose shot. Pneumonia. He sold his Winchester to pay passage on the San Francisco coach, and when he climbed down in the Market Street Terminal of the Wells Fargo and Overland Express, he headed straight for the nearest gunshop. He sold his backup Colt and both his Remington derringers. He was sick as hell, he was going to be off his feet for a while and he didn't want to die on the street.

The cheapest room he could find was on Leavenworth Street—just a block west of Chinatown. Here, for a dollar a day, he could lie alone in a tiny room and sweat out his sickness. Every morning and evening, the bald Chinaman who owned the place looked in with a bowl of rice-filled soup. Sometimes John Slocum could get it down. More often he was raving. Once each day, the bald Chinaman took a dollar for the room and fifty cents for the soup from Slocum's diminishing pile of silver. He never took more than his due and he never touched the Colt that lay beside the helpless, delirious white man. The Chinaman was honest in his way.

Just like the gambler Slocum would play with tonight.

For a month after he came out of the delirium, he was too weak to move and he couldn't do anything but watch helplessly as his stake dwindled.

As soon as he could walk, he went looking for a game. He was down forty pounds from his fighting weight of one-eighty and he wasn't too steady on his pins, but he needed a game to stay alive. Sure, he could have taken his Colt down to the waterfront one dark night and jackrolled some drunken sailor, but jack-rolling wasn't exactly John Slocum's style. Not Captain John Slocum, late of the 114th Mississippi Rifles, CSA.

He found his game. With a real highroller. Every night for the last two weeks, John Slocum had played nickle-dime, table stakes poker with a Chinaman who was eighty years old if he was a day. Sometimes the games were short, sometimes they went on until dawn. They lasted until John Slocum had won a couple of dollars, just barely enough to last him until another game. As soon as Slocum was two dollars ahead, the ancient Chinese gambler would smile his enigmatic smile and bow out—almost as though he wanted to keep Slocum on a string. Slocum never lost these games, but he never won more than two dollars either, and once the ancient Chinaman stood up from their private table in the back of the gambling club, that was it. Slocum could never find another Chinaman who wanted to make a friendly wager, though the club was filled with Chinese betting against each other.

Two dollars a day. Laborer's wages.

Tonight there was a hint of spring in the air as Slocum ambled through the crowds of Chinese, past the markets with the live turtles and goats tethered outside.

The grocer got a dollar for a turtle that weighed twenty pounds. Slocum could have eaten a few terrapin steaks that night, but he needed every damn cent of his meager stake for tonight's game. He wished he wasn't so hungry all the time. A hungry man can't really think straight.

The lamplighters were firing up the gas lights as Slocum turned in the door of the gambling club. The doorman stood aside to let him in, though he was the only white man who was ever allowed to play, and if another had presented himself at the door with a fistful of money, the doorman would have directed him elsewhere. "Down street, sir. No gambling here. Inside is temple. Very sacred."

Inside were a hundred Chinamen, all babbling a mile a minute in their heathen tongue. Four large tables, all of them busy. The players had dominoes for markers and circular tokens they used as chips. They played pretty much like any bunch of players Slocum ever saw. Some were stoical, some wept openly when they lost.

John Slocum had learned to gamble during the war. He was a fair hand with stud, draw, faro, red dog, and black jack. He knew the roulette wheel but avoided it out of preference. He'd played showdown with riverboat gamblers and tossed the bones with Sioux warriors in a Lakota camp in Canada. Usually he stuck to simple five stud. Usually he had more than four dollars to play.

The tables were arranged according to stakes. Nearest the door the tables were reserved for low-ballers—laborers, poor men losing their pay before their wives could get hold of it.

The Chinese casino wasn't decorated like any casino Slocum ever saw. The tables were plain wooden affairs, no baize, no crushed velvet. The houseman wore no uniform, but he was just as careful to collect the house rake-off as any Occidental dealer would have been. As one player got lucky and the chips started to flow, other players got more excited, elbowing each other, shouting encouragement to friends or relatives, urging different betting strategies.

Then they all fell silent. In a split second, all the players lost their tongues. Slocum thought it was a raid and his head snapped around toward the door.

The ancient man in the doorway had skin the color of old parchment and he was dressed like a Mandarin, in a long red silk robe with elaborate Chinese figures in gold down the front. On another man, the gold figures would have seemed gaudy. This man wore them as a right. Like most of the other Chinamen, he wore the neat black cap, and his thin gray hair was braided in a long, long queue. Slocum was reminded of the Blackfoot warriors who let their scalplock grow until it dangled halfway down their back. A scalp to brag about—if you were warrior enough to take it.

The Chinaman had a heavy ebony cane, entwined with fine gold wire in the shape of a climbing serpent. The way he held the cane made Slocum think it was a badge of office.

Calmly, the man inspected the room, his eyes lingering at each and every player. When he turned his gaze on Slocum, it was as if an electrical current had been set up between them. The hair on the back of Slocum's hands stood up, and involuntarily he smiled. A wolf smile. His game had arrived.

Two bodyguards were at the Mandarin's side. The bodyguards were dressed in black boilerplate suits and each of them kept his hand jammed into his pocket while he scanned the room. Slocum wondered if they'd come here tonight to kill. After he saw how nervous they were, Slocum wondered who wanted to kill the Mandarin. The bodyguards looked like men who might quit their job at any minute.

The Mandarin came down the three steps onto the casino floor and moved sedately through the crowd. A path formed automatically for him. Once Slocum saw a similar path open for an ordinary cowhand in a crowded Cheyenne bar. The cowhand had cholera.

He stopped beside John Slocum and murmured. "Ah," he said, "you have come to play again. Perhaps you will have great good luck."

Slocum's belly growled, "Among us," he said, "a man makes his own luck."

"So I understand." The Mandarin's accent was flawless, very slightly British. "No round-eye believes in fate."

The Mandarin's eyes were hard and black as obsidian. Like obsidian they seemed transparent but were not. There was nothing behind this man's eyes, except a black backdrop.

Slocum knew a fair amount about fate. He knew perfectly well he'd never live to an old age. He knew he'd never have children gathered around him. He knew he'd never own any more land than the six-foot hole where they'd plant him. He raised his eyebrows, that's all.

And the Mandarin held his eyes for a long moment before he passed on through the crowd. He found his customary place at the high stakes table at the back of the room. The men who'd been playing there apologized and rose from the table. The displaced gamblers doubled up at the next table, which was already crowded. The Mandarin whispered to a bodyguard and, after a curt nod, the man vanished. As he passed by Slocum, the bodyguard was tugging at his tight western collar, relieved to be going elsewhere.

The other bodyguard stationed himself against the wall, his eyes constantly roving the crowd. Whoever he was afraid of would be a stranger to him.

The old man's hands rested calmly on the bare wooden table. A deck of cards lay in front of them like an invitation.

Slocum thought he smelled something funny. Something like the reek of angry flesh inside a catamount's den. His belly growled again and reminded him that tonight he meant to raise his grubstake. Tonight he meant to play the old man until he had what he needed. Briefly, his vision blurred and the old man's smile faded in and out. Slocum shook his head, angry with himself for his weakness.

The Chinaman removed an ornate change purse from the recesses of his robe and carefully counted out short stacks of dimes—five in each stack. The sight of the small change brought an angry flush to Slocum's cheeks. He hadn't played for stakes like this since he was a kid, yet here he was, night after night, playing good careful poker for dimes.

The Chinaman's smile was surprisingly warm. "Do sit down, sir. I frankly crave your companionship tonight, and more of your instruction."

Slocum wanted to put together five hundred dollars. Five hundred would outfit him and fatten him up enough to tackle something more his size. He sat. He set his four silver dollars on the table before him. "Don't you wish some of your own people would play with you?" Slocum asked.

The Mandarin ignored Slocum's rudeness. "Children fear what they cannot understand," he said sadly.

Slocum didn't like the seating arrangement very much. If Hickock hadn't proved anything else in his life, he'd proved beyond the shadow of a doubt that only a fool or a suicide left his back exposed in a strange gambling hall. True, the bodyguard was on watch, but Slocum never once met a Chinaman who could shoot straight. Slocum moved over beside the Mandarin and felt a little better about it. "Stud needs five players," Slocum reminded him.

"But we play with two," the Mandarin said.

"Sure. But it's a different game."

This time the man's smile was mightily amused. "I am accustomed to the game," he said.

Slocum shrugged. "Your funeral."

"Shall we put a limit on the game or play table stakes?"

Since Slocum had just four dollars to his name, he said, "Life has no limit."

The Mandarin's head bobbed up and down. "You are a man of understanding," he said.

This close, Slocum recognized the smell that bothered him earlier. It was the stink of fear. The elegantly dressed Chinaman was shit-scared. None of Slocum's affair.

At first the play was very slow. The Mandarin always played cautiously and Slocum never bet much until he sensed the run of the cards. Slocum's luck was turning good and soon his four dollars grew to six. And, for a change, the Oriental kept on playing. Everybody playing cards over a period of time gets about the same number of good hands and bad hands. But the professional wins more with the big hands and loses less with the bad. Carefully, Slocum started setting the man up for the kill. Once, when he guessed that the Mandarin had a king in the hole to match his king on the board, Slocum bet half his pile on the strength of two queens showing. Slocum also tugged at his ear. When the Mandarin called his bet, Slocum flipped his cards over ruefully. "Thought I could bluff you," he said.

The Mandarin eyed him warily, then with amusement, as he raked in the pot. An hour later when Slocum had another plausible bluff, he bet high, tugged at his ear, and once more, the Mandarin took the pot.

The way Slocum's luck was running, either he'd win big or just bleed the Mandarin to death. He'd already won twenty dollars and the Mandarin plain wasn't getting the cards.

Their game occurred in almost dead silence and the casino habitués kept a twenty-foot space between them and the two players. It was as if they were playing on another planet, immune to the rules that governed ordinary men.

When the first bodyguard returned from his mission and approached the table, the Mandarin gave a quick command to the other one who left on a mission of his own. The returning bodyguard, at a sign from the Mandarin, approached the gaming table and whispered to him for a minute or so. Slocum wished he knew what the man was saying, but, hell, he didn't understand Chinese.

When the bodyguard took up a post between them

and the crowd, the Mandarin apologized. "Please excuse my rudeness. If business wasn't necessary, I would not let it interrupt our sport. . . . Ah!" The second bodyguard returned, bearing a tray with a bottle and two glasses. When he set the bottle on the table, Slocum inspected the label.

"Yes," the Mandarin said, "Napoleon Cognac. It is very, very old. Napoleon himself might have tasted the fruits of this vintage."

Slocum had tasted fine cognac before but never anything like this. It touched his tongue like faint smoke. It was so soft, it might not have any alcohol in it at all. He raised his glass in a toast. "To your taste, sir," he said. It crossed his mind that he'd be better off with a thick, meat sandwich, but he dismissed the thought.

"To your luck, John Slocum."

Slocum felt as if somebody had just walked over his grave. How the hell had the old man known his name? But the Mandarin's smile was easy and friendly enough.

"You have me at a disadvantage, sir," Slocum said a bit stiffly.

The Mandarin bowed his head, imperceptibly, "Chang Tao," he said.

Slocum nodded briefly and shuffled the cards.

Behind the backs of the Mandarin's bodyguards, the two men continued their play. Bit by bit, Slocum's pile of coins became bills, two or three hundred dollars' worth. The level in the cognac bottle dropped very slowly. No one but a fool would gulp this stuff. It seemed awful warm in here and Slocum asked the time. Nearly three A.M. The chinaman was as calm and collected as if he'd just come in this minute, fresh from his dressing room, but that unmistakable odor of fear never left him.

Finally Slocum had the hand he'd waited for all night. His first two cards were aces back to back. The Mandarin had a jack showing. Slocum bet fifty dollars and the Chinaman stayed in. The next round, the Mandarin got Slocum's ace making him ace-jack showing and Slocum drew an eight. Slocum bumped the bet up to a hundred, confident his luck was running strong. He had aces; the Chinaman only had jacks, at best. The third card was another seven for Slocum, making him two pair, and the Chinaman pulled another jack. Slocum just plain *knew* the Chinaman didn't have the other jack in the hole. This time, he bumped the pot up to two hundred. Now the Mandarin was looking at a pair of sevens with an ace kicker betting against his pair of jacks. He stayed.

The fourth card was no improvement. The Mandarin pulled a ten and Slocum got his jack. Slocum looked at the cards very carefully as if a long stare could give him some new information that he didn't already have. His hands drummed on the table. He tugged at his ear. He pushed his entire winnings into the pot, all he had in the world. His stomach grumbled—a reminder.

The Mandarin didn't glance at his hole card. He sat immobile. Then he laughed. It wasn't a nice laugh. It sounded like somebody grinding up glass. He looked Slocum dead in the eye, terribly amused. "Mr. Slocum," he said. He laughed again. And then, very deliberately, he tugged at his ear. "We are a very old people, Mr. Slocum," he said. And folded.

So Slocum's setup had failed. The Mandarin had seen it coming. Establish a habit of tugging at the ear every time you bluff and then you bet everything on a lock hand. Slocum had used the trick before and usually it worked—if the player he was facing was sharp enough to spot the habit. The Mandarin had spotted the habit and knew it was a trick. Slocum scooped up the modest pot, feeling as if he'd lost more than he'd won.

Don't fuck with your luck. The gambler's maxim. Well, John Slocum had pushed his luck too far, and now, he knew, it was going to be coming back on him with a vengeance. And so it did.

If he had a pair of kings, the Mandarin had aces.

If he had two pair, the Mandarin had three of a kind.

When he dropped out of a pot, the Mandarin didn't have anything. When he stayed, the Mandarin beat him.

In no more than an hour, three of Slocum's four hundred were heaped up in front of the ancient Chinaman. Slocum was pretty hot under the collar.

And the maddening thing was, he had nothing to bitch about. John Slocum knew all the tricks that made a man's luck run stronger than it rightly should. He could deal seconds, bottoms, false cut, and recut with the best sharpers alive. He knew all the ways of marking and shaving a deck. And John Slocum knew this game was straight. The Mandarin was simply getting all the cards. Slocum asked the time. Five A.M. When he turned in his chair to look at the rest of the casino, it had pretty well cleared out. A small group of players was at the low stakes table, but everybody else had gone home.

"Play, Mr. Slocum?" the Mandarin asked politely.

Slocum grunted, rubbed his head and poured himself another snifter of that brandy. "Yeah," he said. The way it was turning out, that cognac was going to be the most expensive booze Slocum had ever drunk.

And he still couldn't get a hand. His money ran out of him like he was bleeding. He had one hundred, then he had fifty, then twenty. He played cautious, close to the vest, tight-asshole poker, and two out of three times the Mandarin took the pot.

Finally, almost too late, his luck changed a bit. He filled an open-ended low straight, seven through jack, and even though his eyes were blurring, he knew the Mandarin only had ace-high. He pushed his last money into the pot. He laughed. He tugged at his ear.

"And two thousand," the Mandarin said, calmly.

It was no-limit poker. The Mandarin had every right to do what he'd just done. Slocum didn't have another penny in his pocket, let alone two thousand, and the Mandarin with his damn ace-high had just bought the pot. Slocum stood up and stretched. Jesus, he was tired. At least he wasn't hungry anymore.

"I'm tapped out," Slocum said. "You bought it."

The Mandarin favored Slocum with one of his rare smiles. "I'll accept your marker," he said. "Is that what you round-eyes call it? A marker?"

Maybe it was the implied insult, but Slocum didn't take a second to think before he said, "Done."

The Mandarin turned over his hole card. It was nothing special. Deuce of hearts. That gave him an eight, duece, nine, ace, and ten. All hearts.

The cards swam around in John Slocum's tired mind. They arranged and rearranged themselves. But every time they came out the same way: The Mandarin had an ace-high flush and that surely beat his straight—any day in the week.

Slocum grinned. "Like the cowboy said to the whore, it sure is nice to get fucked by an expert," he said.

And the Mandarin nodded at him, finally a little weary. "Mr. Slocum," he said quietly, "I have a little proposition to make to you."

"You know," Slocum was still grinning, "it's funny, but I thought you might."

The Mandarin stood up, briskly, despite his years. He dismissed his bodyguards, and the two stocky Chinese left the casino. "Will you be my guest for breakfast?" he asked. "After a night of gambling I require some light nourishment."

"Sure," Slocum said. "Lead the way."

Outside the Chinese casino, the streets were quiet. Six A.M. The early morning fog was lying soft and easy over the San Francisco streets, and gas street-lights didn't do too much good against it.

All the markets, so bustling the evening before, were closed and the windows covered with thick wooden shutters. The street smelled of fog and fish. Without a word, the Mandarin led the way to a little restaurant on Kearny Street. Not a fancy place. It was busy with teamsters, cable car conductors, a few fishermen on their way home, and one or two other Orientals.

"Not every Occidental restaurant likes to serve us, you know," the Mandarin said at the door.

They took a table in the back, and this time, Slocum didn't object when the Mandarin put his back to the wall. Nobody was looking for John Slocum—not in San Francisco anyway.

The Mandarin ordered a simple meal of scrambled eggs and toast. Slocum asked for a big platter of steaks, eggs, and pancakes, but when the food arrived, he could only eat a few bites. He guessed his stomach had shrunk. While he picked at his food, the Mandarin reminded him of all the Territories where John Slocum's face graced a wanted poster.

Slocum was wanted in Nebraska, Utah, and New Mexico, and the Texas Bankers Association had a ten-thousand-dollar price on his head. He'd never done too much business under his own name, and the Pinkertons never really got a handle on him. He'd ride in, take the money, and run. In between times, he liked to play a little cards.

Slocum was appalled that this Chinaman knew about his past. Besides, he'd lost his appetite. He pushed the plate away from him. "How do you come to know so much?" he snarled.

The Mandarin smiled his tired smile. "We have a mutual friend," he said. He sipped at his glass of water as if it were a fine cognac. "Leland Stanford."

"Stanford?"

Again that smile. "Mr. Slocum, you may recall that it was the Chinese who built the railroads. Thousands of my countrymen lie now beside the tracks that created Leland Stanford's fortune. Naturally, I have had dealings with him. As, I gather, have you. He did mention something about his son and a Shanghai parlor. He was surprised to hear you were in the city. He said he would have helped you if he'd known."

"Didn't care to beg," Slocum said. "You mentioned a proposition."

"The cards weren't favoring you tonight," the Mandarin said. "Though I have gambled all my life, these last few months my luck has been extraordinary. It's a compensation, I suppose."

"Compensation for what?"

The Mandarin's eyebrows rose in surprise. "For my death, of course. Surely, with your experience, you can tell that."

Slocum only knew that he could smell the man's fear.

"I am, uh, 'involved' with one of the Chinese protective associations. . . ."

"A tong."

The Mandarin looked away, his eyes passing over the restaurant, dismissing each one of its occupants one by one. "That is the term you Occidentals use, I suppose." His voice was bored, like a man admitting to a trifle. "And our group has had, uh, difference with another group, the Hop Sings."

The fights in the Chinese community were rarely mentioned in the San Francisco papers unless the killing reached the point where whites might get involved. Slocum hadn't heard a word of any trouble.

"They're out to get you?"

"Quite. And since the Hop Sings are so much more powerful than my group, my group has withdrawn its shield of protection. I can only count on members of my own family these days and they, regrettably, often find reasons to be unavailable when I most need them. We Chinese, Mister Slocum, are an eminently practical people."

"So you want me for a bodyguard?"

The Mandarin barked a laugh. Then he coughed. He wiped his lips with his handkerchief and cast a mischievous eye at Slocum. Though he must have been at least seventy, his eyes were very young. "No. Not quite that simple. I must die. If I die, the Hop Sings will be satisfied. There is only one other in the direct line of my family. When I am dead, the Hop Sings will allow the rest of my people to prosper."

"One other?"

"My daughter, Mr. Slocum. Lee, my only daughter."

That was it. The Mandarin wished to remove his daughter from the very real possibility of harm and had decided to put her with his cousin in Butte City, Montana. Once he was dead, and some time had passed, she might return to San Francisco safely to claim her legacy; but now she was in mortal danger. "Men's memories are short, Mr. Slocum," he said. "And the Hop Sings are men, whatever else they might be."

"And you want me to get her to Butte City?"

"I forget about your marker, and . . ." The Mandarin found his purse and counted out a thousand dollars in specie. "It will not be easy," he said. "The Hop Sing have agents in all the gold camps, and you must avoid them."

"And on the trail?"

"In the settlements, Mr. Slocum, you should beware of the Hop Sing killers. On the trail, I am assured that no Chinese executioner would be your match. And once you're in Butte City, my estimable cousin can guard Lee. We are more powerful in Butte City than the Hop Sing."

The sun was doing its best to burn off the fog

from the sidewalks outside the little restaurant. The air had a bite to it. It was spring. He'd never been to Butte City, and it had the reputation of being the roughest boomtown the West had ever known. Hell, he was ready. So that very morning, he visited the outfitters along Sutter Street, provisioned two pack-horses, and bought two stout mountain ponies for him and his charge. At the Mandarin's instructions, he took the ferry to Oakland. He ate a big meal at the hotel, bathed, laid out his new clothes, and slept until the clerk banged on his door at four the next morning. With his horses he waited at the terminal while the big blunt-nosed ferry docked. Slocum felt full of piss and vinegar. The Mandarin had warned him that Hop Sing killers would pursue him all the way to Butte City. He jingled the coins in his pocket and grinned. Let 'em come.

He didn't know exactly what he expected to see when the passengers got off the ferry, but a tiny, sixteen-year-old Chinese girl who didn't speak a word of English wasn't what he had in mind. Still, when the bundled-up girl made the agreed-upon recognition signal, he shrugged and mounted up. At least she knew how to ride, her bundle wasn't too large, and she wore a sensible pair of gabardine pants.

The high country was still locked in winter. Bannock Pass crossed the Bitteroots at 7,500 feet. It was the lowest pass between Idaho and Montana and the only one open so early in the year. The other passes were frozen under twenty-foot snowbanks. A man might get across them on snowshoes, or skis, but never a man with four horses and a sixteen-year-old girl. So Slocum chose to try his crossing at Bannock, though generally he preferred the higher passes, known only to him and the Indians.

Bannock Pass wasn't so bad. The trail was firm, they could detour around the deep snowbanks, and it never warmed up enough for the spring avalanches to be much of a problem.

It was beautiful country, the high white peaks of the Bitteroots, the narrow winding trail, the dark green—almost black—of the douglas firs. The girl couldn't have seen anything like it before, but she rode behind Slocum quietly, without a word or a glance at the stunning vistas that opened up at every turn in the snaky trail.

Her business. Slocum didn't hold with a lot of useless chatter himself.

They camped out on top of the pass and the temperature fell to ten below during the night, but Slocum's ample supply of buffalo robes and the small reflector fire he'd built in the shadow of a fallen ponderosa kept them warm all night though he had to get up at three A.M. to add wood to the fire.

Slocum wondered if the girl knew any English at all. Ever since they left San Francisco, she had signaled her wants by the quick gestures of her small brown hands.

Every meal, Slocum ate well. He felt the beef returning to his bones.

As they descended into Montana, the snow got less. On top of the pass it was dead winter. In the foothills it got warmer and by noon, when Slocum dismounted beside the Big Hole River, it was spring, all right. The river was brown, muddy, and fast. The ground off the trail was soft and treacherous and he walked, leading the horses. A horse could go down to his hocks in this stuff and snap a delicate fetlock.

There was browse for the horses, and they took to the new green grass eagerly, tired of the carefully rationed oats Slocum had been feeding them through the high country. The girl dismounted too and stretched and smiled at Slocum. They'd traveled together the better part of two weeks, and this was her first real smile. It lit up her face and changed it.

She was a pretty little child, with solemn, wide dark eyes and high cheekbones like a young Indian. Her hair was knotted up in the longest braids Slocum had ever seen. And every evening, once he'd finished his grub and fired up a smoke, she'd sit by the fire, combing those long braids out and rebraiding them, humming to herself all the while. A sad tune.

"Can't you sing anything cheerful?" he'd asked once. She looked at him puzzled and went on singing as before.

Oh, well, they'd make Butte City tomorrow afternoon sometime, and once he delivered the girl, he'd find himself a good steak, a game, and a woman. The prospect cheered him. "C'mon, girl, time to ride."

The trail passed between the spindly trunks of the jackpine: not much use for anything but firewood and not much good for that. Patches of snow under the trees where the sun hadn't penetrated yet, but not so much of it. Along the streams they crossed, the ground was black and smelled of that funny early spring smell of fertility and loss. It was a pretty day, sun high in the sky and doing its best to warm them. Slocum was enjoying the ride. He still found it strange to ride anywhere in the West without constantly checking his backtrail for Indians, and he still checked from time to time, but that was old habit. The cavalry nailed Sitting Bull four years ago, and he was the last of the great warrior chiefs. Still, habits die hard, and every now and again Slocum pulled over where he had a good view of his backtrail.

Routine—until he spotted the two men following behind. They never closed up when Slocum slowed, never dropped back when Slocum picked up the pace. Maybe just a couple of punchers trailing the same trail and as leery of Slocum as he was of them. Maybe.

Slocum clucked to the horses. Might as well pick up the pace a little. Make it hard for them to get around in front of him if they had a mind to and knew this country better than he did. He'd ridden these trails once with Clubfoot George Ives, back in '68. George had known this country like the back of his hand, but he was dead now. Vigilantes strung him up.

No sense worrying about it. Still, Slocum slicked his Winchester out of the scabbard, jacked a round into the chamber, and let the hammer down. He hadn't lived as long as he had by taking foolish chances.

The light stayed longer than a month ago, but it started getting cold about the same time, around four o'clock. He'd been avoiding all the towns ever since he left San Francisco. The old Chinaman warned him there might be trouble, and besides, he had a few too many posters out on him to be comfortable in any small town but he thought he might make Silver Star the exception. The town lay along a small creek that looked as if it had been eaten by a great mole and then spit out again. Rough gravel banks on both sides of the creek and the scraps of old sluice boxes. It had been a gold town once. Maybe it had been prosperous too, but from what remained it was hard to tell. Two buildings were the town. Two low log structures. From the flashes of firelight, Slocum figured one for a smithy and maybe a livery stable too. The other had a couple of lamps in the windows, and to Slocum that spelled saloon. Why not? After a couple of weeks alone with the silent, Chinese girl, he figured he could use a little talking company.

The saloon was a one room affair. It was pretty rough and it smelled like old farts, spilled booze, and beargrease, but at least it had a real wood floor, not the packed dirt Slocum half expected to find. The big potbelly in the center of the room looked like a donkey locomotive boiler set on end, and Slocum headed directly for it, grateful for the warmth. The girl came inside with him, got her back to the wall, and stared straight ahead as though she didn't see Slocum or the greasy bartender either.

The bartender looked like he'd wintered in his clothes, and smelled ripe as a dog who's been rolling in cowflops. "Howdy," he called out. "How's the trail?"

"Poor," Slocum said.

"Well, I would have closed up half an hour ago, but, hell, I hoped that a couple boys from the Donovan Ranch might stop in for a drink or several. Hell, it's Saturday night. Sometimes it gets real busy in here Saturday night."

Slocum had lost track of the days. "Whiskey," he said.

The bartender poured his shot out of an unmarked bottle. It was about as good as it should have been. It traveled down Slocum's throat like molten lead, and when it hit his stomach it set his ears to ringing.

"Another," he said hoarsely. Delicately, he coughed. He'd had worse but not often. The old traders used to cut their Indian whiskey with gun-powder, and it appeared this gent kept to the fine old customs.

The second shot made him forget his troubles for a moment. "You cross the Bannock or Lehi?" the saloonkeeper asked.

Slocum tossed four bits on the bar. "The smith any account?" He could hear the ringing of the blacksmith's hammer across the street.

"Oh, sure. He's a fine fella. Best work this side of Dillon."

One of Slocum's packhorses needed a shoe, and though he could probably last to Butte City, there was no sense chancing it.

The Chinese girl had moved over to one of the saloon's tables and sat. She had some kind of book she'd been reading at night, and she had the book out now. Once Slocum had asked to see it, but it was Chinese to him.

"You got any beer?" Slocum asked.

The saloonkeeper did. It was warm and no better than his whiskey. Slocum leaned back against the bar and looked the place over. The only decoration was a few old calenders tacked to the unfinished log walls and the initials carved into the logs.

"Doesn't look like much now," the saloonkeeper volunteered, "But you should have seen Silver Star in seventy-two. Hell, on a Saturday night there'd be so many men in here, you couldn't turn around. Miners, prospectors. Hell, Wild Bill Hickok rode through here once. Had a beer at this very bar."

Slocum had known Hickok. Somehow he couldn't imagine the fastidious gunfighter having a real good time in Silver Star.

When the two horsemen rode up outside, the bartender brightened some. Maybe he'd have a good Saturday night after all.

Slocum cocked one heel on the bar rail and let his right hand dangle loose. Maybe these riders had been following them by accident. But John Slocum didn't really believe in accidents.

They played it pretty well. The kid's eyes barely touched Slocum's and the nut-brown man didn't look at him at all. Both of them stared at the Chinese girl.

The kid was pock-faced, blond-headed, maybe twenty years old, and had the plump lips that his plump face demanded. He was only middling tall and from the way he walked, Slocum guessed he'd be a pretty good horseman. His jacket was open and Slocum saw the white butts of twin Colts stuck under his belt.

The nut-brown man was older, maybe forty, and he dressed in a simple linen duster. His dark face was cut with deep weather lines and his thin mouth stayed impassive. Somewhat negligently, he had an old Sharps buffalo rifle tucked under his arm. The Sharps threw a .69 caliber slug, and though it only threw one of them at a time, one was usually plenty.

The kid walked over to the table and eyeballed the girl before he strolled back to the bar. The nut-brown man set his Sharps on the bar and turned loose of it before he ordered his whiskey. Manners. He favored Slocum with a slight nod though his face stayed expressionless. One always recognizes another.

The kid leaned over the bar and sneered, "You always serve redskins in here? How many white men will take a drink in a place that serves redskins?"

"She's Chinese," Slocum drawled. Keeping the record straight.

So the kid turned to face him. "Ain't a whole lot better," he said.

The nut-brown man didn't like the look of things. He eyed John Slocum openly and what he saw didn't reassure him any. The nut-brown man had first sniffed gunsmoke and blood riding with Quantrill, and he'd tasted his share of that curious elixir since.

The quiet man at the end of the bar was a mite taller than average. Over six feet, maybe a hundred and eighty pounds. Tremendous wide shoulders, long arms, long hands, and thin-hipped with a horseman's small ass.

John Slocum's hair was black as a raven's wing and had some of the same dark natural gloss. His eyes were green. Usually still and untroubled, now they were narrowed down a notch, watchful and still as a bobcat's. His coat was open, and his right hand just sort of naturally lay near the opening. He wore a faint smile on his face, but it wasn't clear what was funny: the two men, the saloon, the Chinese girl, or all the vagaries that a man can run across.

The girl closed her book and put it away. She kept her eyes on the newcomers at the bar.

The saloonkeeper poured them each a healthy jolt of whiskey. The kid tossed his right off. The nut-brown man's hands never touched the glass. He'd seen a few hardcases in his day—Hell, he'd known the James brothers when they rode with Quantrill—and he knew the tall gent had been cut out by the same stamp. The nut-brown man sighed and unbuttoned his linen duster. He wore his gun for a crossdraw. You couldn't ride and wear a six-gun buscadero fashion unless you wanted the hammer to cut your leg to pieces. Maybe the crossdraw wasn't so fast and maybe it took a lot of practice to loose off a shot just as your Colt was passing your target's belly—it was the reverse of leading a duck: moving gun, still target; but the crossdraw was fast enough in the hands of an expert. The nut-brown man hadn't figured to run up against an expert. He'd been hired to follow a Chinese girl and kill her. A couple of years ago, when he was younger, he wouldn't have taken the job, but he'd fallen on hard times. The kid was always talking about the fun they'd have with the girl before they killed her, but the nut-brown man drew the line right there.

When the kid turned off the bar, he had his drink in his left hand, and his right hand casually brushed against one of his ivory gunbutts, just checking.

The little smile never left Slocum's face. He didn't move an inch either. One foot on the bar rail, he leaned against the bar, his unfinished glass of beer at his elbow.

"You the squawman?" the kid asked loudly.

Slocum kept still.

Disgusted at Slocum's silence, the kid turned back to the bar and ordered another shot.

The nut-brown man eased himself back away from the bar a few steps. He left his Sharps on the bar, but his hands were empty. He'd left his whiskey glass there, too.

The tension in the air reached the girl and she anxiously examined all four men: the fat bartender, the nut-brown man, the kid leaning into his whiskey, and John Slocum, her laconic guide.

"Next round's on the house," the bartender said with forced cheerfulness. "On the house. Name your poison." And though he rarely drank, he poured himself a shot of his own rotgut. Just to be democratic.

Slocum didn't move. The bartender brought Slocum's shot to him and set it beside his untouched beer.

"Obliged," Slocum said, but didn't touch the drink.

The light was getting poor outside and the yellow kerosene lanterns in the window cast a yellow glow.

The nut-brown man didn't like having the lanterns behind him. Slocum smiled. The kid didn't know any better.

While he waited for the kid to start pushing again, Slocum ran his tongue around his mouth. Yep, getting dry. He wondered why it was his mouth always dried up before the shooting started.

The kid was getting excited. Slocum didn't scare him. He had five hundred dollars in his jeans and another five hundred waiting for him in San Francisco when the job was done. He drank his drink and felt the faint flush of excitement touching his nerves. In another few seconds, he'd be ready. The kid had killed six men, the first three as a "stock detective" —men he'd laid for outside their homes at night and shot in the back. But he had a genuine knack for gunplay and he'd practiced plenty. The last three men he killed face to face and he liked that better. He liked to see the light go out of a man's eyes as he died. He licked the whiskey off his lips and turned to face the girl. She was a pretty little thing. He wondered if it was true about slant-eyed pussies. He'd never had a Chink before.

"Another drink, gents?" the bartender said hopefully. Though it galled him, he added, "Another round on the house. Hell, it's Saturday night."

He was hoping the three men would take their quarrel elsewhere.

The kid tossed off the bartender's free shot and went over to the girl. He stood half facing Slocum, ready for the quiet man's move if he made any.

Hell, the girl was a pretty little thing, no question about that. And he'd never had a Chinese. He wondered if maybe they could keep the girl alive for a couple of days after they killed her bodyguard. He didn't see any good reason why not. He thought about a few of the interesting things they could do. The thought excited him. When he reached out to touch her face, she jerked her head back. "What's a matter, girl?" he jeered. "Little skittish, are you?"

The nut-brown man's eyes never left John Slocum. The bartender edged along the bar. His sink was a deep zinc-lined affair. It was a fine place to lie behind when the Colts started talking.

The kid was ten feet to the right of the nut-brown man. Not for the first time, John Slocum wished that he'd learned to work two six-guns at once. Not too many times a trick like that came in handy, but this was bound to be one of them. "Friend," he said to the nut-brown man, "you've seen this sort of whipsaw before. This time, you misread it." And he smiled, a gentle, forgiving smile.

The nut-brown man once saw Ben Thompson smile that way, one blustery night in Abilene. Some Texas trailhand had won the biggest pot of the evening and was crowing about it, while Thompson smiled that smile. Ten seconds later, the kid had three neat red-rimmed holes in his belly and he had his hands wrapped around his middle so his guts wouldn't fall out, and Thompson never lost his smile the whole time. Like he was playing a private game. Like nobody, not even the kid, was quite real to him. But the nut-brown man had killed his share. He shrugged, "In for a dollar, in for a dime," he said. "Bartender! One for my friend there."

The bartender liked standing behind the sink, and when he moved to fill the nut-brown man's order, he scuttled like a mouse from one bit of cover to another.

"Much obliged," Slocum said, and tossed the drink at the back of his throat. "You got a handle?"

While they spoke, the kid was stroking the girl's cheeks. She stared straight ahead, from time to time wetting her lips with her tongue.

"Murphy. Jack Murphy."

"John Slocum."

The name didn't mean anything to the nut-brown man or to the kid either. It wasn't supposed to. John Slocum always used another name when it looked like he was heading for a wanted poster.

"What the hell are you two jabbering about?" the kid snarled. He had one big hand on the girl's throat, one thumb in the soft hollow above the collarbone.

The nut-brown man sighed. "Just good manners," he said. He didn't bother to explain that good manners consisted in knowing the name of the man you were trying to kill, because the kid wouldn't have understood. He didn't give a damn who he killed.

The girl's eyes were wide and blank as the kid traced the veins in her throat. Her skin wasn't yellow, more like an ivory color, like the keys of an old piano. She wore some sort of blouse, fastened at the throat by a chunk of dark green carved jade. When you looked closely, you could see it was some kind of snake or dragon maybe, but until you got close it seemed like Chinese writing. He fastened his hands around the brooch and jerked it away, tearing the top of the girl's blouse. While his left hand held the pin, the kid's right trembled close to his belt and his eyes never left Slocum. Slocum leaned against the bar rail, relaxed, as if he was taking a drink at some fine hotel somewhere. The bartender slowly dipped below the precious zinc sink. When no shots came, he peeped out above the bar again.

Slocum's mouth twitched with annoyance. The kid misread the tiny twitch for fear. "You like her, huh?" he asked. "She hot stuff?"

Slocum would have spared the nut-brown man if he could. Professional courtesy. Though the nut-brown man was the more dangerous man, he was thinking about taking the kid out first. But he hadn't used his Colt in four months. He decided to play it conservative.

"She's a sweet kid, all right," he said quietly. "Some kind of princess, I reckon, with her own people."

"She any good in bed?" the kid demanded.

"Never asked her," Slocum replied mildly. He spoke like he didn't give a damn for the girl, and that wasn't misleading. He didn't.

Like all of the really great gunfighters, John Slocum had an ability to empty himself of all feeling, for others or himself, before a fight. He became, when he was committed, less than a man and more than a man and would kill so long as he had a breath. The kid, like most beginners, made the mistake of thinking you had to be angry at a man to kill him. John Slocum knew better.

The air in the stuffy log building tasted sweet to him, maybe a hint of something else, like the faint stink of a distant fire, but that was probably just the blacksmith forge across the street. He heard the first of the dusk birds start a tentative call. Sounded like a spring warbler to him, but he wasn't that sure.

The kid spread the girl's blouse open with his left hand. She wore a white camisole under the blouse, some kind of lacey confinement for her breasts. He slipped the straps off her shoulder, a little awkwardly, and shoved the lacey material down over her breasts.

The bartender gasped, but he was the only one.

His eyes ate up the girl's lovely, small cup-sized breasts with their dark long nipples. None of the other three men were noticing them. "Gawd," he said. He came up above his sanctuary, pulled by the girl's beauty.

The girl stared straight ahead as the kid pawed at her. Her eyes were a little narrowed and her gaze was flat. But when the kid grabbed at her perfect small breast and squeezed it, she cried out softly, hurt.

"Don't like that too much, huh?" the kid said. "Well, you'll like it well enough by the time I get through with you."

Still the quiet man leaned against the bar, quite immobile.

Somewhat awkwardly, the kid grabbed the girl under the armpit and hauled her to her feet. The bartender was practically drooling. With his left hand, the kid pushed her against the back wall of the saloon and pinned her there. The kid's left hand was at the buttons of her gray cavalry twill trousers. The pants were high-waisted with half a dozen buttons and he was having trouble getting them open. Soon he revealed a triangle of yellow silk, the girl's drawers. The bartender was half across the bar. He'd forgotten about the gunmen altogether. Roughly, the kid hooked his hand into the waistband of her trousers and shoved. The pants hung up on her sleekly flared hips, but the kid kept pushing at them.

"Will you look at that," the bartender breathed.

And for a moment the nut-brown man did look.

Slocum came off the bar rail as his hand darted for his heavy Colt .44. He was going into the gunfighter's crouch as the gun snaked out, hammer drawn back and finger firm on the Colt's hair trigger. This took place about as quick as you blink your eye. The shot followed Slocum's move, almost overriding it, the heavy bullet smashed into the nut-brown man's left chest—high, just where his heart was. The nut-brown man was pretty quick. He actually got his hand on his gunbelt before his eyes flared wild with blood and died.

Slocum rushed his first shot as much as he dared because he still had to swivel to drop the kid and the kid was pretty close to the Chinese girl. Close, hell! He had one hand inside those yellow silk knickers of hers, and if he got any closer he'd be inside of her. So Slocum took his time with his second shot. He tagged the kid high in the right shoulder.

The .44 caliber slug weighs eighty grains, and when propelled by a hundred twenty grains of hercules black powder, it works like a freight train. It ain't fast, but it's got punch in reserve.

The slug shoved the kid away from the girl and spun him half around. About now, the bartender realized that war had commenced and dropped behind the bar.

The kid had his Colt out, but he couldn't do much with his shoulder smashed. He just couldn't lift his arm. But he was game. He checked his involuntary wheel and started for his other gun. Slocum waited until he had the gun out before he broke the kid's other shoulder. The kid had time to look bewildered before Slocum's next bullet made a hole where his right eye had been. The back of the kid's skull exploded like a watermelon and his head snapped back on his neck so fast, the bullet probably broke his neck, too.

The bartender was groping under the bar for the old muzzle-loading shotgun he kept there. Hell, a man had to defend his place of business, didn't he?

The crash of the bodies hitting the floor. Silence while all the dust motes danced around the room, aggravated as bees. When the bartender peeked over the bar, he looked right into the eye of John Slocum's Colt.

"You sittin' in?" Slocum asked, pleasantly enough.

"No!" The bartender dropped the shotgun at his

feet, and when Slocum's Colt motioned him, he stood up real tall, his hands stretched out over his head.

The bartender opened his mouth and closed it again. The girl was rebuttoning her trousers and trying to pull her blouse back together. The kid sat in the corner where the force of Slocum's last bullet had thrown him. The nut-brown man was lying flat on his face. His boots kicked the floor, once, twice, again. An awful smell filled the room as he voided himself.

Slocum opened the loading gate of his Colt and punched out the four brass cartridges he'd used. Carefully, one at a time, he replaced the bullets with new ones from his cartridge belt. He spun the cylinder to check it and holstered the gun. Then, and only then, he turned his attention back to the bartender. "Drop your arms, man," he said. "The killin's done."

When the bartender dropped his hands, he realized how sore they were from holding them up there, every muscle strained. Shakily he poured himself a shot of whiskey.

"You keep their guns and horses," Slocum said. "And bury 'em. I don't expect there's any next of kin." Slocum's voice came out cracked and strange.

The girl was waiting for him at the door, quite composed, though her eyes never touched the two bodies that lay on the streaked wooden floor. "Sorry it went on so long," Slocum said. "I was worried you'd get hurt, too."

The girl smiled very, very faintly. "You certainly didn't rush things, did you, Slocum?" she said. Her English was clear and unaccented except that she broke Slo-cum into two distinct syllables.

Damn! Slocum had been on the trail with this girl for two weeks, and she had never let on she spoke anything but Cantonese.

Outside, the Western sun was doing its best effects on the horizon. Bands of pink, red, and gold. Streamers of cerulean blue, interspersed with the pink clouds like the bellies of long, peaceful fish. The shadows were deep at the side of the saloon and reached from the smithy across the street. The smith stood in the doorway of his forge. He had a rifle propped against his doorsill but didn't look too anxious to use it. "Anybody hurt?" he called out.

Slocum patted the necks of the dead men's horses. "A couple pilgrims had a little trouble," Slocum replied. He untied the broken-gaited packhorse. For some reason, he was tired and he figured that maybe they'd done enough traveling for one day. He led the packhorse across the street, its bad foot making it bob like a cork in the water. "Like to take a look at this horse of mine," he said. "Frog's gone on the right rear shoe. Think the hoof needs paring, too."

"Bring her in under the porch here where I can get a light on it."

The blacksmith was a short, powerful man with huge veins on his forehead and hair on the back half of his skull. He handled the horse calmly and knelt down by her offside rear to inspect the hoof. The horse lifted her hoof readily enough. It wasn't exactly a first.

"Those two fellows who followed you in there . . ." the blacksmith said.

"You gonna be able to work that hoof?" Slocum asked.

"Yeah. Those two fellows . . ."

"You might put a bid in on their horses. They'll probably be going cheap."

The Chinese girl put the other packhorse between herself and the blacksmith. She peeled off her soiled blouse and took another from her baggage.

The blacksmith pulled a short stool, like a milking stool, from the smith and sat down to carve away the horse's bad hoof.

Across the street the saloonkeeper was dragging the dead men outside. This was Saturday night, and if some local ranchhands did stop by, dead men on the floor might dampen the festivities. He propped one body up against the outside wall and went back inside to get the other one. The girl looked at the body with no more interest than if it had been a cigar-store Indian.

Slocum called to her, "Now that you can speak English, maybe you can be of some use. Go get me a bottle of that fellow's whiskey." He laughed. "Tell him to put it on my tab." Wordlessly the girl obeyed.

The blacksmith finished trimming the packhorse's hoof and took fifty cents for his trouble. The saloonkeeper had both the dead gunhawks outside now, propped against his building like some sort of bizarre advertisement. The girl mounted up with some grace and waited for Slocum. Slocum didn't feel any great need to ride all night. They were an easy day's travel from Butte city, and he figured he'd had enough excitement for one day.

Just the faintest light left in the sky, a pink tinge on the horizon. Slocum rode right past the first creek they passed, because it was too obvious a campsite, but he drew up when another one—a wet weather spring from the looks of it—crossed the trail. He dismounted and led the horses over around a bend in the creek where the campfire wouldn't be visible from the trail. While the girl gathered firewood, he unsaddled the horses and humped the pack saddles to the side before carefully brushing down each one of the mounts. Slocum had learned to take care of his horses before he took care of himself.

By the time he was finished, the girl had a small cookfire alight.

Slocum sharpened a couple of forked sticks and a crosspiece. He opened a can of beans and a can of tomatoes. He sliced up a couple of chunks of beef jerky and tossed it into the beans for flavor. The girl sat down beside him, hands clasped around her knees, staring into the fire. After a while she said, "I wonder if he is dead now."

There wasn't any real good answer Slocum could make to that. "Your father was a brave man," he said.

She didn't seem to think that was real important. She ate her beans without another word and when the meal was finished did the washing up with sand from the edge of the little creek. Slocum unloaded his Colt and, unwrapping a chamois skin pouch, extracted his field cleaning kit. That old black powder would pit a barrel quick as a wink if you didn't keep the steel clean. The girl watched him as he used the brass rods and brushes on the barrel and each cylinder.

"I wish I knew how to shoot," she said.

"Woman's got other weapons, if she knows how to use 'em right," Slocum said. "I only knew a couple women knew how to use guns, Calamity Jane and Big Nose Kate, and they never killed anybody with 'em that I ever heard tell."

"If I could shoot, I would protect my father," she said fiercely.

Slocum put down the pistol and looked into her dark eyes. "Reckon you would at that," he said. "But he wanted you to stay alive. That was his wish. Now don't you go wishin' you'd defied him."

Her head lowered, slowly and more than a little reluctantly. "We Chinese women are taught to obey," she said.

"Sorry I had to let that kid get at you," Slocum said. "I needed his attention distracted a little, otherwise I couldn't guarantee nothing."

She raised her head then. "Do I have beautiful breasts?" she asked.

"Well, ma'am, to tell you the truth, I wasn't noticing."

And quickly, agile as a deer, she got to her feet and unbuttoned her blouse and shrugged it back over her shoulders. "Are they beautiful?" she demanded.

They were. Little damn things, no more than a handful, but the nipples were long, brown, and erect, and he didn't think they were just reacting to the chilly air.

"I've seen bigger," he said thoughtfully. "But they do look like fun."

She unbuttoned her trousers and pushed them down to lie in a heap at her ankles. "And my legs. Are they not slender and firm?"

Slocum rolled a quirly. He managed to keep his hands from shaking tobacco all over the place, but it was a near thing. "Can't see 'em all," he remarked. "You're still standin' in your pants."

And then she giggled at him and lifted one leg quickly so her twill pants flew across the fire and wrapped around his head—and ruined his quirly.

He tossed the pants aside and uncoiled to his feet. Defiantly she stood, waiting for him, her mouth mock-angry and her hands clenched at her sides. He walked around her like a wary buyer inspecting a horse. "Not too much meat on 'em," he observed, "but they're a good-lookin' set of pins, all right."

Her legs swooped down from the curve of her buttocks, slender as a doe's. Her hair was tightly braided on top of her head, in place with two hefty wooden pins. When he tugged at the pins the whole length of it tumbled down her back.

She must have felt the tickle of her hair, but she looked dead ahead and her fists remained clenched at her sides. The black hair rustled against her brown skin. The skin gleamed in the firelight.

Completing his tour of inspection, Slocum came around to the front of her and put his hands on his hips. He meant to say, "I think you'll do," in a neutral voice, but it came out sort of husky somehow.

Her yellow silk underwear covered her small belly. Gently, he tugged it down, below her hips and buttocks.

Just a faint dusting of hair at her juncture and her belly popped out, bowl-shaped, like a child. Her navel pushed out, not in.

"Yeah," Slocum said and took her into his arms. Her mouth found his—quick and easy and hot. Her eagerness surprised him and the way she pressed herself against his groin, like she wanted to be glued to him, now, now.

She wasn't satisfied with the way Slocum unbuttoned his shirt, and she damn near tore it off him trying to help. She was trying to kiss him while he kicked off his boots and her hands got in his way when he tried to unbuckle his belt. "I can take 'em off myself, thank you," Slocum said. Then he said, "Mmmmph" as she kissed him again.

When he was naked, she pushed away from him and quite deliberately dropped her gaze. She ran her tongue over her lips nervously, "I don't think . . ." she began.

Now it was his turn to come to her, and slowly he stepped forward. "It can't fit," she said. "You are too big. It won't fit." She clasped his cock between her hands, delicately, like butterfly wings.

"Oh, we'll make room for it somehow," Slocum said. But the girl was still frightened, and when he drew her to him, his cudgel between her thighs, he could tell she was cooling to the idea.

"I . . . it is my first," she whispered. And then she relaxed in his arms, her breasts pressed against his chest hair.

So he lowered her to the blankets beside the fire and kissed her long and deep. He busied himself with her breasts until her nipples were pebble-hard under his callused hand and he traced the curve of her cunt until the moisture came and her little hips, with a will of their own, pushed against his hand.

"Now," she said, in a small voice, "now I am ready."

But Slocum didn't want to hurt her, though his cock felt like a cannon with a hair trigger. He slipped a finger into her, probing gently, stroking her in and out.

"Oh," she gasped. "Oh, please."

Gently, smoothly, he slipped the finger in and out until her pussy relaxed enough for him to work two fingers in. She winced with the second invasion, but desire was clouding her eyes and her hips were bouncing against the blankets in the age-old rhythm.

Her hand started flailing about and found his cock and gripped it. Slocum didn't think that was such a hot idea. He rolled between her legs and pushed forward, as gently as he could. She was very small and the head lodged right in the opening, despite his careful preparation. Maybe she realized the difficulty because, for a moment, her eyes cleared, and she drew her face back from his. Then a determined look passed over the girl's face and she tossed her hips upward. Her mouth opened in surprise as he sank into her.

Then she started dancing around the maypole, her young hips working and twisting. He sank into her slow, and it seemed like a very long time before her upthrust buttocks slapped against his balls. She was coming steadily, tossing her sweat-streaked face from side to side and crying out in a language that Slocum didn't know and didn't know if she did either.

He drove into her just once, with all his strength. Just for a second their belly hair mingled before he groaned his seed into her.

2

From the top of the Continental Divide, Butte City looked like one of the mountains of the moon. The voracious smelters had stripped all the timber for twenty miles around the Hill and the ground was yellow and bare. The smelters cast a steady pall over the Hill itself, black and ominous.

"There she is," Slocum said. The girl had ridden next to him all morning and now, wordless at the desolation that was to be her new home, she reached out and took his hand. He took it though he couldn't offer her much comfort.

Slocum was travel weary and glad the end was in sight. Last night, what strength remained after the weeks on the trail had pretty much been drained off. "Remind me," he thought to himself, "to stay away from unbroke horses and virgins." After her first, the small Chinese girl was insatiable. She wanted to try everything and anything, right now. Man'd have to be less than a gentleman not to oblige. But today Slocum was feeling the toll and his cock rested inside his pants like a battered warrior.

They rode down into the long flats below the Hill and passed a few scruffy teepees and log huts, all that remained of the Indians who'd been here when the first gold strike had been made on the Hill. Slocum didn't know the name of the tribe, and since they'd been decimated by smallpox and poverty, maybe they didn't either. They were a poor, pock-marked, shabby bunch, and the kids came out to the road with their hands out. Slocum tossed 'em a couple of silver dollars. Hell, they had to eat too.

The road was straight as a die and dusty as hell. Slocum had heard they were going to put a railroad into Butte City—a branch of Jim Hill's Northern Pacific—but the railroad builders hadn't got around to it yet, so the refined gold, silver, and copper were hauled south to the Union Pacific railhead. The road was rutted deep where the wagons had passed, and the ruts were hard as concrete. Slocum traveled slowly. He didn't want to break a horse's leg in those ruts, and he figured that if he hurried, that's just what would happen.

As they neared the Hill, they passed a few shacks and the odd gallows frame—the tall wooden structures that winched the cages up and down underground. The cages dropped the miners in and brought the raw ore out. Not that so much of it was raw. Butte City had a history of wide veins of native silver and copper —almost ninety-five percent pure.

Main Street started at the flats and rose straight up the Hill. It was wide enough for three ore wagons at once, and there seemed to be a hell of a lot of them. The teamsters bullied their way past each other with language their mothers hadn't taught them, and a couple of times Slocum had to back off his horses in favor of an ore wagon skating downhill on the thin edge of control—the driver standing in the wagon box, hauling on the brake and cursing the air blue.

The air was bad. A lot of sulfur in those smelter fumes and more than a little arsenic too. A few of the miners' wives planted tiny garden plots behind their shacks, but it wasn't any use. The smelter fumes killed everything that tried to grow.

The Chinese quarter was on Main Street, halfway up the Hill. Three blocks of fairly prosperous-looking buildings, most of them brick, with Chinese ideograms on the parapets and medallions.

Slocum reined in before a brick building that announced in English: "The Canton Block." As many miners as Chinese were on the bustling sidewalks. Slocum told the girl to wait with the horses while he located her kin. He stepped into the first Chinese restaurant he found. The trade was half Chinese, half Occidental. Noisy as hell and it smelled pretty good. Apparently the whites here didn't object to Chinese cooking because they were certainly chowing down cheerfully enough.

Slocum caught a harried waiter's sleeve and asked directions to Chang Tung's place. The waiter gave him a funny look, like he wasn't too fond of white men who asked for Chang Tung's, but, maybe Slocum was imagining things.

Turned out Chang Tung lived right around the corner in the same building. Slocum wondered how many Chinese lived in the big brick structure. He guessed quite a few. On the quieter side street, Slocum noticed where the building's foundation had cracked and buckled. Nothing too serious yet, but one day the constant underground tunneling would drop the surface here and the building would come tumbling down.

Slocum stopped before a plain, heavy oak door and patted the girl's shoulder reassuringly. He banged the thick iron knocker and after a few seconds a peephole slid open. Slocum spoke to it: "I'm John Slocum. And this here's Chang Lee. We're looking for Chang Tung. He's her cousin."

The eye that had been briefly visible in the peephole disappeared and they were left to wait on the stoop. The girl nervously patted the travel dust out of the skirt she'd insisted on wearing today. "Pants aren't proper," she'd said. And maybe she knew Slocum was thinking she hadn't been all that proper last night, because she blushed when he looked at her.

The Chinaman who opened the heavy door was a shifty-eyed, bandy-legged runt. Roughly, he urged the girl at the narrow flight of stairs that was the only way out of the otherwise featureless hall. He tried to push John Slocum back outside, but, having come this far, Slocum wasn't about to leave before he had the girl delivered proper, so he pushed back. The Chinaman didn't insist. He closed and bolted the door with a wide steel bar and two steel bolts.

Enough security for a bank, Slocum thought.

The hall at the top of the stairs had two doors. The Chinaman babbled something to the girl and urged her toward one of them. "He says I must come alone with him to meet my honored relative," she translated. "After I have made my appearance, you will be asked in."

"All right." Slocum leaned against the wall and tipped his hat over his eyes. When the two were gone, he tugged his pants away from his sore groin and sighed as he leaned back again. His eyes narrowed to slits and he halfway dozed off. He wondered what the girl was discovering about her new life. He wondered if there'd be any dragons in it. Like the dragons he'd seen on the Chinese New Year. Big scarlet dragons with scales that clashed and glittered like blood. Slocum shook his head awake. He sniffed. Sniffed again. "Oh, Jesus," he said. When he tried the door the girl had passed through, it was locked, but the other door opened easily enough.

Heavy curtains over the windows filtered out the daylight in the long shoebox room, and the candles that guttered in wall sconces didn't do much to dispel the gloom. Sounds: men murmuring, like they were dreaming with their tongues. The shuffle of the slippers of the old emaciated Chinese crone who came toward him. In the dim light, Slocum couldn't be sure it was a woman. He didn't suppose it made much difference. Not here.

The figure was hissing at him. When it was evident that Slocum didn't understand Chinese, the crone hissed, "Close door, please. Light most unsettling. Most unsettling."

Slocum closed the door behind him and waited for his eyes to adjust to the bad light. The crone tugged at his sleeve. "Five dollars," she said. Slocum wanted to know a bit more, so he dipped five silver dollars out of his pocket and watched them disappear. This time the crone's hiss was one of satisfaction.

The shoebox room was lined with double deck wooden bunk beds. No mattresses or blankets. The beds were simple two-story wooden shelves.

It was eerie, but it didn't scare Slocum much. He'd been in a doss house before. The sweet smell of burning opium. It was almost incense but not quite. Just standing in the room made Slocum's head ring with the first effects of the opium smoke.

So this was Chang Tung's business. The source of his wealth and authority. Slocum wasn't altogether pleased.

An incredibly thin hand plucked at his sleeve. The crone had a wooden opium pipe in her hand and a ball of black opium in her fingers. She held the gummy little black ball up for Slocum's inspection and favored him with a cackle that meant: As a connoisseur, I know you'll really appreciate this; it's the best!

Slocum smiled briefly and allowed the crone to lead him down the narrow aisle between the bunkbeds.

Probably half the occupants were Chinese, mostly elderly Chinese. Some sat cross-legged, smiling at their visions. Some crooned softly to themselves. Most lay on the harsh wooden pallets, lost in their dreams.

It surprised Slocum to see how many of the bunks were occupied by whites. These were generally younger than the Chinese, and most of them were dressed as workingmen, but they sat on their bunks dreaming just like their Oriental brothers.

Near the end of the room, the crone started directing Slocum toward the empty shelves they passed, but Slocum wasn't really very interested in smoking the stuff, he just wanted to give Chang Tung's business the once-over.

Just at the end of the room, where the heavy, close-woven curtains covered the windows, a white man sat on the edge of his bunk, his feet on the floor. Slocum drew up, ignoring the constant plucks of the crone who wished to get him and his pipe settled before returning to whatever her own dreams were.

The man was a gent. Elegant gray pants and brightly shined handsome shoes. When he leaned forward to put his head in his hands, Slocum noticed that his shirt was of the finest linen. He wore an ascot at his throat. His floppy hand brushed against his opium pipe, and the wooden stem shattered with a tiny ping when it hit the floor. This enraged the crone, who scooped up the pipe, waved it in his face, and plucked at the bosom of the man's expensive shirt.

"You pay," the crone shrilled.

Blankly, the gent stared at the broken pipe, but clearly he didn't have any idea what the pipe was or what it was for. Vigorously, he shook his head from side to side. He was a handsome man—long, narrow face, big, arrogant nose, and dark eyes. His hair was dark—in this light Slocum couldn't tell if it was black or brown—and thick and rumpled. The gent ran his hand through his hair. "Damn," he said. Then he said, "Stop pulling at me, Chin. I'll talk to you later."

The gent's coat was folded up neatly at the head of the bunk, and it looked like he'd made a pillow out of it while he was traveling through opium land. Now he reached into the coat and pulled out a fat wallet. Without checking the denomination, he passed the bill to the crone. The crone was more particular and held the banknote very close to her eye before accepting it. From the sound of the crone's chuckle, the gent had bought the opium pipe fifty times over. The gent reached up to the rail of the bunk above him trying to haul himself to his feet. He had all the strength of a kitten, and after a moment of struggle, he let his arms fall back and dropped his head into his hands again.

"Slocum," a voice hissed at his elbow. It was the other Chinese, the one who'd led the girl away. "Slocum, come with me. Chang Tung is looking for you. Slocum, come."

John Slocum shook the man's hand off him but followed readily enough. He didn't worry too much about the well-dressed gent on the bunk. Now that the crone had seen that fat wallet Slocum figured he'd get all the attention he needed.

Halfway back toward the door, Slocum's feet got a little wobbly. Damn air was full of opium smoke. Slocum ordered his legs to behave themselves, and they did the best they could.

Even the stale air in the hallway smelled good to Slocum, and he took a couple of deep, deep breaths, shaking his head to clear the cobwebs. The Chinaman made no comment. He'd seen a few men trying to clear their heads. *Wonder what he'd do if I punched him?* Slocum thought. The thought made him giggle and he shook his head again. He'd have to watch himself for a few minutes.

The Chinaman opened the other door and motioned Slocum into Chang Tung's sanctum.

Two men waited with the girl, Lee, in one of the most opulent rooms Slocum had ever seen. Floor-to-ceiling red drapes covered the wall. The room was bright with oil lamps—odd-shaped ironwork pieces with oil cups burning inside their hollow bellies and casting strange flickering shadows over the faces of the Chinese. A large desk gleamed with the deep patina of aged wood lovingly cared for. The desk was ornately trimmed, and the bowed legs of the piece transformed themselves into lion's paws at the floor. A few massive upholstered chairs lined one wall, and the boss Chinaman was urging Slocum to make himself comfortable. "Do sit down, sir," he said.

But Slocum had his attention fixed on the other Chinaman: the giant.

The giant had his arms folded inside his simple brown robe and his gaze reminded Slocum of some statues he'd seen. John Slocum stood a couple of inches over six feet tall himself, and this Chinaman made him feel small. He must go six-ten, at least, Slocum guessed.

The boss Chinaman kept asking him to sit. "I'll stay on my feet, thanks," Slocum said. He wanted to be ready if the giant suddenly got mean.

All the while the girl was docile and submissive, her head lowered, paying no attention to John Slocum.

The giant wasn't just tall, he was wide. He might have weighed three hundred and fifty pounds. His neck was bull-thick and his shaven head was as big as a good-sized pumpkin.

"I see you are impressed with Io, Mr. Slocum."

"Yeah," Slocum said. "I never seen anything like that outside of a zoo before. Still, I suppose he makes a handy hat rack."

Something guttered deep in the big Chinaman's eyes. Something nameless and terrible. Slocum wondered how many .44 bullets he could get into the man before the Chinaman killed him.

"My relative tells me you met some opposition on your journey," the other Chinaman said.

Slocum forgot about the big Chinaman and inspected the girl's kin. Even if he hadn't been a doss-house operator, Slocum wouldn't have been too impressed. Chang Tung was a medium-sized gentleman with a king-size smile. The smile reminded

Slocum of the smiles sometimes found on bleached skulls in the desert. He wore his hair in the traditional braid, but his suit was Western and draped off his knobby body like it was hanging on a bumpy coat hanger. The man's cheeks were narrower than his smile and Slocum wondered how that could be. Chang Tung had his hand stuck out. Slocum decided he didn't see it.

"A couple gunhawks," Slocum reported. "I suppose they were hired by the Hop Sings, but they'll never tell us anything about it now."

"My humble relative says you acquitted yourself well," Chang Tung insisted.

"They were in the wrong business." Slocum shrugged off the praise. "They was in the gun business when they should have been in the corpse business." His smile was wolfish, and Io, the giant, looked at him with more interest than before.

"Please sit, Mr. Slocum," Chang Tung urged again. "I will have Io bring tea." A flick of his fingers sent the giant on his way. "The Changs, it appears, owe you a debt of gratitude."

Slocum sat down. He tossed his filthy gray Stetson on the polished wood desk. His head was clearer now. "You don't owe me anything," Solcum said. "I took a fee for the job."

"My esteemed cousin."

"That's the gent that paid the bill."

"Ah, yes." The Chinaman looked both sad and gleeful at the same time. "We will not see his like again."

Slocum's eyebrows went up, but he didn't ask the question because Io returned, bearing a lacquered tray in his huge stubby hands. The giant's hands carried calluses the likes of which Slocum had never seen before: His knuckles were flattened into circles about the size of a double eagle and a horny ridge ran along the outside of his hands. When the giant noticed

Slocum's gaze, he smiled like a man who's triumphant over a small matter.

"Io, that will be all," Chang Tung said. "You may take my relative to the house. Instruct my wife to begin her training."

The giant bent at the waist in a medium-respectful bow before pulling the curtains aside to reveal another heavy door. The girl never once looked at Slocum. They left.

"Training?" Slocum asked.

Again that gleeful smile. "Yes. The daughter of my cousin is a very, very important person, Mr. Slocum. If you'd known how valuable she is, perhaps you might have been successfully approached to, uh, abandon your commission."

Slocum let that one slip by. Sometimes John Slocum was impervious to insult. Other times, of course, he was as touchy as a medieval lord. "How valuable?" he asked.

The Chinaman smiled, as if he'd put something over on somebody. "Oh, I suppose the Hop Sings would have paid several thousand dollars in gold for the maiden."

"If they'd been willing to spend that much, they could have hired a couple better gunhawks," Slocum said.

"She will be married to the best Chinese family in either Denver or Seattle," the Chinaman said. "After her training is complete, of course."

"Training?"

"How to be a dutiful wife. My cousin was a good man, an important man, but I fear he neglected his duty when it came to his daughter. She must learn to put her husband first, in all things, to serve him before she serves herself, to pass on our traditions. My wife and daughters will soon train young Lee in the proper ways."

"And then you marry her off."

That smile again. "No, Mr. Slocum. Call it an alliance. You see, there are many Chinese scattered through the gold camps of Western America. Several, uh, associations, dominate the scene."

"Like the Hop Sings."

"The Hop Sings are dominant in San Francisco," the Chinaman snapped. "They have no authority in Butte City and very little in Denver and Seattle. The Hop Sings are fools. They would organize laundry men."

Slocum sipped at the tea that had been poured out for him. Usually he didn't much care for tea, but this stuff wasn't too bad. "While you organize the whores and the dope peddlers?" he inquired mildly. Slocum didn't give a damn about any Chinese tongs, but he enjoyed baiting the self-assured man who sat across from him.

"I see you visited our parlor," the man said.

Slocum shrugged, "I seen 'em before."

"It is a very lucrative business," Chang Tung said. "With my people, the use of opium is a very old custom. But miners who spend all day underground, surrounded by danger and the constant possibility of death, enjoy opium dreams, too. And, from time to time, one of the wealthier classes decides to give it a try." His mouth shaped itself into the lines of contempt. "Too jaded by life, they take their pleasures in the rare and exotic."

"Of course, they pay."

Chang Tung said, quite happily, "Why, yes, they do, Mr. Slocum. As long as they can."

"And when they can't, your ape beats the money out of them?"

"Io?" The Chinaman was shocked. "Oh, no. Io is too important to my family to be used for such small purposes. I see that you didn't care for Io. Did you wish to fight him?"

Slocum took a sip of tea.

"It would be forbidden," Chang Tung explained carefully. "Io is one of the main treasures of my family. We would not waste him on such a one as you."

Slocum let the insult pass again because he was curious about the Chinese giant.

"When Io was a very small boy, he began training in a remote mountain monastery where he learned his skills. He can kill very quickly, Mr. Slocum. Quicker than you, even with your pistols. In the ancient times, when China was ruled by the Mongols, these monks developed skills at fighting with their hands and small, easily concealed weapons. Those skills have not been surpassed to this day. Io is a very great master. There isn't another like him in this country. Io is my army, and he goes forth to do only my bidding."

"Uh-huh."

"And now, thanks to you, I have Lee, too. That maiden and Io make me very powerful. My family is now the most important Chinese family in the West. Do I bore you, Mr. Slocum? You look bored."

"Oh, I suppose it's all right," Slocum said. "Every time I hear that kind of bullshit slung around, I like to keep my head down."

The Chinaman flushed. "My cousin is dead," he announced. "The night you left San Francisco, he was beheaded in his own house. His servants claim to have heard nothing, but my agents are questioning them now. Of course, the servants opened the doors to the Hop Sing hatchet men. I wish them to admit that simple fact before I make them beg for death. We are a very ancient people, Mr. Slocum. And some of our amusements are very ancient, too."

"Yeah." Slocum put on his hat. "Well, give my best to Chang Lee," he said and turned to leave. After ten minutes in the same room with this man, Slocum felt like he needed a bath.

He was strolling down the stairs with not much on

his mind when somebody started banging on the front door. Whoever wanted in had very big hands. The doorman backed up and put his hands to his mouth.

"Open up in there, you bunch of damn heathens. Open up or I'll take this door off its hinges!"

The doorman was backed as far into the corner as he could get. Slocum jerked him aside and pressed his eye to the peephole.

Seven, no eight, men outside. Burly Irishmen from the looks of them. Two blue suits: city police. And the others wore badges on their coats. One man, a slender blond fellow with a grenadier's waxed mustache, was shouting instructions. "Get back from that door, Harrington. They ain't gonna open up. Use the axe on it."

Before the axe smashed into the door, Slocum was halfway up the stairs. He nearly trampled the frightened doorman who was scurrying ahead of him.

"Open up in there!" the deputy commanded, and the crash of their axe smashing through the door made command redundant.

Slocum didn't rightly know what the officers of the law wanted. He wasn't known in Butte City. He'd been in Montana Territory before, but no warrants had been issued from his last visit.

But John Slocum didn't figure they meant him any good. A man who had as much money on his head as Slocum did couldn't welcome any contact with the law, no matter how innocent. Too many lawmen would be able to decipher the maze of aliases on the wanted posters, and some of those wanted posters advertised hanging offenses.

So he was ready to make tracks.

Outside the opium room, two frightened Chinese stared at Slocum, and the well-dressed white gent Slocum had seen before was trying to gather his wits. The gent was pounding the side of his head with his hand, as if he were trying to beat some sense into himself and swearing, "Goddamnit. Goddamnit!"

The door to Chang Tung's office was locked, and the doorman was scratching at it and whining piteously. Remembering the heavy bolts and bars on the inside of that door, Slocum decided to give it a pass. He charged into the long room that housed the smokers. A couple were sitting up on the edge of their bunks, alert enough to guess that the noises they were hearing weren't part and parcel of their opium dreams, but most of the smokers lay as he'd seen them before, pretty much indifferent to life or death. At the end of the dim shoebox room, Slocum ripped the heavy curtains away from the window wall. And saw bricks.

Some mean-spirited son of a bitch had bricked the windows up. Every one of them. Angrily, Slocum banged at the bricks before he turned back toward the hallway.

He didn't have too much time to spare. Downstairs, the axe was tearing long pieces out of the door, and it couldn't be too much longer before they had enough space hacked out to draw the bolts. "Get in there," someone was shouting. "I want that damn Heinze. He's worth a hundred dollars gold to the first man who lays hands on him."

The doorman was still whimpering outside Chang Tung's door. The dapper gent eyed Slocum and grinned wearily. "How'd you like to make an easy hundred?" he said.

"You the one they're after?"

"I'm Heinze. F. Augustus Heinze." He spoke in a curiously stilted way, but his accent was American enough.

"What do they want you for?"

The man grinned and shrugged. "So they can steal me blind while I'm locked up with a bunch of dumb

Chinks who don't speak English. Ain't it a hell of a life?"

And though the man was weak as a kitten, he managed to find a grin. Slocum eyed him carefully.

Below, the axe stopped. "Get those bolts, Harrington. Get inside. You can't do no good out here."

F. Augustus Heinze came up off the wall and brushed some of the lint off the lapels of his coat. He buttoned the coat. "Might as well go down like a gentleman," he remarked.

That made John Slocum smile. The man might be nothing but a dandy and a hophead, but, hell, he had style.

Swiftly, Slocum knelt to examine Chang Tung's door. "Put your shoulder against this," he said.

Heinze obliged. He was too weak to push the door hard enough so Slocum could locate the bolts.

"Shit," Slocum said. "Well, we can always try the hinges." Quickly he set his big hands on the top edge of the door and measured down two spans. If he remembered right, that's about where the hinges should be. Unless Oriental carpenters hung their doors different.

A rush of air. A square of light, swiftly blotted out. The clatter of feet on the stairs. Half a dozen deputies were charging up the stairs, two by two by two. Quickly, Slocum took the Chinese doorman, swooped him off his feet, and while the banty man squealed in terror, hurled him down the stairs at the phalanx of deputies.

He slammed into them. Nobody fell down, but they jammed up good when the Chinaman hit them.

"What do I do?" Heinze asked.

"Bring me some more Chinks," Slocum snapped. He grinned. He was having a good time.

Heinze was mostly recovered now, and in just seconds he was holding a comatose drug addict by the scruff of his neck. Slocum tossed a second Chinaman at the deputies. The deputies couldn't budge on the stairs. Their eyes were enraged.

"You son of a bitch," one shouted. "I'll remember you."

"Friend," Heinze said, "if those boys reach us, they aren't going to be too gentle."

Slocum could have used his Colt, but he didn't think it was a good idea. He didn't want to kill any lawmen. Slocum had enough men on his trail without adding any more. So he used his Colt on the hinges of the office door, placing two shots where he figured each hinge would be. The gun jumped hard in his hand and the holes he made in the door weren't very large, but Slocum knew they'd be the size of silver dollars by the time the deformed bullets tore through the other side.

"Christ!" one of the deputies yowled, "he's firin' on us," and went for his own gun.

"C'mon," Slocum urged Heinze. "Together now."

As one, they smashed into the door, putting their shoulders into it. When they hit, it didn't burst open, but it gave an inch or two. Again they crashed into the weakened door.

The deputies in the stairwell were tangled up in Chinamen. One of the rear rankers got off a shot, but since he didn't want to hit any of his mates, the shot went high and the bullet embedded in the plaster of the ceiling.

"Shit," Heinze said. The two men hit the door again and this time it swung drunkenly open. Slocum's bullets had broken the top hinge but missed the bottom one, and they stepped through the triangular opening awkwardly. Slocum kept his pistol in his hand. If he was going to meet the Chinese giant, he wanted to shoot first and explain afterward.

But Chang Tung's office was empty. Heinze, who'd never been in this part of the building before, stopped and exclaimed, "Damn. Ain't this something."

Slocum was already tearing at the curtains that concealed the back door. Heinze picked up a piece of jade from a shelf and whistled. "Will you look at this? Genuine Ming Dynasty, if I'm any judge."

The deputies had passed the Chinamen over their heads and were coming up the stairs again. Slocum had the back door open and yelled at Heinze, "Damnit, stop daydreaming!"

Heinze jumped to follow the tall gunman. But the little Ming figurine went into his pocket before he left.

The back door opened on a circular, very narrow stairwell, almost a ladder. A single kerosene lantern high overhead. Slocum hurried down the circular stairwell with one hand on the stairs above him. The damn thing dropped so fast it made him dizzy. He hoped Heinze didn't fall and take him along for the ride.

The door at the bottom opened into a dim passageway. Here, light that filtered through sidewalk grates supplied the only illumination. The walls were big chunks of cut stone and Slocum thought he heard the roar of a steam boiler ahead.

A faint voice behind him, "Down here, boys. The rats found a back way."

Slocum ran down the passage trying to put a little distance between him and the deputies. And he started to get mad.

This wasn't his quarrel. He stood to gain nothing from it. No man here was his enemy. Yet he was scuttling through an underground tunnel like a damn fool. What really burned him up was the remark about "rats."

Heinze was doing his best, but his coordination wasn't very good and he was bouncing against the wall, first to one side, then to the other. Slocum kicked open the door to a boiler room—the heating system for this building and, from the looks of the pipes, another two or three as well. The boiler was an enormous black cylinder, with a brass nameplate that said: "Boelitz of St. Louis." The boiler room door was fairly stout and could be barred from the inside. Slocum smiled his quicksilver grin. He was tired of running.

A quick glance at the steam gauge: Two hundred and twenty pounds—just twenty pounds under the red line. It was cooking pretty hot. Slocum's grin grew broader. He had about three minutes' lead on the deputies. Unless he ended up in a blind alley down here, he could surely get clear.

But he wanted to give them a little something to remember him by.

He spun back to the boiler room door. Another few seconds had it bolted, and a length of pipe he braced against the door added a few seconds of lead time.

Heinze was leaning against the stone wall, still pretty shaky and sweating. His elegant gray suit was smudged and one sleeve was ripped. He was mopping his sweaty forehead with a handkerchief. "Friend," he said in a muffled voice, "let us not linger."

But Slocum was having too much fun to hurry. Two great steam lines disappeared into the stone wall— heating the three story brick building overhead. The valves that fed steam into those pipes were frozen, and Slocum had to bang on them with the coal scoop to close them down snug. The shovel rang, steel blade against brass. As soon as he had the lines shut off, the steam gauge started creeping upward toward the red line.

Through foggy eyes, Heinze watched the lanky gun-man as he scooped coal into the fiery boiler and banged the boiler door shut. He looked like some maniac out of hell with his coal-smudged face lit up by the boiler flames.

Someone slammed against the door. A voice cried, "They've locked it. Harrington! Put your shoulder to it, man!"

Heinze started to run. He couldn't figure out why Slocum wanted to feed the furnace in the middle of a pursuit, but he didn't see any reason why he should be taken because of his rescuer's eccentricities. He had too much to lose.

With one quick move, Slocum slipped a length of brace wire over the steam escape valve and tied it down. The temperature gauge was quivering on the red line.

He darted out of the boiler room and bolted the opposite door.

This door was good and stout. Slocum couldn't hear the deputies crashing against the other door though he knew they were. The grin was fixed on his face like it was part of his personality. "I believe it's time to dust," Slocum said with a laugh. And the two men hurried through the tunnel, which, as Slocum had guessed, connected all the buildings in Butte City's Chinatown. They passed staircases leading to the buildings above, but Slocum had some instinct about all of them and passed three of them before he mounted another (no different to the eye from any of the others) and pushed into the kitchen of the Chinese restaurant he'd been in only an hour before. Had it just been an hour? Christ!

When they stepped out into the bustle of Main Street, a few men shot glances at the odd pair. Slocum's face was streaked with coal dust and soot, and his partner looked like somebody'd dragged him through a refuse heap. Heinze brushed at his ruined jacket.

A muffled thud. The sidewalk jumped a few inches and settled down again, leaving only a dust haze to mark its odd leap. At sidewalk level, the building had acquired a new and alarming bulge. A few voices called out. One man howled. Then the babble of excited Chinese voices filled the air and all along the length of the building, windows were hurled open. Slocum inspected the curious faces, but he didn't spot Lee or her nasty relative either.

A good smile spread across Heinze's features, chasing his dazed expression before it. "Damn, man," he said. "That's rough."

"Probably didn't kill any of 'em," Slocum said.

"Probably not."

"But," Slocum laughed out loud, "I'll bet it singed their tail feathers."

"I expect it did." Heinze looked at Slocum, a little owlishly. "Friend, I believe I owe you a drink."

"You do."

Because it was close by, Heinze led Slocum down the Line: Butte City's infamous street of cribhouses and brothels. The girls at the open windows flashed their charms at the miners passing by. From the looks of it, they were doing pretty good business, though it wasn't but three in the afternoon.

John Slocum had seen plenty of red-light districts before. Hell, in Abilene's heyday, whores outnumbered respectable women three to one. But usually the red-light districts were a little more discreet. Here, just riding down the street was a shopping expedition. And some of the girls didn't look half bad. Oh, well, time for that later.

The house where Heinze stopped was a little more imposing than the rest: a frame two-story, freshly painted white, with the windows painted a contrasting green. As soon as Heinze looped his horse's reins over the hitching rail a flunky rushed out. The flunky wore some sort of uniform, halfway between an ordinary black suit and the long formal coat of an English butler, but his ruddy face was Irish as paddy's pig. "Afternoon, Mr. Heinze," the lackey said. "Jeez, it's good to see you. How long's it been now, two, three weeks?"

"Something like that." As Heinze passed the reins he dipped into his pocket and Slocum saw the glitter of gold change hands. Big spender. "Me and my friend here are going inside for a drink. I want you to make sure some jackanapes doesn't run off with our horses, and I'll be wanting a cab when I come out. I won't be long."

"Sure thing, Mr. Heinze." The flunky touched his cap.

No sign marked the door, not even the red-shaded kerosene lantern that usually served as the whorehouse trademark.

Inside, the house was cool. It was a well-built house: closing the hallway door muffled the street noise like somebody'd dropped a heavy blanket on it. In a moment, the parlor door was opened by a tall, gracious-looking woman, dressed to the nines. Her hair was braided and coiled on top of her head and not a single hair was out of place in her impressive coiffure. Her gown was muted brown silk, with lace at the throat and collar. She stuck her hand out, like a man. "Afternoon, Heinzy," she said. "Good to see you again."

Heinze turned to the rangy gunman but hesitated, embarrassed. "Friend, you did me a very great service back there, but I'm afraid I didn't catch your name."

So Slocum introduced himself to the handsome woman. "I'm Blondetta," she said simply. "Welcome to the Irish World."

She went on to say that whatever they were looking for, they could probably find it here.

Heinze smiled reluctantly. "Not this afternoon, Blondetta," he said. "Hell, not even one of your kids could get it up for me today. I been slammed around so much I don't know which end is up. Some other time. We'll just require a glass of your best whiskey."

No disappointment crossed the woman's face. "Why, Heinzy," she said. "You know I'm always glad to see you. You don't have to drop by only when you're looking for a girl."

Slocum thought her smile was mostly genuine and entirely practiced. From the look of her—her fine high breasts and narrow hips—he also thought she'd be a fine woman to tumble. Some other time.

The parlor was a quiet room, white plaster with simple walnut chair rails and ceiling molding. The couches were plush red brocade, and the tables had that sort of fake Indian decoration they'd been putting on all the furniture lately.

"I'll send Mattie in with drinks," she said before sweeping gracefully out.

Heinze put his boots up on the couch and leaned back. "I owe you a favor, friend," he said after a moment. "If they'd got a hold of me, there would have been the devil to pay."

Slocum had long ago noticed that the very men who cried out most eagerly for help usually minimized their debt once the trouble was past. So Heinze was a little refreshing.

"Nothing," Slocum said. "I didn't want to hang around myself."

A young Indian girl brought them their whiskey— a Nez Percé, by the looks of her.

Slocum flashed his thank-you in the sign language all the Plains tribes understood. The girl understood all right. She blushed and retreated in some confusion.

"Any time you need anything I can give," Heinze said, "just ask."

"Well," Slocum drawled, "that's kind, but it doesn't seem to me to be much of a thing. Hell, every man's gonna get picked up sooner or later in a whorehouse or gambling house raid. I don't see where this is much different."

"Trouble is," Heinze explained, "there's two judges I haven't been able to buy."

He didn't want to say anymore. Slocum sipped his whiskey and didn't press for an explanation. His business.

3

The favorite was a big Alsatian hound. It must have weighed in at ninety-five pounds, and it was half starved and all mean.

Slocum sat right at ringside, wondering if he'd just lost himself a hundred dollars. The Alsatian was a long-jawed bastard, narrow in the hindquarters, quick to duck whenever its handler booted or cuffed it.

"This here dog's the fightin'est dog in the territory," the handler announced. "He's been in forty fights and never lost one of them."

The dog's muzzle had a dozen slash scars that gleamed white against his brown fur. Slocum thought he might have won forty fights, but he didn't win them without a little cost.

The dogfight was held on the main floor of Walker's saloon, and it promised to be a big event. The big old-fashioned barroom was packed with miners, tinhorns, pimps, and swells, the color of different social classes all reduced to the color of the money they were willing to bet.

The Alsatian was whining with excitement, and the handler kept him muzzled so those great slashing teeth wouldn't start on the men crowding around the dog, inspecting him. Even with the muzzle, nobody quite dared to pat him, and it wasn't hard to understand why. The dog was a bolt of energy and a single wrong move could set him off. Slocum had seen a few gunfighters like that, but most of them were dead. Billy Bonney was like that. Hell, drop a teacup near him, and like as not he'd come up shooting. But

Billy had been dead for seven long years now. It made Slocum feel older than he was.

Some barricades had been set up in the middle of Walker's floor for the dogpit. The barricades were only six feet high, and Slocum thought that either of the dogs could jump those walls in a second if they lost interest in chewing on each other.

Slocum had seen plenty of dogfights in the Klondike, during the gold rush at Dawson City, and he'd learned a few things then. That's why he bet on the Alsatian's opponent.

This dog wasn't attracting quite so much attention, and fewer bettors examined him. He was a long-haired white dog that looked to be part malamute and part mastiff. A little smaller than the favorite, he had great ruffs of hair along his neck and back. Under all that hair, it was hard to spot the configuration of the animal's muscles, but Slocum thought he was solid, all right, and he was impressed with the dog's handler, too. A grizzled old prospector from the looks of him, he knelt by the dog's head and spoke soothingly.

The Alsatian kept heaving against his restraining chain. He was ready to get at the malamute and end the fight here and now.

The malamute stood steady, eying the other dog fearlessly but calm, waiting for the other dog to start the ball rolling.

Slocum liked his attitude. That's why he'd put money on him.

The crowd was bigger today than the fight promoters had expected.

Every damn mine on the Hill was closed down, and a couple of hundred unemployed miners thronged Walker's, making bets and drinking. The bar was doing a landrush business, the four burly bartenders perspiring as they moved the mugs of beer and the shots down to the thirsty excited customers. Walker himself was behind the bar, and Mr. Walker never tended bar in his own tavern except on special occasions—like Saint Patrick's Day or dog fights.

In common with most of the fancier saloons, Walker's had a long mahogany bar, polished brass bar rail, and an elaborate leaded glass backbar that wouldn't have looked out of place in a corner of a cathedral. Carved filigrees and a fancy roseate of stained glass adorned the center of the backbar.

The rest of the room was plain: chairs, tables, blunt dusty walls, and a four-holer outhouse out back. Beer was a nickel. Whiskey was a dime, and it wasn't bad whiskey either. Most men liked to have one of each.

At length the bettors withdrew from the makeshift ring and retreated back into the crowd. Slocum gave one tinhorn a sharp jab in the ribs when he placed himself right in front of him. After one long look at the rangy gunfighter, the tinhorn murmured an apology and moved to block somebody else's view.

Soon, nobody remained in the ring except the two handlers and their dogs.

The instant the Alsatian's owner removed his muzzle, the dog set up a growl that made the hackles rise on Slocum's neck. It was the sound of an animal that means to kill, and Slocum had heard that sound too often to ever be comfortable with it. The malamute didn't return the compliment, but Slocum noted that the dog set himself to take a rush: chest forward, rear feet apart, forepaws flat.

When the miners weren't talking about the fight, they were talking about Heinze. Apparently F. Augustus Heinze was a man to be reckoned with in Butte City. Slocum didn't care and didn't listen very closely to the talk about the man he'd rescued until the talk got ugly and the words "necktie party" came up. That perked up Slocum's attention.

From what Slocum overheard and pieced together, he guessed that Heinze was an independent mine owner and that his mine was called the Minnie Healy. Since every other mine on the Butte Hill was owned by the Amalgamated Copper Company, Heinze's position was unique. And dangerous. Men spoke of Heinze's judges, so apparently he owned him a few. Others spoke of high-grading and the Apex Law. Slocum couldn't make much sense out of that but understood that somehow Heinze was stealing the Amalgamated ore and that an obscure mining law was involved. The legal battle was being fought in the territorial capital, where neither Heinze nor the Amalgamated had a clear majority of judges. Each side, however, had enough judges to slap an injunction on the other. And when Heinze received an injunction against mining any more ore out of the Minnie Healy, he'd responded with an injunction of his own. Two could play that game.

So just this very morning, the paymasters of the Amalgamated Copper Company had paid off the five thousand miners working for them with the words: "This is the last payday you'll know in Butte City. That damn Heinze has closed us down and thrown you all out of work."

Most of the miners were mad as hell. There was plenty of angry talk in every saloon, and men who'd never been known to travel "heeled" had suspicious-looking bulges under their coats.

One of the real big talkers was a man Slocum recognized. He was a big Irishman who wore a wide soiled bandage around his head. Slocum heard him called "Harrington," confirming that he was one of the deputies who'd chased Heinze and Slocum through Chinatown. He kept his face turned away from the man, though he didn't think Harrington had seen enough of him to recognize him.

"The hell with you, Harrington," a miner called out. "You want to lynch Heinze, do it yourself. You're nothing but a damn Pinkerton anyway."

"I say the son of a bitch should dance at the end of the rope," Harrington retorted.

Further conversation stopped when both dog handlers released their animals.

The Alsatian advanced slowly to the center of the ring, low slung, the hair bristling from his neck to the base of his tail and his lips drawn back in a grimace. The malamute didn't move.

One drunk complained, "Hey, what kind of dogfight is this? I don't see no fight!" Soberer men knew the two dogs were just sizing each other up.

When the Alsatian held the center of the ring, he stopped, dead still, and once more gave forth his low, dangerous growl. Slocum leaned against the low wooden barrier, pressed from behind by every manjack who wanted to get a better look. When someone squeezed him too hard, Slocum used his boot heel on the offending party's foot. That gave him a little breathing space.

Slowly, the malamute stepped forward, oddly delicate, always on balance. Slowly, presenting his muzzle to the other dog, he circled the Alsatian; once, twice, three times.

Maybe the Alsatian was a little dizzy. For sure, when he did make his move, he didn't connect the way he'd intended. The Alsatian spun, a trifle faster than the malamute and jumped at him. If the Alsatian had collided dead on with the smaller dog, the malamute would have been thrown, perhaps rolled over on the floor, belly exposed to the kill.

But the white dog simply dropped down a little lower and used his shoulder to break the rush of the other dog, who glanced off him like a badly placed billiard shot. It was too quick for most men's eyes to follow, but John Slocum saw that malamute extend his sharp muzzle and rake the other dog's shoulder as he went rushing by. The Alsatian's muzzle got nothing but air.

But the Alsatian was very fast and came around (almost as if his body were reversing itself) even as he rushed by. He hit the malamute before the white dog could turn to meet the threat. The Alsatian smashed into the malamute's side and his teeth seized at the white dog's throat, counting on a quick kill.

But the heavy mat of fur around the malamute's throat prevented any such conclusion, and the Alsatian got nothing more than a mouthful of fur as he bore the smaller dog over. The malamute tried to twist his jaw to get a piece of the Alsatian, but the larger dog was already past him, over him, had rolled him over by that grip on the top of his neck.

The Alsatian set his jaws and heaved. Perhaps he hoped to jerk the malamute into the air and snap his neck, but the white dog was too heavy and a little too quick. The scalpellike teeth of the malamute slashed at the other dog's nose, again, again. And the Alsatian released him.

Before the Alsatian could make up his mind what to do next, the malamute was head on again, muzzle protruding out of a mass of protective fur, broad shoulders set to take the next fast rush.

For a time, they circled each other. So far the only damage was to the malamute's pride and to the Alsatian's snout, which bled drops of dark blood onto Walker's floor.

Now the malamute was an even odds bet with the Alsatian. The Alsatian's owner was screaming at his dog, "Tear the bastard apart!"

Still the two dogs circled, warily. Apparently, neither had any illusions this was going to be an easy fight.

A man near Slocum said, "I heard that malamute fought thirty fights in Canada."

That made Slocum's hundred-dollar bet feel a little better.

This time, not even Slocum's quick eyes could tell which dog had moved first. The Alsatian and the malamute became, suddenly, a tangled mass of snarling snapping dog. Each was trying to get a grip on the other's throat or, failing that, the other's soft underbelly.

Then the Alsatian made one mistake. Forgetting the thick ruff of protective fur, he went for the malamute's throat. The other dog let himself be bowled over, let himself be shaken, and when his jaws came around he closed them on the Alsatian's leg, clamping down until he hit bone.

The Alsatian hung onto the malamute's ruff like grim death, but the sharp snoot was snapping at his side now. The blood came so that each time the malamute whirled around, it spattered the by-standers and the room stank with the rich, hot odor. And that smell made the malamute crazy. Though the strain on his ruff made his eyes bulge, he dug that little muzzle into the other dog's flanks, where the kidneys are. One, two, three deep bites and the Alsatian turned loose of the ruff and tried to face the white dog again, but it wasn't any use. As the stuff poured out of him, the malamute circled him, and when the Alsatian's bag leg trembled, the malamute was on him again, fast as a striking snake. He knocked the larger dog off his feet and, when he went down, followed him. One quick snap at the brown dog's throat. Even John Slocum closed his eyes when the malamute's jaws closed on the Alsatian's throat.

Both handlers vaulted into the ring. The Alsatian's handler was shouting for somebody to pull "that damn wolf" off his dog, although, by now, it didn't make any difference. The malamute was still worrying his dying enemy and eyed the Alsatian's handler with the same concentration he'd used on the Alsatian. The handler made a grab for his coat and came out with a little stubby bulldog pistol. "If that dog goes for me, I'll be the last one he goes for," he snarled.

But now the malamute's owner was beside the dog,

down on one knee, arm around his neck. Slocum was reminded of the way two pack wolves get side by side to defend each other. The man whispered to his dog and the malamute gave him a little shake of his bushy tail before limping after his master.

Slocum caught up with the man who'd bet him at the door. Slocum was one of the first creditors to reach him, but he was already crying poverty. The man said he didn't have enough to pay everybody. Slocum didn't care, as long as he got his.

Maybe it was the stink of dog's blood in the air, but when the bandaged Pinkerton started yelling, "We've all been cheated out of our work. Let's go tell that damn Heinze a thing or two," a growl went up from the crowd in Walker's Saloon.

Another stooge chimed in, "Let's get the bastard," and that was that. Slocum was borne along in the crowd of men, crushed so tight he barely had room to get his hands in his pockets. He kept his hands on his money. He'd seen a couple of dips working the unwary.

Other Pinkertons had been talking it up in other saloons along Park Street. When the Walker's bunch started up the Hill to Heinze's house, other men poured out of the 1,2,3, the Board of Trade, and the Bucket of Blood.

Slocum hadn't seen so many angry men together for one purpose since the gathering of the Sioux tribes in '77. Many of them carried short clubs and pipes. A few slung rifles under their arms. Most of them carried shortguns under their coats, and a couple of men had lumpy bundles under their arms that had to be dynamite.

The Pinkertons were orchestrating the whole thing. Slocum saw three other faces from the abortive raid on the doss house, and every one of the Pinks was urging the rope for Heinze.

"He threw five thousand honest miners out of work."

"He's a damn cheat."

"He's takin' bread out of every man's pocket and fattenin' his own purse with it."

Heinze's mansion was a low, wide affair. With its portico and second-story porch, it reminded Slocum of the mansions the Yankees had burned when Sherman marched from Georgia to the sea. Heinze's home was lower than most of the millionaires' mansions in Butte City, but it had the usual squares of stained-glass windows set high in the walls, and the usual gingerbread decorations dangling along the porch rail and forming the roofpeaks.

"Let's burn the bastard out of there."

A high iron fence surrounded the mansion. The yard behind it was cobblestoned. The first man to reach the gate shoved the latch and it sprang right open. Clearly, Heinze hadn't been expecting any trouble.

For some reason, the men paused before stepping up on the porch. The rear of the crowd pressed against the front and compressed it.

"Come on out, you son of a bitch!"

"Let's see your face, you damn highwayman."

As cool as a cucumber, F. Augustus Heinze stepped out onto his second story porch and examined the mob. He wore the rough denim trousers and work shirt of a working miner and the checked wool jacket favored by many workingmen. His shoes were work shoes, laced up tight and muddy. He leaned on the porch railing, surveying the crowd like a man watching a Fourth of July parade.

The bandaged Pinkerton was very near Slocum. He cupped his hands to shout, "Come down from there, you gutless son-of-a-bitch!"

Behind Heinze a woman's face was pressed against a window. She had red hair and pale, pale skin. Slocum thought he'd like to get a slightly closer look at her sometime.

Heinze raised his long arms, like a boxer declaring his triumph. "I'm glad you came," he shouted.

"I'll bet you are!" the Pinkerton shouted back.

A few men laughed, and this eased the mood a bit. If they'd gone right in the front door, no doubt they would have strung Heinze up from his own porch railing. Slocum had seen lynch mobs before. But now their essential sense of fairness insisted they give the man a chance to speak. A few of the Pinkertons kept shouting, "Get the son of a bitch," but at first a few, then more, miners outshouted them: "Let him talk. He's got a right to tell his side of it."

Heinze lowered his arms slowly, and as they came down, the men quieted. For a long moment he said nothing. Then he said, "I hear the bastards gave you your walking papers." And then he laughed.

Slocum had to admire that laugh, because in the mood the miners were in, that laugh could have gone either way for the confident man on the balcony.

"Well, they're tryin' to give me my walkin' papers, too!" he shouted. "Damn Amalgamated Copper anyway! They want every damn dime that comes out of this Hill, no matter who breaks his back to dig the ore out. And you know where all that money goes?"

Slocum was kind of enjoying himself, so he shouted, "Where?" playing Heinze's stooge.

Heinze's finger shot out. "Right back to New York and the pockets of J. P. Morgan. That's where it goes. And while you men are heavin' muck for two dollars a day, they're drivin' around in hansom cabs and buyin' up half the museums in Europe. You know me. You know I pay fair wages. You know I never wanted to throw anybody out of work. Hell, the Minnie Healy isn't doing anybody any good shut down."

Slocum had an eye on the nearby Pinkerton, and when somebody slipped through the crowd and handed the Pink the little bundle, Slocum moved up on his blind side.

The bundle was eight sticks of twenty percent, capped and fused. A few men near the Pinkerton drew back from him. Slocum eased in closer.

Heinze raised his arms again. "I've got work," he said. "I've got enough ore at my smelter to keep men working for a month or longer if the damn judges don't turn me loose. And I'll need good men to smelt the ore and get it to the railhead. How many of you want to go to work tomorrow morning?"

The miners raised a cheer. Tentative at first, once it picked up steam, it was something to hear. The Pinkerton struck a match and touched it to the dynamite fuse. Slocum pushed his Colt .44 into the man's side. "I wouldn't do anything sudden, if I was you," he said in a soft voice. With the pistol half concealed by his coat, nobody nearby spotted the move, but Heinze's eyes flickered onto the man, his deadly package, and Slocum. With his free hand, Slocum tipped his hat.

The fuse was about six inches long and looked to be a five-second fuse: that is, five seconds per inch. Slocum was having a real good time. The Pinkerton was frozen in place, the dynamite bundle sputtering in his arms. "My God," he said in a voice like a prayer.

"He's in St. Louis," Slocum said cheerfully. "Can't help you here."

"I pay three dollars a day for honest work," Heinze shouted. "And you all know the Minnie Healy's a good mine to work and nobody gets hurt at my smelter!"

This time, the cheer that went up was even louder. Though the miners must have known Heinze, with only one operating smelter, couldn't hire them all, he had given them some hope, and what he'd said was true: He was better to work for than Amalgamated.

Inexorably, the dynamite fuse sputtered along. Little spurts of smoke came off the fuse as it marched toward the caps. The Pinkerton had a Colt .44 grinding into his ribs and death in his hands, and he stared at his bundle as if it were a coil of rattlesnakes he'd picked up by mistake. "Please," he said.

"Hell," Slocum said cheerfully, "you still got a few seconds to say your prayers."

Though Heinze was saying something about "the Amalgamated," he had one eye on the smoking bundle, too—probably wondering if it was going to land in his lap when the fuse got short.

An awful stench suddenly struck Slocum's nose and he realized that the Pinkerton had fouled himself. It was that stink as much as anything else that made him reach out and pinch the fuse, just three inches and fifteen seconds from an explosion that would have reduced the Pinkerton and him into scraps for the ragman.

The man's eyes stayed bugged out, still staring at the bundle, as if it might yet kill him. Slocum shrugged and stepped away. The man smelled too bad for company, and he was harmless now anyway.

Slocum slipped his Colt back under his jacket and only Heinze saw the flicker of metal as the gun disappeared.

Heinze's voice was booming now. "Now, I'd hate to say anything against the Amalgamated Copper Company"—he paused for the chorus of hoots and jeers—"but ain't they the devils to deal with?" He let his pointing finger rove over the crowd, and it seemed to each man like Heinze was speaking to him, particular. "It isn't that they cheat you," he said, and the irony never left his voice. "It's that you let 'em do it. They cheated you yesterday. And tomorrow, when they come to cheat you again, you'll just say, 'Yes sir' and 'No sir' and 'Can I please get me a rustling card?' "

(The Amalgamated issued rustling cards to applicants at its main office over the company store. These cards were given only to men who didn't look like troublemakers—not to aliens, or Jews, or men who didn't have their hats in their hands. With the card, a miner could apply for a job at Amalgamated Copper's hundred mines. Without it, he couldn't find work—unless Heinze hired him.)

This time, the noise of the crowd was a roar, like an angry, wounded predator. A few men waved their arms around. Some of those arms had pistols in them. Slocum slipped back through the crowd—no easy feat against the crush of men who wanted to hear every word that dropped from Heinze's lips.

Heinze made a gesture of mock disgust. "All right, all of you. Get out of here." He aimed his finger at the cobblestones outside his mansion and said, very loudly and very distinctly, "You bastards are trampling my prize rose bushes."

And this time, when the crowd roared, it was laughter and a cheer all at once. Slocum had reached the rear of the crowd when, once more, he found himself at the head of it. The crowd was flowing again, away from Heinze's mansion, and Slocum was in the van. A few runners broke from the crowd, tearing hell for leather down the street.

"Stop 'em, they're Pinks," somebody shouted, and soon the whole crowd was running after the Pinkertons and it was worth a man's life if he slipped and fell under those thousands of boots.

The Pinkertons had a little lead, but some of the younger miners were pretty quick, too, and were gaining fast, their arms windmilling for more speed and their heads thrown back, sucking in the oxygen.

The Pinkertons were running for their lives, and they knew only one place in Butte City that'd surely give them refuge: the offices of the Amalgamated Copper Company.

These offices were at the corner of Granite Street and Main, about halfway up the hill. There wasn't anything fancy about them. The Amalgamated offices took up the second story of a long brick building above the company store. Here men could exchange their pay vouchers for dry goods, groceries, meats, Bib overalls, carbide for their lamps, and, as the sign outside advertised, "a hundred other necessaries, great and small."

The store was painted a peculiar shade of flat white, and the miners, in jest, had started calling it and the company offices "the White House."

A single staircase at the right of the store led upstairs to the company offices. You wouldn't find the company president there. He was J. P. Morgan, and he lived in New York. But the mine superintendents were there and the accountants and the security men the company hired to keep order in its vast, far-flung Montana properties.

The Pinks darted up that staircase two and three steps at a time. The nearest miner made a dive for the heels of the last of them but just missed.

Upstairs, the Butte City Superintendent of the Amalgamated heard the trouble coming before he saw it. His name was Kelly, Marcus Kelly. Kelly had the clear, bland complexion of a young Irish tenor, the brows of a hawk, the manners of the mucker he'd been for years, and the guts of a Texas warthog protecting its brood.

He stood at the big windows overlooking Granite Street, his hands folded behind his back, and swore, "Those fucking crazy paddies. Those fucking crazy paddies. Goddamn it! Break out the Winchesters!"

When his chief clerk handed him the rifle, Kelly smashed the window out with the gunbutt as if it were a silly, useless encumbrance.

Slocum had been in too many wars to get dragged into another man's fight, willy nilly. Hell, he'd sided with Heinze once—twice—but now that was just the luck of the draw. He was just an interested bystander.

Even before the pursuing miners made their last grasp at the Pinkertons, Slocum peeled off at a convenient saloon. It was three o'clock in a hot afternoon and he wanted a beer. The bartender was at the door watching the men run by. His neck was craned trying to make out what was happening at the head of the mob. Without a word, Slocum stepped behind the bar and drew himself a schooner of beer, holding the glass at a very slight angle so the head wouldn't be too high. He put a nickel on the bar and came over to stand beside the bartender.

Nobody could ever say Marcus Kelly lacked courage. With only forty employees, mostly clerks, he waited until the mob of five thousand cheering men were almost on the sidewalk in front of the company store before he curtly ordered, "Fire."

Forty Winchesters spoke. Footsteps pounded up the narrow stairs as the hard-breathing Pinkertons gasped and wheezed their way into the offices.

As packed up as the miners were, those Winchesters did more damage than a charge of grapeshot. It didn't require a marksman: just someone willing to lever another shell into the chamber and touch it off, lever, and fire until the hammer fell with a click on empty metal.

The first volley dropped ten men dead and wounded fifty more, the bullets passing through one miner's flesh to rest in the flesh of the man just behind him.

The Winchesters spoke again, again, again. And despite the pressure of the crowd behind them, men were diving for cover in doorways or behind the fallen bodies of their friends, and a few were swimming against the tide of men that threatened to trample them into the bricks of the bloody street.

The weary Pinkertons joined Kelly at the window and emptied their own revolvers at the miners. Without a word—without removing the cigar from his mouth—Kelly cuffed the nearest Pinkerton. With one ham-handed blow, he laid the man out. "This is how you hang Heinze?" he snarled. "This is how you follow instructions?"

Then he threw the Winchester back to his shoulder to tag a miner named Frank Burke he'd known years ago when Burke was a powderman at the Neversweat. Kelly had never liked Burke anyway and figured he might as well make his shots count.

Some of the armed miners were firing back now. Pocks of dust jumped from the boards of the company building. The clerks downstairs in the company store decided that discretion was the better part of valor and scurried out the back.

Just as well. The miners' bullets focused briefly on the company store—probably because the glass was unbroken. Bullets seemed to concentrate naturally on a female mannequin wearing what Butte City considered to be the height of Eastern fashion. Several bullets destroyed her flamboyant black hat, and more than a few slugs smashed her bosom and trunk into plaster dust. The bullets broke the mannequin in two and the trunk sagged over, held together only by the rags of her once glamorous clothing.

The saloon Slocum had chosen was two hundred yards from the company office, and as soon as he saw Kelly's gunbutt smash through the window, he stepped back and drew himself another beer. He was too old to get shot by accident. It wouldn't be so bad getting shot intentionally, but an accidental shooting would be awful embarrassing. He sat on the bar with his schooner of beer as the miners met Kelly's first volley. Men dove through the door—one bowling the saloonkeeper off his feet in his hurry to put something between him and the bullets. One or two pulled stubby pistols out of their coats, pointed their popguns around the corner of the door, and popped away.

Slocum sipped at his beer. It was pretty good beer, too. He'd rarely had better.

The crack of the Winchesters. The sputtering barrage of the miners' six-guns.

Seeing Slocum sitting on the bar, idly swinging his heels, an angry red-faced miner confronted him. "How come you're not helpin' out, man?" he demanded. "Maybe you're one of those Pinkertons."

"Nope." The dark-haired man smiled and there was laughter in his green eyes.

"Well, why you sittin' there havin' a beer?"

"It ain't my party." And there was something in his flat voice and something more in the flicker in his funny green eyes that backed the miner off, though he was angry enough to chew nails and had seen two of his friends cut down by the Amalgamated's Winchesters.

Pretty soon it was a sharpshooting contest between two ill-equipped armies. Generally, the Amalgamated had the best of it. Their Winchesters had the range and the Pinkertons up there had some skill, at least. The miners who stuck their heads out for an aimed shot heard the nasty snap of lead beside their ear, and the ones who stuck their pocket pistols out and fired away blindly didn't hit anything.

The florid-faced miner stepped back from the doorway, cursing and rubbing at his head where a splinter had gashed his forehead. His blood was very bright red, almost iridescent, and it gushed like the splinter had cut an artery. Slocum wondered where all the blood came from. He'd never seen a man hurt so little who bled so much.

Slocum's beer was gone. He swiveled around on the bar and drew himself another one. Feeling mildly hospitable, he drew one for the wounded miner, too.

The miner was ashamed of having said Slocum was a Pinkerton. "Jesus," he said. "They're cutting us to pieces out there. Those murdering bastards."

Slocum didn't mention that the miners hadn't come down the street to politely exchange views. He contented himself with a nod.

"It's those rifles. Hell, we'll never get near the place." The miner was dripping blood into his beer, and Slocum looked down at his own schooner and suddenly wasn't very thirsty anymore.

It was the look of that beer as much as anything else that made him speak. "Now, if a bunch of you boys was to get around the side of the building with a little dynamite . . ." he mused.

The Butte City miners weren't any great shakes as gunmen, but every manjack had used dynamite a time or two, and Slocum's quiet suggestion took hold at once. The bloody-headed miner grabbed a couple of the men at the door, explained the idea, and in a moment, half the saloon poured out the back where an alley would take them alongside the Amalgamated Building. Slocum crossed and uncrossed his legs. The saloonkeeper shook his head at him. "You're a cool one, aren't you," he said.

Slocum just smiled.

When the miners' fire slackened off, Kelly believed he'd won the fight. His Pinkerton riflemen were still keeping the street clear of miners, and minutes ago, they'd finished the last miserable son of a bitch who'd tried to take refuge behind another man's body. The bullets hit the man, passed through him, and cracked the bricks in the street so when the body bounced, it looked as if it were lifted on a cloud of brick dust.

Kelly could count fifteen men out there, and damn sure, every single one of them was dead. Maybe a couple of others his men had wounded would die, too. Cost? Bullet pocks in the façade of the Amalgamated building and new glass in all the windows. Old J.P. wouldn't be too happy about the shooting, but, hell, they'd weathered worse. Morgan'd get the reporters to write about an angry, drunken, armed mob who attempted to smash company property and order a couple of his pet senators to angrily deplore the same mob.

Kelly leaned his rifle against the wall and turned to Harrington, leader of the men he'd sent to get Heinze. "Okay," he said. "You didn't do it. How come you didn't do it?" Then he noticed the smell. "Christ!" he said. "You stink. How the hell . . ." Kelly pushed the man away from him.

Kelly's riflemen weren't finding many targets out in the street, and the return fire was no more dangerous than the pop of firecrackers on the Fourth of July.

"It was that lanky, black-haired fellow. I had the dynamite all ready to throw when he stuck a gun in my ribs. I told you about him. He's the same one who got Heinze out of the doss house. I seen him there."

"He Heinze's bodyguard? That don't seem like his style. He never had a bodyguard before."

"Well," the Pinkerton said, "it looks like he's got one now."

"Until you kill him," Kelly said. He spoke as if he was already thinking of other matters.

"Until I kill him." The Pinkerton's face broke into a smile.

Outside, the miners were arguing. They'd rounded up thirty sticks of twenty percent and they had plenty of fuse for whatever they might desire, but there were too many experts. Some wanted to plant a huge charge in the center of the building. Others wanted to toss the stuff up on the roof and drop the ceiling. Finally, one old powderman was elected to do the job. To a stranger, his appearance might not have occasioned very much confidence: His right arm was gone and he was missing three fingers on his left hand. But the miners knew he could do the job if anybody could.

He placed the sticks of dynamite thirty-two inches apart on the ground. The wall studs would be sixteen-on-center, and this much dynamite would cut the wall like a knife—cut it and crumple it. He asked the others to pack mud on the sticks of dynamite while he fused them. The mud would direct the force against the building.

Marcus Kelly was getting worried. The miners were too quiet. Had they broken into a hardware store for rifles of their own? Were they coming around back? Did they intend to fire the place? . . . Dynamite?

The instant Kelly's mind formed the word, he knew the answer. It was what he would have done, and he knew plenty of men thought the same way he did.

Most of the clerks had retired from the windows, replaced by the more accurate Pinkertons. Amalgamated's clerks and accountants were a pretty rare commodity in the territory. Every one of them had been hand-picked by Morgan's office manager and sent west. Miners were plentiful in Butte City, but a first-rate bookkeeper was worth his weight in gold. They stood around in their shirt sleeves having a smoke. Some of them had killed a man or two that day and were regaling the others with details. Kelly clapped one man on the back. "You boys done a fine job here this afternoon," he said. "I think you better go home now. Hell, take the rest of the day off—with pay."

The clerks didn't really want to leave, until Kelly reminded them they could tell their stories of heroism and derring-do more comfortably at Walker's over a tall whiskey. He told them to use the back stairs, and they did.

Kelly counted the Pinkertons at the windows. Eight. They were a pretty sharp bunch, all right, but hell, the Pinkerton agency could have a dozen more of them in Butte City in four days from Denver, or three days from Salt Lake. The Pinkertons were shooting whenever a miner shoved a pistol into view, which wasn't that often.

Kelly walked down the back stairs himself. He

would have taken Harrington with him, but the man smelled too damn bad.

The thirty-two sticks of dynamite cut the wall out of the Amalgamated building. Hurling debris in front of the blast, it smashed most of the internal walls of the company store, depriving the upper floors of whatever support those walls provided.

With the wall gone, the roof lifted from the blast, then slid downward into the street, pulling the other outside walls with it.

The blast didn't totally destroy the Amalgamated building. When photographers came the next day for the newspapers, the north wall was still standing (at least one story of it).

It took volunteers the better part of the afternoon and night to drag the eight bodies out of the wrecked building. Many of the bodies were dead from the crushing weight of the beams. One or two had blood splotches at their ears, eyes, and mouth. The concussion had killed them. Two had been standing in an upstairs doorway when the blast went off and they got the full benefit of the building's wooden construction. The splinters from a hundred shattered timbers impaled them and shredded them as easily as a housewife shreds cabbage.

4

On a Thursday night, Slocum sat in the parlor of Irish World, inspecting the merchandise. He'd been shown in by the same Indian girl who'd brought him his whiskey the last time. Slocum understood the first rule about whorehouses: never on Saturday night. On Saturday, the girls were hurried and careless. On Saturday night, drunks scuffed up the parlor floors and picked unnecessary fights with other men who weren't sure which kind of gun the occasion demanded.

Slocum had been sitting in that parlor almost an hour and was sipping his second glass of whiskey. One at a time, the girls had come down the stairs to join him, hoping to drum up a little trade.

The girls wore variations on the standard whorehouse costume: a loose-fitting kimonolike dress with nothing underneath except their charms. They'd lean over near Slocum so their pink-tipped breasts would peek out at him. They'd cross their legs so the silk fabric drew away from their delicate thighs. One or two of them let their hands stray to rest on Slocum's leg. One casually let her hand trace the outline of his cock. Though it was a practiced technique, she involuntarily drew in her breath sharply. Slocum grinned at her.

For a moment, the girl, a pretty brunette, lost her whore's charms. "Mister," she said quite seriously, "you could likely wreck a girl with that."

"Oh," Slocum smiled back at her, "I don't get too many complaints."

Of the girls he'd seen, he liked the brunette best.

She had a good slender figure and, underneath her manner, Slocum suspected her motor was powerful and ready to go. But he wanted to see all Blondetta's stock. The night was young.

Still, she was a good-looking filly, and Slocum marked her name in his mind as she swayed out of the door. Her hips gave a little twitch as she left, and Slocum shook his head admiringly.

He got up and wandered around the room, inspecting the pictures as he waited for the next girl. A few reproductions of Remington's Western paintings; a couple of oil originals—one over the fireplace—of nude women whose proportions spoke more for the artist's lust than his eye for detail. Slocum was inspecting a simple pen-and-ink sketch when Blondetta came in behind him. The sketch was a simple thing: a cowboy trying to haul an old mossbacked longhorn out of a coulee; but to Slocum's eye, it was subtly right. The strain on the cowboy's horse, the fear and power of the longhorn. The cowboy, hauling with all his weight but ready to abandon his saddle in a moment if the longhorn came at him. A little signature on the bottom read "C. M. Russell."

As Blondetta approached, he turned. "I like that," he said simply.

"Uh-huh." Blondetta's expression was neither here nor there. A faint tinge of anger was in her eyes. She dismissed the picture with a wave. "He came in last winter. A cowboy. No money for a drink. No money for a girl. He said he'd draw himself a girl and a drink. He stayed here three days and must have pronged every girl at least once. I don't know why I let him do it. That was the drawing he made. A couple sports have wanted to buy it, but once I told 'em what it cost me in girls and booze, they weren't so interested anymore."

Tonight Blondetta wore a subdued, almost matronly dress. The fabric was velvet and the color was a dark purple, almost blue. There was no lace at her sleeves, and a simple gold lady's watch dangled at her throat. "You've been here quite a while, friend," she observed.

"Yeah," Slocum drawled. "Just talkin' to the girls gives me pleasure."

And that was true enough. Slocum was one of the fairly rare men who truly enjoy talking to women. He could sit with them, fascinated, for hours at a time.

"Well, this isn't exactly a house of pleasure," Blondetta said. "I'm a businesswoman."

Slocum looked around the room, empty except for the two of them, "For a businesswoman, you don't keep too busy," he noted.

"Friend . . ." Blondetta began warningly.

But Slocum cut her off. "I've seen all the girls then?" he asked.

Something in Blondetta's tiny hesitation gave her "yes" the lie. Slocum gave her a polite smile, making it obvious that he didn't believe her.

Blondetta sighed. "Yeah," she said, "I've got one other girl. Lucy. Some think she's the best of the bunch. But she's busy right now, and she'll be busy for another hour. She has, uh, a special engagement."

Slocum's eyebrows went up. "Special?" He twirled the whiskey around in his glass and held the glass up to the light.

"That's what I said." Blondetta had said all she meant to.

Well, one habit a good madam needs is discretion, and Slocum wouldn't press her on the matter; but his curiosity was piqued.

As he was thinking these thoughts, he got a whiff of the perfume Blondetta wore. It was very delicate, very feminine, and probably very expensive. "You're a mighty handsome woman yourself," he noted.

This wasn't the first time Blondetta's charms had been so appraised, and she had her stock answer: "I don't go with the sports." She had to turn her head to speak to Slocum because he was walking around her —at a respectful distance, to be sure—appraising her.

"No. No. Of course, you don't," he said absently, reducing what she'd said to nothing at all. "Still you are a remarkably handsome woman. You remind me of Lily Langtree. I heard her sing in El Paso once. Of course," he added, "Lily didn't have your eyes."

A blush spread over Blondetta's cheeks, and she wasn't a woman who blushed very often. "You can stop that kind of talk any time now," she said.

Slocum was surprised. "Why? I'm sure that more than a few men have found your charms . . . considerable," he said. "There's nothing like a young girl for freshness, I'd have to admit that. But when it comes down to it, a man wants a woman."

Unaccountably, once more, she blushed. But during her confusion, she was eying Slocum. He wore a neat blue suit, cut by a good tailor. His gold watch chain was fine and thin. He wore no rings. His hair was black as hell, and the laughter in his eyes suggested that he'd been there a time or two. He wore a gun under his coat, inside a pants holster or simply stuck under his belt. Blondetta was something of an expert on what made a man bulge, and this bulge could only be a Colt. He looked like a prosperous tinhorn gambler, except his hands were too weatherbitten for card tricks. He might have been a plainsman, or a scout on the town, but his hair was too carefully trimmed and he had none of the broad expansive gestures that marked an outdoor man in the confines of her parlor. He might have been a rancher, but he was too soft-spoken. Puzzled, Blondetta broke another of her personal rules. "Mister," she said, "just exactly what do you do?"

The mantel clock softly chimed the half hour. Outside, some teamster bellowed to his horses and the sound filtered through Irish World's thick walls.

And damn, the man had a fine smile: wild and carefree as a boy's. "Investments, ma'am," he said. "Risk investments."

Maybe she was embarrassed at having asked the question or maybe she was angry he'd turned it aside so easily, but she snapped, "Well, if you hang around with Heinzy, that's the only kind of investments you'll make. Dead risky."

His raised eyebrows invited her to continue. His hand tugged at the bell rope and when the Indian girl entered his hands flickered signs at her before she was fairly inside the room. She left on his mission, real quick. "Hell," Blondetta said, "how long do you think Amalgamated is going to leave Heinze run loose? They can buy more gunmen and more judges than he can. They've got the Pinks working for them." Her mouth got small and mean to show her opinion of the Pinkertons. "And they're the worst killers in the West."

Slocum flashed his peculiar smile again. "They've murdered a few," he noted mildly. "I've known some of them."

And that was true, he had. And John Slocum's picture—though not his name—was on permanent file at the Pinkerton office in St. Louis.

When the Indian girl returned she bore a tray with a bottle of Monopole and two crystal glasses. Without a glance at her mistress she set the tray on the parlor table. Slocum dipped into his pocket and tossed her ten dollars in gold.

Blondetta said, "What the hell . . ."

"Unless," Slocum said, "you'd rather continue this discussion upstairs."

Gracefully, Blondetta picked up the tray and turned to face the man she'd decided to love. "You bastard," she said. The softness in her voice took all the sting out of the word.

As she preceded the black-haired man up the stairs,

she was wondering just why and how she'd got herself into this. Usually when she felt the need for a man, she picked one of the miners who came in on a Saturday night, and it was always the same. She always dressed more garishly than usual and never told the miner who she was or that she owned the place. Exactly twice a year Blondetta took a lover, and now she was marching toward her own private bedroom with this disturbing man on her heels. And she was blushing like a damn schoolgirl. Once inside, she set the tray down on a table beside her bed and turned angrily. "If you think . . ." she began, pointing her finger at Slocum.

"Ma'am," he said softly, "I try not to think. It slows me down somehow."

Once more caught off balance, she didn't object as he pulled the cork out of the champagne with his strong fingers and poured her a glass. And she didn't object when he clinked his glass to hers.

Blondetta's bedroom was a study in scarlet. Scarlet brocade wallpaper, scarlet velvet settees. Only her bedspread was startlingly white in that red, red room. The light cast a romantic hue over her pale lovely complexion.

Slocum sipped his champagne, thoughtfully. "Do you mind?" he asked, terribly polite. Before she could object, he'd shrugged out of his neat blue coat and folded it neatly over a chair. His ebony gunbutt jutted out from his waistband, and Slocum pulled the gun out, clip holster and all, and laid it on the bedtable. "You know," he said lightly, "that damn thing gets a mite heavy sometimes."

The Colt was angled so a man on the bed could get at it in a hurry. Blondetta noticed that as she noticed that Slocum's chest, in his white cambric shirt, was very broad and his shoulders were wide enough to lay an axe handle across them. She began to feel like a young girl. She liked the feeling.

When she kissed him, she kissed him like that, too, the way a young girl kisses, lips barely apart and tremulous. She tasted the champagne on his lips, tart and exciting.

He unbuttoned her velvet dress, one button at a time, the velvet tickling the palms of his hands as she strained against him, as if she would devour him with her kiss. When the dress was open to the waist, he pulled it aside. A thin, ivory-colored slip, barely concealed her heavy, pink-tipped breasts, and as he kneaded them, the tiny nipples grew hard as diamonds. He tugged at the slip, and she moaned and pulled away from him. "You first," she said, hoarsely. "I want to see you."

He slipped easily out of his shirt and pried his boots off one at a time while the woman watched, her tongue at the corner of her mouth, her eyes dazed.

She gasped involuntarily when she saw the scars on his chest. On his left arm a puckered scar marked the spot where a Yankee bullet had smashed him off his horse. A knife cut across his upper chest ended in a jagged zigzag above his belly. If he hadn't taken that knife away from the man who was trying to kill him, Slocum would have been gutted like a deer. But the knife fighter was long dead now. They'd buried his knife with him.

And when he turned, neat as a cat, to drape his pants over the chair, she saw wide white stripes across his back. She'd never seen anything quite like them, but, then, she'd never seen a man who'd escaped from the cells and whipping posts of Yuma Prison. Not too many ever escaped, and of those who did, most died in the desert.

Blondetta thought about asking him if anybody else had survived the train wreck, but she decided that wasn't very funny. And, besides, he'd turned now to face her; calm, confident of his manhood. She restrained a gasp. The word "stallion" came to mind and she felt a funny weakness deep in the pit of her stomach. Calmly, Slocum poured himself another glass of champagne. "Now you," he said.

Wordlessly, she unhooked the buttons from waist to hem, and the dress fell away from her. She let the straps of her slip fall from her shoulders and it rustled softly to the floor.

She was a full-figured woman with big breasts and generously rounded curves. Her hips were low-slung and her legs near the top of her thighs were almost plump. Her triangle was blond as her hair and full. She was a woman in her prime, and, almost mockingly, Slocum offered her a toast before picking her up and depositing her in the center of the white sheets in the red, red room.

He came into her very quickly. She was wet and ready for him but, even so, she groaned with his size and he let himself slip into her an inch at a time until their hair mingled and their belly sweat ran together. He scooped her full buttocks in his hands and pulled her to him to drive deeper and, right away, she began to come, her muscles squeezing him, milking him, and the ripples running across her belly. Tossing her head from side to side, she put her knuckle into her mouth to hold her cries. She gnawed at that knuckle as her hips convulsed and she bucked against him.

Slocum held still. He was the lance on which she was determined to impale herself. She bucked under him like a colt who'd never been broke, and he simply rode her, as easily as he could. She dropped her hands to her side and grabbed his ass, scratching him hard, digging in her nails.

It seemed that she came for a very long time, though probably it was no more than five minutes before she gasped, "Enough, Jesus, enough." Slocum lay still, feeling her flutters subside along his cock.

"Christ." she said. "I . . . I . . ."

"My pleasure," he said amiably.

In a minute she pushed at him and he withdrew, his

cock hard as bar steel. She admired it for a moment. She gave it a loving pat. She took a long sip of champagne and when her mouth closed on him it was cool and tingly from the champagne bubbles.

Afterward, quite naked, they sat and talked. She told him some stories about the whorehouses up and down the Line, and he told some outrageous lies that kept her giggling. They finished the better part of the bottle of champagne before he mounted her again, this time using her, driving hard against her, having his will. She cried out this time, so loud that the girls down the hall heard her and several of them teased her about it a week or so later.

Slocum washed his hands in the washbasin and slicked his hair back. She lay on the bed, legs still apart, unable to move.

"You tell 'em I'll be down later," she said, her voice slurred.

"Sure," he said, slipping into his pants. When he clipped the holster onto his waistband, she said, "I suppose you know how to use that thing."

Slocum didn't say anything, just smiled.

The upper hallway in Irish World was deeply carpeted, and Slocum's footfalls made very little sound. A man and two women stepped out of the room at the head of the stairs and Slocum advanced noiselessly. The man was familiar. He was walking tiredly, like a man who could do no more. Slocum felt some sympathy. The women flanked him and he had his arms over both sets of shoulders as they made their way downstairs. One of the women was dark-haired, her tresses almost as black as Slocum's. The other, the taller, was a redhead. The man was Heinze.

At the bottom of the stairs, they paused, unsure whether to continue together or not. As they decided to enter the parlor, Slocum called out, "Evening, Augustus."

Heinze's strong-featured face revolved slowly to examine Slocum. His eyes were slightly dazed, as if he'd been smoking opium again. A tentative smile spread across his features. "Evening, Mr. Slocum." He made a gesture that somehow embraced the two women, the whole of Irish World, and the stairway where Slocum was standing. "Didn't know you went in for this sort of thing."

Since Slocum hadn't met many men who didn't, he made no reply.

"Come in," Heinze urged, "I think I owe you another whiskey."

Slocum followed the trio into the parlor. He didn't really need another whiskey, but he wanted to meet Heinze's women.

The black-haired girl had some Mediterranean blood in her. Her eyes were as black as her hair; her skin was swarthy; her expression petulant. Her body held the hint of ripeness, so strong it was almost an animal presence, though it was a quality of her age (she wasn't yet twenty) and already the faintest aura of decay hung about her. Her lips were smudged; her hair was touseled, and a strap from her gown hung loose on her arm. The gown itself seemed to have spent a couple of hard hours, though it looked expensive and was clean enough.. She wiped her forehead while she returned Slocum's blatant inspection, checked the palm of her moist hand, and rubbed it dry on the side of her gown.

"Slocum, meet Lucy," Heinze said briefly. He was tugging on the bell rope like a man who needed a restorative.

Slocum nodded to the girl. She didn't deign to reply in kind but said, "Where the hell's that redskin? I need a damn drink."

"Charming girl." Heinze observed, with just the faintest hint of mockery.

"Yes, charming," the redhead agreed.

The redheaded woman was slightly older, but no more than twenty-five, and she carried herself like a patrician. Her skin was the color of skimmed milk, and just under the skin of her hands and neck the veins were blue. Her eyes were green, like Slocum's, but where his eyes were deep and remote, hers were blank with only a hint of the fires that could be fanned there. Her gown was cut low at the bodice. A deep red fingernail scratch marred the perfect surface of one rounded breast, and Slocum found himself wishing he'd made the scratch. When she caught the movement of his eyes, the woman flushed and pulled her wrap over her shoulders.

The Indian girl brought in the drinks and set them down. Though her eyes never sought Slocum's, before she left her hands flickered in a brief signal only he could read.

Slocum burst into a laugh. Heinze's eyebrows were puzzled.

"She said that Irish World would be a happier place for two days," Slocum said. "While Blondetta recovers."

Heinze's grin matched his own.

Slocum put his eyes on Heinze's women, one at a time. "I'd say you know how to keep yourself busy, Augustus," Slocum noted.

"No fun having money unless you know how to spend it." Heinze's grin was that of a hooky-playing schoolboy. Both women seemed to be too interested in their whiskey to meet Slocum's eye.

Heinze pushed back a lock of curly brown hair from his forehead, which was streaky with dried sweat, and Slocum found himself thinking absently, that Heinze should have washed up before he came downstairs. "I been meaning to thank you again," Heinze said. "Whooee." He downed his whiskey with a single toss and poured himself another. "That damn mob out there clamoring for my ass and me talking just about as fast as I could. Hell, I knew I just couldn't stop yarnin'—not for a minute—and that damn Pinkerton ready to blow me to hell and my house with me."

When Heinze pushed his hand out, Slocum shook it. He didn't want to make anything more of the incident than it merited, but he couldn't very well turn down the mine owner's thanks. "Why don't you introduce me to the lady," Slocum said.

Heinze's eyes flicked briefly from the dark-haired girl to the redhead. "Oh," he said. "Sorry. Miss Clare Scott. Mr. Slocum."

"John," Slocum insisted.

The girl didn't wish to be introduced to a dangerous-looking man in the parlor of a whorehouse, but she couldn't ignore him. "Charmed," she said faintly.

Heinze met Slocum's look and winked. "Oh, yeah," he said, "Clare is quality, no question about it. Why, her fathers came over on the pilgrim boat, or maybe," he paused, "maybe they was here waiting for it."

The girl tossed her head, failing to see the humor.

Heinze's face dropped its mocking pose. "Hell, did you see what that mob did to the Amalgamated? Now, wasn't that a hell of a thing? Half the papers I seen said I incited them to riot. Now, what do you think about that?"

Slocum didn't think much about it. Or care, either.

Heinze said, "It's terrible. Radicals and anarchists, blowing up the office of a 'respectable' company and murdering, too. Did you hear they found eight bodies in the ruins? Clerks, no doubt. Simple wage earners."

"Family men, with babes to support," Slocum finished the joke.

Heinze nodded. Clare was impatient to be gone and tugged at Heinze's sleeve. Lucy said she had to go back upstairs to change.

Heinze's face twisted. "That's my Lucy. Always the businesswoman." Angrily he reached for two double eagles, which he handed to the dark-haired beauty. As soon as she had the money in her hand she said, with a professional lick of the lips, "That's Heinzy. You come back and see me, now."

His nod meant he didn't want to but knew that he would.

When the girl was gone, Heinze helped the redhead into her coat while they waited for a cab. "John," he said as he wrapped his silk muffler around his neck, "I've been meaning to talk to you. I have a little deal that might interest you."

Slocum hadn't been thinking very much about work. When he had money in his pockets, he didn't tend to worry, and when he was low on funds, he simply got some more. But he was curious to see what the mine owner had in mind.

"Why don't you come with us up to my house? I'd prefer to talk private, and there ain't no noisier place to talk than a whorehouse."

The night was dark. The moon only a thin wedge into its first quarter, and the rapidly scudding clouds dispelled what little illumination it could give. Since the smelters and mines were still shut down, the air was clean. Slocum missed the reek of arsenic and sulfur he'd come to think of as Butte City's own smell.

The cab was driven by an enormous fat man who flowed all over the driver's seat. In the night outside Irish World, something was very subtly wrong. Slocum peered at the fat man but didn't know the man's heavy face and long handlebar mustaches. Still, John Slocum had learned not to ignore premonitions. He inspected the street up and down the Line, but since the night was blustery and cold, not many roisterers were about and no one offered any danger to the party boarding the cab. Slocum didn't know why but his hackles were up. He loosened his Colt and unbuttoned his coat before he got in the cab. Apparently Heinze noticed nothing. He was babbling about Lucy's body. At some other time, Slocum might have been interested in Heinze's detailed description of Lucy's intimate charms, but right now he was watching for trouble.

Clare sat between the two men, dead quiet, though she could hardly have enjoyed hearing Heinze describe the other girl's movements and artifices in such glowing terms.

Slocum's nervousness faded as the cab progressed north up the Hill, the horse's hooves clattering on the brick streets.

Though it was spring, there was a deep chill in the air, and after a bit, Clare came out of her solitude. "Have you known Augustus long, Mr. Slocum?"

"Nope."

She smiled a bitter smile. "When I first met him, I thought he was the finest-looking man I'd ever seen. He quite turned my head."

The bitterness from her voice moved into her face and stayed there long after she fell silent.

The cab pulled up in front of Heinze's mansion, where two lamps illuminated the portico. Heinze jumped out to hold the door for Clare, who swept by him as if he didn't exist. Behind her back Heinze permitted himself an ironical grin.

The porch columns were quite massive but were fitted wood, not stone. Sidelights beside the door glowed their inviting glow. A large octagonal lantern hung from chains overhead. The door was heavy paneled walnut—a good four inches thick—and swung back noiselessly to welcome them.

"Evening, Murph," Heinze spoke to the tall elderly Irishman who took his hat, his gold mounted cane, and his scarf.

"Good evening, sir," the man replied in a voice mellow as an old violin.

The entry hall was impressive but bare. Light filtered in from big stained-glass windows during the day, but now only the lamps outside gave them any color. The walls were paneled in burled walnut, arranged in eight-inch squares that rose higher than Slocum's head, their soft colors trapping and casting back the light in a glow. The ceiling was sculptured plaster and a good-sized candle chandelier dangled above their heads. For furniture, there was a ratty wrought-iron hat rack, nothing else.

"Come on," Heinze smiled, "I'll show you the joint."

Clare draped her coat on the hat rack and when it slipped off the hook and slid to the floor, she simply didn't notice it. She wouldn't. "Darling, I've seen the house, several times. I believe I'll have a bath now. I'm filthy." She didn't mean dirty, she meant filthy.

"Sure," Heinze said with his most charming smile. "Maybe we'll join you later."

Her blue eyes were weary and cold. She ran them over Slocum's angular body and face. "Thanks, but no thanks," she said.

John Slocum felt some anger, though he hadn't made the suggestion and wasn't all that interested anyway. "Wash good," he said briefly. "You need it."

With an angry toss of her head she swept out of the hallway and up the main staircase. The staircase was wide enough for four people abreast, or maybe two horses, and she occupied it all, every inch.

Heinze's glance was questioning. "Why do you want to make her mad?" he asked. "Hell, a man doesn't get anything that way."

Slocum's smile was as brief as his speech had been. "If she was my mare, I'd trade her," he said. "I do hate a hardheaded filly."

Heinze shook his head. "Damn fool," he said. Together they strolled into the big dining room. The walls were paneled in cherry, and tiny squares of blue tile framed the shallow fireplace. The fireplace was doing its best, but the ceilings were too high and all the heat went up there instead of staying lower where it could have done some good. Heinze rapped the paneling fondly. "I had this shipped all the way from Connecticut," he boasted. "Cost me a mint. The cabinet-maker who did the work wanted to age the planks in the room for a year before he shaped them. He said that way the wood would never crack or check. I told him I didn't know if I was going to be here in a year and couldn't wait. He was real disappointed."

The woodwork was elaborate, but Slocum had seen finer—plantation houses in the Old South where the wood had been rubbed dark by generations of house slaves. This wood had a century to go before it'd lose its raw, new look.

Like the hallway, the room was almost bare of furniture. For dining there were a couple of cheap wooden tables that looked as if they'd been bought at a restaurant distress sale; they even had a few sets of initials carved into the battered wood. Four chairs, part of some much-abused Grand Rapids set, had dusty, torn cushions, one of them puking its springs. Heinze dragged up a chair and parked himself with his boot on the table.

When Slocum heard a tiny sound behind him, he spun around. He'd been spooky ever since he left Irish World, and there was nothing in this barren house to make him any easier.

It was Murphy, Heinze's man. He had a bottle in one hand and three glasses. His fingers were stuck into the glasses. He set the bottle down and poured Heinze's and Slocum's glasses brimful before he filled his own and withdrew to the far end of the dining room, where he took a seat, his glass cupped in his hands.

Heinze noted Slocum's glance. "Oh, don't worry about Murph," he said. "He's one of the three monkies. He hears no evil."

True. The old manservant was sipping at his whiskey as if it was the only interesting thing in the world.

Slocum moved over by the fireplace. The flames dancing up the chimney in two-foot spears.

"You got a damper on this thing?" he asked.

"Yeah, but if you close it, the chimney smokes. See that black mark over the mantel? Hell, the smoke comes pouring out." Maybe he sensed Slocum's disapproval because Heinze added, "Money doesn't buy everything, you know. Just fun."

"Fun?"

Heinze's boyish grin. "Hell, Slocum, a man's got to have his fun."

Thinking about the two women Heinze had just had, Slocum could understand what he meant. He didn't have to like it to understand it. "You got some sort of deal to talk?" he asked bluntly.

Heinze waved his hand negligently. "Plenty of time. Plenty of time. I want to drink my whiskey, and then I'd like to show you the house. You know, there's a different kind of rare wood in each one of the rooms. And the whole third floor's a ballroom. Parquet floors."

"I've seen houses before," Slocum said flatly.

Heinze put his glass down but didn't lose his smile. "Yes," he said, "but this is my house."

The way he spoke was the way the King of England might have spoken about his palace. Slocum didn't go for it. "I ain't a very patient man," he said. "There's times you got to be patient, when you got to bide your time. I waited once on a ridge in Arizona for three days and never moved a muscle. I was lookin' to kill me a Chirachua. He was pretty good, but he got impatient. So he moved. I guess he thought I'd slipped away somehow. But I don't care to wait on another man's pleasure, and I don't give a damn for this barn of yours."

For a second, the black thunderclouds gathered behind Heinze's eyes, but he laughed. He got up and clasped Slocum's arm. Slocum didn't much care for that either, but he let it pass. "Hell, man," Heinze said exuberantly, "I like you. You know that?"

Slocum shrugged. In the process he managed to dislodge Heinze's hand. "Good," Heinze said, shaking his head as if he were agreeing with something Slocum had said. "Good. Let's go upstairs, to my study. That's where all the real work gets done."

As Slocum followed Heinze out of the cold dining room, he saw that Murphy had lowered the level of his whiskey about a sixteenth of an inch. The man's eyes were closed but the whiskey glass was locked in his hand.

Heinze took the stairs in bounds, like a kid. Slocum followed more slowly. The house was dead quiet, like a tomb. An elaborate grandfather clock stood on the landing, but the pendulum chamber was still filled with the shipper's excelsior. It had never been wound.

Heinze's study was a smaller room and different altogether. Slocum wondered if the reason for the bareness elsewhere was because everything was concentrated in here. The study was in the front of the house and had big French doors leading out onto the balcony where Heinze had faced the mob. The room lacked the fancy paneling that adorned the rest of the house. Furnishings: a couch, covered with cartons of books and papers, a straightback wooden chair, a desk, a swivel chair and bookcases that lined the walls. Some of the glass fronts were opened, some closed. Books in heaps on the floor and piled carelessly on top of more neatly stacked books in the cabinets. Many of the books had German titles. Some were about "Bergwerken" and "Metallurgie." The English books were also about mines and metals, though there were a few law tomes, and several cases were filled with books on stock issues and bonds.

Proudly, Heinze waved his arm at the mess. "My sanctum sanctorum," he said.

Well, it wasn't much for looks, but it was a lot more

comfortable than downstairs, and the floor grate let in enough heat to fight off the chill. Slocum perched on the edge of Heinze's desk and repeated, "Your deal."

Heinze fancied himself a shrewd judge of character —and he wasn't far wrong either—but he liked to spend a little time getting to know a man before he tailored his proposition. "Slocum," he said real seriously, "what do you want out of life?"

Slocum's frayed patience snapped, but his voice stayed mild enough. "I'd like to mind my own business," he said.

Heinze took no offense. His brows were puzzled. "Hell," he said, "a man like you can have most anything he wants, it seems to me."

Slocum laughed.

Heinze's puzzled eyes gazed over his whiskey glass. Slocum had lost his brother and father in the war, along with his home and his way of life. Since then, he'd had perhaps half a dozen real friends (all dead) and as many loves (mostly gone their own way). He remembered his lovely Blackfoot wife and how he'd buried her after the cholera killed her and the baby, too. She'd never been a big woman, but when she died she couldn't have weighed more than eighty pounds. And that's why he laughed. "Sure I can," he said. "I can get anything I want."

Heinze had the good sense to know he was in over his depth. He coughed. He drank his whiskey and rolled it around in his mouth before he swallowed. He uncapped a circular humidor and pulled out two cigars. One he tossed to Slocum; the other he bit with his strong white teeth. "Okay," he said. "Okay."

Heinze eyed the quiet, tall man, trying to make up his mind. He liked the cut of the man, but he sure as hell didn't know him. Oh, well, a man has to take a chance sometime. He gestured behind him where a couple of photographs were hanging. "Take a look," he invited.

Slocum couldn't see much special. One was a stiff photo of a couple, taken fifty years ago, standing ramrod-straight in the tintype. A wedding picture, from the looks of it. The man wore the yarmulke and the woman the formal gown of the Jewish wedding ceremony. Heinze and the man had the same jawline and Slocum figured he was Heinze's father.

The other picture was a photograph of a mine. Not the workings, of course, just the headframe and engine house. It looked like a one-skip operation.

There was something peculiar about the picture. Slocum wasn't a mining man, though he'd done a little prospecting in his day. He'd been part of Bill Fairweather's party when they made their strike at Virginia City, but while Fairweather was making his name and fortune, Slocum was trying to get four very scared prospectors clear of a Sioux hunting band that'd stumbled across them and figured they were easy prey. Slocum had filed a claim late, but it never brought him anything but grief and after he'd gunned three claim jumpers, he'd given up the mining business for good.

The photograph had a cramped appearance, and when Slocum leaned over close, he noticed that the engine house had a funny shape to it. "Hell," he said. "It looks like some inventor made some changes."

Heinze tapped his own chest and grinned. "I did it, friend. I did it all."

Born in New York City, Heinze had been educated as a mining engineer in Heidelberg, Germany. The ore bodies that lay under Butte City's fabulous Hill excited mining men all over the world, and once Heinze had his degree, he traveled due west. He didn't have two nickels to rub together.

His first job was managing the Boston-Montana properties. Instead of a salary, he asked for a percentage. Heinze said he'd manage the mine free if he could keep all the ore that ran under ninety percent pure silver. Since the main ore bodies were running close to ninety-five percent, the owners readily agreed. And as soon as Heinze took over the mine manager's job, the percentage dropped to eighty percent and stayed there.

Heinze shrugged. "Hell, I just added a couple tons of country rock to the high grade. Boston and Montana kicked about it, but they'd made a stupid deal and couldn't wiggle out of it."

With the money he'd made from the venture, F. Augustus Heinze bought himself two territorial judges and a lawyer.

These were the stakes: The famous Hill, which dominated Butte City, was the richest mineral find ever made in the United States. Huge veins of high-grade silver and copper ran beneath its unprepossessing surface, and there was just enough gold mixed in with the silver to pay for all the costs of mining and smelting.

In 1878 they mined 18 million dollars in silver, 27 million in copper and 4 million gold.

And one Eastern-backed company controlled it all: J. P. Morgan's Amalgamated Copper Company.

Originally, the Hill had been a maze of conflicting claims. Some men owned no more than fifty feet; some had several working mines and were millionaires in their own right. One by one, Morgan bought up the claims until, finally, with the purchase of the Alice properties, he owned every claim on the Hill. The Boston-Montana, a small operation, was allowed to operate on the flats east of town, but it was there on sufferance.

Heinze's lawyer had a first-rate mind. The lawyer told him about the Apex Law.

The Apex Law said if a man owned a piece of property where a vein of ore apexed, that man could follow the vein, *no matter where it led*. If it led onto another's claim, well, that was too bad.

Heinze's survey crew reported that there had been one tiny site on the very top of the Hill that hadn't been claimed by anyone. The confusion of claims, and counterclaims—some carefully surveyed, some merely paced off—had created a fifty- by forty-foot section, right in the middle of the Morgan properties that nobody owned.

Heinze claimed it.

He called it the Minnie Healy, after a girl he knew at Blondetta's. By all accounts, she was a pretty thing.

Then he claimed that all the veins on the Hill apexed on the Minnie Healy property. And his two judges agreed with him.

The property was so narrow that his engine room's steam engines were custom-built with vertical rather than horizontal cylinders. There wasn't room for the cylinders to run sideways.

And while the lawyers fought in the territorial courts, F. Augustus Heinze mined ore. Three shifts, twenty-four hours a day.

"The Amalgamated wants to get me," Heinze shrugged. "And they aren't too particular how they do it."

"So," Slocum said, "somebody gave you a license to steal. So what does that have to do with me?"

Heinze leaned back in his creaky swivel chair and eyed the gunman speculatively. "Ever been east?" he asked.

"I was in St. Louis once. I ain't been further than that since the war."

"What do you know about J. P. Morgan?"

Slocum shrugged. "About as much as I want to." He knew that Morgan owned a piece of almost every profitable mine in the West. He knew that Morgan bought, bribed, or simply outgunned the original owners. J. P. Morgan had a reputation in the East as a fine, upstanding man, a patron of the arts and a world-famous collector. Slocum didn't know him this way. He knew him only as a thief.

Heinze made a bridge of his fingers as he talked. "Morgan and Amalgamated. They're the big fish in Butte City. Except for the Minnie Healy, they own every damn piece of decent ground on the Hill. They been taking millions out of here. Millions. They own the governor, the state, hell, for all I know, they own the whole damn country."

"So you're puttin' the squeeze on 'em?"

Heinze grinned. "Yeah. Now, ain't that a hell of a thing?"

Slocum scratched his head. "Don't seem too smart to me."

"Probably not. Probably not." Solemnly, Heinze puffed at his cigar, and his features disappeared behind the thick gray cloud of smoke.

"And it sure ain't smart to spend your afternoons in a doss house and your evenings in Irish World with one woman who'd cut your throat soon as not and another one who'd sharpen the knife for her."

"Oh, hell," Heinze said. "It ain't no fun to fuck 'em when they like it."

Slocum didn't agree. In fact, he'd held the opposite view most of his life. He said so.

"No matter. No matter." Heinze waved the difference away. "I'm goin' to Helena tomorrow afternoon to see if I can get the injunction lifted. The Minnie Healy ain't making me a dime unless it's hauling ore. I've already got two judges out of five. I only need one more. And when I'm operating again, I want to go back to New York City."

"Why?"

"To talk to Morgan. Hell, you don't think I'm stupid enough to buck him forever?"

Slocum didn't think Heinze was stupid. Crazy, maybe.

Heinze dropped all pretense of banter. "Morgan's

man at Amalgamated, Marcus Kelly, left Butte City two days ago, as soon as they blew up his offices. Hell, he didn't even wait around to see the Pinkertons buried. He killed two horses riding to the railhead. He'll meet with Morgan in New York. That's good and it's bad. Good, because I can go up to the territorial capital and get that damn injunction lifted. Bad, because him and Morgan've only got one way to go. They'll have to break me, or kill me. And they've got the money to pretty much do whichever they choose."

Slocum began to see the outlines of Heinze's idea but he waited for the men to spit it out.

Heinze pointed his cigar at Slocum as if it were a pistol. "I need somebody with me. Somebody who can keep the wolves off. That's you."

"Bodyguard?"

"Well . . ." Heinze's brow wrinkled. "If that's all I wanted, I could hire a half-dozen bully boys from the detective agencies. I need somebody who can think."

"You done all right on your own so far."

"I was lucky," Heinze admitted candidly. "Kelly's a fool and Morgan's in New York. If Morgan was here himself, I'd be selling apples on the street corner."

"Or pushin' up daisies."

"Maybe that, too. Look, if I pull this off, if I keep yanking the ore out of the Minnie Healy for another couple months, I'll be a very rich man."

Slocum thought about it. "I don't like to work on salary," he said. "I never did much like workin' for the other man."

Heinze shrugged, very quick, the way a duck shakes water off its back. "It's a wager. If I'm alive in a month, I pay you, say, five thousand in gold. If I'm dead, you don't get a dime."

"Try ten thousand."

They shook hands at $7,500 and Heinze asked

Slocum to meet him at the Minnie Healy in the morning. Slocum might as well get acquainted with the hole in the ground that was going to make them both rich. Then Heinze yelled to his peculiar manservant to bring more whiskey. His voice boomed in that empty house. Slocum didn't want any more booze and said so. Tell the truth, he didn't want any more of F. Augustus Heinze either.

Murph was off doing his master's bidding, so Slocum found his own coat.

Slocum pulled the door behind him. Something almost ripped his head off. He drew and fired four times while diving behind one of the porch pillars.

That's how fast it happened. Slowed down, it went like this: Slocum, left-handed, was pulling the heavy door closed behind him when something set him off. Later Slocum wondered what warned him and decided that it must have been the smell. Likely, the assassin had been on Heinze's porch earlier, perhaps even pressed his ear to the dead quiet door, heard nothing, and slipped back into the darkness, leaving only the disturbed air behind him and the faintest, faintest smell.

Heavy clouds blanketed the narrow moon, so it wasn't movement that altered Slocum—not in that poor light. And though it might have been sound—the rustle of the assassin's clothing, perhaps, as he raised his arm for his throw—the throw itself raced the sound to Slocum's ears and he was moving before the steel star whizzed past him, just near enough to slice the lobe of his ear. At the time, it didn't hurt, not a bit— the steel was so sharp and Slocum was moving so fast—but it hurt later. The lobe of his ear was sliced nearly in two and it hurt like the dickens. But he was already moving when the steel sliced him, otherwise it would have split his face in two, just as it split the four-inch walnut planks of Augustus Heinze's front door.

It must have been the smell that warned him. If Slocum hadn't been lucky, his bones would be moldering in some forgotten grave like so many of his friends'. And Slocum had lived too long with Indians to deny the power of the spirits of the earth. But he didn't think it was a spirit that warned him. He thought it was the faintest scent that commanded his body to move, bypassing the brain altogether.

He turned loose of the heavy door, and his knee crumpled as his right hand stabbed at the edge of his coat. His long fingers found the ebony-handled butt of his banker's Colt. Something, he didn't know what, grazed his cheek and his eyes were seeking a target as he fell forward. His Colt was on the rise and he was desperate for a target. For the better part of twenty years, John Slocum had practiced the simple art of draw and fire so that they'd be one act, not two. By now, his hands didn't understand any other way. Once his hand started for his Colt, the damn thing was going to go off, if he was hit or not, if it was all a mistake. He'd sometimes thought, ironically, it'd still be firing when he was dead, his heart or head shattered by another man's bullet. He'd seen it happen that way. He'd seen more than one man, dead on his feet, still firing back until his brain lost control of his nerves and gave over to the purposeless jerking of a corpse.

His eyes were swinging quickly from side to side in the rapid sweep that picks up the slightest movement, but he saw nothing, nothing at all, and the Colt was on the way.

As his long fingers tugged the butt, the barrel slipped out of the stiff leather pouch he had clipped inside his waistband. His thumb had the hammer drawn back an instant before his finger was inside the trigger guard. The hammer of Slocum's Colt was specially broad and short. It cocked a minisecond quicker than the factory model and his thumb couldn't miss it. When the gun was level, he touched it off. His leg was gone from under him, and he was into a long dive for the nearest cover. The gun flashed while he was in flight, and the gun crash deafened him. Instinctively he'd fired at the spot where the whatever-it-was had come from. His bullet traveled parallel with the ground and about three feet high. The Colt bucked up and to the right, like they all did, and his thumb had the hammer back and his second shot rolled out, same as the first, a little to the left, before he hit the ground behind the heavy white pillar that supported Heinze's porch. He didn't feel anything at the time, but he'd torn hell out of his elbows landing that way, and he ruined a jacket that still had a couple of years' good wear in it.

Because the assassin would be expecting a right-handed gunfighter to poke around the right-hand side of the pillar and fire, Slocum executed a border shift, right to left, and fired a third and fourth time around the left side of the pillar. He'd never thought of himself as any great shakes with the left-hand gun, but he was better than most, and his last two slugs whined along parallel tracks. If the assassin had stayed put after hurling the whatever-it-was, at least one of Slocum's bullets would have taken him in the mid-section, and maybe two.

Slocum didn't fire anymore. The roll of the firing echoed back to him and he knew it'd be just a few seconds before voices were raised and lights came to the windows that overlooked Heinze's mansion. He hoped Heinze had enough blessed sense to stay indoors. Like any rational man, Slocum never carried a bullet under the hammer of his Colt, which meant he only had five and just one left at present. He lay there, his eyes roving the shadows, wishing his vision was night-ready, wishing the son of a bitch would make a move.

The voices. The lights. The sound of someone

pounding toward the front of Heinze's house. "Stay back," Slocum yelled. He guessed he'd yelled loud enough, anyway, because the footsteps stopped coming.

Then his ear started to hurt. He knew he'd been tagged, but it didn't feel too bad. Funny how blood could be cold running down your face. Funny how loud your heartbeat could be. After ten seconds, Slocum eased the hammer down on his Colt, because if he didn't, his hand was going to start to cramp, and he didn't want to give that hand any more bad habits than he could help. He wasn't a natural lefty on the best of occasions.

When a couple of lanterns started coming toward the front of the house, Slocum got up and brushed himself off. He wanted to be damned sure the assassin was gone before he showed himself, so he waited until the lantern light reached the cobbled courtyard. Then he holstered his Colt and stepped easily from behind the pillar.

"Come on out, Augustus," he called. "He's gone."

But when Heinze shoved on his front door, it was stuck and it took both him and Murph to push the heavy door open. The whatever-it-was had forced the wood apart and swelled the door into the doorframe. Slocum drew his Colt again, long enough to punch out four bright cartridges and reload.

Murph had a heavy goosegun in his hands and was waving it around. Slocum took care to step behind him. "Take a look out there," he said. "I don't think I tagged him, but you can look for blood."

Heinze was carrying a nickel-plated pistol in his hands—from the looks of it, one of the new Smith and Wesson Russian .44's. The way he held it didn't inspire Slocum with any confidence. Heinze had his fingers wrapped around the bird's-neck butt as though it was an odd, unfamiliar shape. "What the hell was all the shooting about?"

Slocum didn't answer. He was kneeling beside the walnut door examining the assassin's weapon. He'd never seen anything quite like it.

It was a five-pointed steel star, razor sharp. Eight or ten ounces of fine-honed steel. The tips of the star were blurred slightly circular so it looked as if it was spinning even when it was at rest. Slocum couldn't see all the weapon yet. It would be half an hour before they hacked the splintered door apart to get it out. Now he could only see two tips of the star.

John Slocum had seen most every weapon a man uses on another man, but once he held the heavy steel star in his hand, he had to repress a shudder. He'd never seen anything like this before: not on this earth.

The next morning, just after dawn, John Slocum rode up Anaconda Road, slipping his mountain horse past the ore wagons that rolled down the Hill from the Amalgamated mines on both sides of the narrow road. He passed the Neversweat, the Anaconda, the Stewart, the Black Rock, the Granite Mountain, the Elm Orlu. Though clouds of overheated air billowed out of the airshafts, no steam rose from the tall stacks of the boilers, and the skips and cages hung quietly on the sides of the gallows frames: no work today.

The Minnie Healy looked even smaller than it had in the photo Slocum saw last night. There simply wasn't much to it; just the engine house and the stubby wooden gallows frame, much shorter than most of the gallows frames on the Hill. Most mines had a cluster of support buildings in the mine yard: machine shops, change rooms, an office for the superintendent, and, if room permitted, often a stamp mill to reduce the ore before it traveled off to the smelter.

The Minnie Healy was so spartan that Heinze's superintendent shared a table in the engine room with the engineers. His pay records were always getting lost under the underground maps weighted by the core samples they drilled to guide the turns the tunnel would take.

Now, with the mine shut down, the superintendent was bent over his table with one of his engineers, puffing quietly on a pipe. As Slocum stepped in the door, they eyed him briefly but went back immediately to a discussion of the tunnel at the 1,400 where their core samples said they'd find a rich vein of native silver.

"Mornin' " Slocum said.

The superintendent raised his head again. He was a salt-and-pepper blond, maybe fifty, with tremendous forearms and shoulders. A couple of his teeth had been knocked out, years ago. The hole was a convenient slot for his pipe bit. "Sorry, friend," he said. "We ain't hirin' this mornin'. Whole Hill's shut down."

"Uh-huh. Heinze here yet?"

Now both men eyed him. "You know Mr. Heinze?" the superintendent asked, quietly, wondering if the tall stranger was here on a rough mission.

Slocum flashed his quick, surprising grin. "Don't worry about it, man," he said. "We're in the same army."

The superintendent kept his eyes on Slocum for a fairly long time before he was satisfied. "He ain't here yet," he said. "Find yourself somewhere and take a load off your feet."

"Uh-huh." While he was waiting, Slocum wandered around the engine room. The Minnie Healy had two hoists—one full-sized hoist for the ore skips and a smaller motor to raise and lower the mancage. Both hoist motors were new. Both glistened with the luster of rubbed brass and blacking. Though the main hoist boiler was cold, the mancage hoist hissed quietly and a big Cornishman tossed charcoal into its boiler from time to time.

The engine room was a tall building and would have

been pretty chilly except for the heat from the boilers. The walls were all glass, divided by iron regular fretwork. It was kind of like being in a rectangular cathedral, except all the walls were square panes of glass.

When Heinze came in, he was ebullient. His mobile face was happy and he looked somewhat younger than his thirty years. "Mornin'. Good mornin'," he called out at the door. Then, peeling his gloves off, he stepped briskly over to the table and examined the map. Wordlessly, his trained eyes noted the veins and faults on the 1,400-foot level and he hefted the diamond drill core and held it up to the light. "Wire silver," he said. "How thick is the vein?"

"It's a little hard to tell," the engineer replied. "It's under the Black Rock, you know. We're trying to drive our workface around the tunnels Amalgamated's already got. This core was taken on the workface, about thirty feet in. But they can hear our drilling in the Black Rock and well . . . ."

"So?" Heinze laughed. "All the big veins on the Hill apex at the Minnie Healy and we can follow them anywhere."

The engineer tugged at his collar and peered at the map as if it held a solution. "I've been told . . ." he began. "Hell, all of us have been told."

Heinze's brows furrowed and, like a flash of summer lightning, his grin was suddenly brighter. "Told what?"

"Well . . ." The engineer was mighty uncomfortable, and only Heinze's persistence made him talk. "Probably just saloon talk anyway." He paused and looked up, somewhat defiantly. "Some of the shift bosses at the Black Rock say they've got orders to fight if we start working Black Rock ore."

"Fight? How?"

"I dunno. Steam hoses, maybe. Dynamite. Guns, I suppose."

Heinze snorted a laugh and turned to Slocum. "Hey,

John," he roared. "You ever get in a donneybrook underground?"

"Can't say as I have." But Slocum remembered the huge tunnel the Union sappers had dug under the Confederate lines at Danville.

The Union soldiers were digging toward the lines, and Confederates drove shafts to intercept them. Once in a while they connected, and some of the most murderous battles of the war had been fought under the surface of the earth. The Union sappers got around the Confederates and blew a half-mile of ground—men, guns, trenches, horses, and dugouts—into oblivion. Slocum had never spent any big part of his life underground. He wasn't any damn mole and didn't want to live like one. Perhaps Heinze spotted his discomfort because he said, "Before we go to Helena, John, we'll go down the hole. I'd like to show you what we're up against."

"Yeah. Sure," Slocum said, not very enthusiastically.

When Heinze finished with the mine engineer, he led the way to a corner of the engine house where miners' coveralls were stuffed into baskets dangling from the ceiling. He pulled down a couple of baskets and peeled off his coat. "Man," he said, "you better change if you want to keep those clothes lookin' fit for travel."

So Slocum draped his coat over the bench and pulled on a pair of coveralls. While he changed, Heinze eyed his Colt. Heinze was curious to know how many men John Slocum had killed with that deadly machine, but knew he didn't have the right to ask.

Slocum tugged off his boots and shoved his feet into a pair of heavy gumboots, and once the two of them had put on the miners' helmets and carbide lamps, they looked like any other two muckers going on shift.

The coveralls were crude, caked with dirt and stiff.

Slocum fooled with his carbide lamp until he had the flame right. Up here, in the daylight, you could barely see the dim flame, but down in the hole the light would be bright enough.

The mancage was a simple wooden frame with a steel grate for a floor. The frame members were pine four-by-fours and the sides were open.

Heinze pulled the cage door shut after them. "Pull your elbows inside," he advised. "If you want to keep them." Then he waved at the engine house and cupped his mouth to shout, "Cut the rope," and the two men dropped like a stone.

They didn't lower the mancage, they dropped it, and the gray walls of the shaft rushed by Slocum's eyes in a blur. His stomach rose to his throat and stayed there until the engine man clamped on the cable brakes and Slocum's knees buckled as all the blood rushed from his head.

Heinze laughed as the cage came to a jarring stop. "Gets to you, doesn't it?"

"Yep."

The two men got off onto the fourteen-hundred-foot station platform. A couple of good-sized carbide lamps were stuck into wall crevices in the big room. Here's where they dumped the ore into the ore skips and turned the mule trains around to return to the work-face, half a mile away. The station platform was an underground roundhouse.

Normally, the men rode mancars into the workface, but since the injunction had shut everybody down, Heinze only kept exploration crews working: deepening their tunnels, searching for rich ore pockets, and timbering the most dangerous passes in the tunnel. Nobody was waiting for the two men with a mule-drawn donkey car, so they had to walk.

Many of the mine mules were born underground, living all their lives underground, and some only saw the earth's surface when they were too old or halt to pull the ore cars anymore and were lifted into the blinding sunlight for their last trip, to the glue factory.

The tunnel was well timbered with twelve-by-twelves. Heinze's miners were the best-paid and safest workers on the Hill. Mining is always a dangerous business, but Heinze's men got the best of everything.

They walked beside the tracks, which led deeper and deeper into the tunnel, their carbide lamps hissing and the sounds of their feet in the muck beside the tracks. "How do you get the water out?" Slocum asked. "I didn't see no pump house up aboveground."

Heinze's white grin was a surprise in the grayness. "Don't need one," he said. "I just dig my tunnels a few feet above Amalgamated's tunnels. This fourteen hundred is actually at thirteen ninety-five, and all the water out of the Minnie Healy is lifted up through the Black Rock where the tunnels connect."

Now, that was a nice idea. Couldn't have made the Amalgamated owners too happy, though.

Heinze stopped from time to time to point out a stope—the big rooms, rock-littered, where his miners had taken out pockets of silver or copper or, less frequently, gold. "Took three hundred thousand out of that pocket," he noted. "And another hundred thousand of the prettiest telluride out of this one here. We're under the Elm Orlu now. You should have heard the Amalgamated howl."

The tunnel stopped at the workface. A slab of solid rock with neat circular drill holes bored into the face. Some of those holes were bored for sampling. Others would hold the dynamite charges, which, when exploded, would drive the tunnel further ahead in search of ore.

A slight black seam ran across the face and Heinze pried at it with his penknife. The shavings he handed to Slocum were dark black where they'd oxidized, but the knife cuts showed the bright gleam of pure silver.

"That's the game," Heinze said. "That's what we're here for."

The shavings were cold and heavy in Slocum's hand. They twinkled in the light from his lamp like newly minted coins. He said, "Yeah, Well, that's fine. Now, if you're done with the guided tour . . ."

"You don't like it down here?"

Slocum remembered the close walls of his cell in Yuma prison. The same blank gray walls, day after day after day. "Not much," he said.

5

George Blankenship was a happy, successful man. In his view he owed his success not to superior abilities or his capacity for hard work but to his singular foresight. He knew when to sell and for how much. As he liked to say to his cronies in the Capital Club, "A man's got to know where the wind's blowing. A man can be too greedy."

George wasn't. He was a somewhat cunning, not too scrupulous man who never made an unnecessary enemy and never endangered himself for a friend. He was set up. His wife, Meg, a pale-faced, long-suffering woman, had given him one live child and one dead one before retiring to the back of their ranchhouse where she read the Scriptures, and never bothered with her husband. His daughter, almost twenty now, was, as many had remarked, "the apple of Old George's eye" and "the spit and image of her mother when she was a girl."

George had been a justice of the peace and a territorial legislator, and now he was a judge in the court of appeals. He didn't know much law. He hired a couple of sharp young lawyers to explain the intricacies of tort and possession, consideration, and premeditation. But he understood perfectly well what side his bread was buttered on. He was Amalgamated's man, always had been.

And now, as he sat drinking his whiskey at the Capital Club, he was feeling pretty damn good. It didn't matter which way the Minnie Healy case came down. Heinze could only score a temporary victory if he scored any victory at all. Heinze had been shrewd enough to buy up two of the five judges before anybody, even Amalgamated, dreamed they'd be useful. But when Heinze made his offer to George, George had been smart enough to carry the offer across the street to the Amalgamated for a counteroffer. If they hadn't matched Heinze's money, he might have gone along with Heinze, but George Blankenship was a great respecter of power and Amalgamated had it. Amalgamated had offered George no more than Heinze. They matched his offer to the penny: $20,000 to be our man for a year. George said he was a little disappointed they didn't outbid Heinze, but the Amalgamated lobbyist knew George and just looked at him until he went away.

Now the judges were balanced two for Heinze, two for Amalgamated, and that old fool Judge Adair who said he was going to vote for the right of the matter. George knew that was plumb foolish. He thought the two Heinze judges were backing the wrong horse, but even so, he gave them the grudging respect due from one professional to another. But Judge Adair was a fool, pure and simple.

Amalgamated's lobbyist had been working on Adair for months, and though the price offered the intractable old man was better than double the price George had taken, George felt no particular resentment. He knew that the price goes up when a man won't sell out. Once he does, of course, he's in a different market. He's somewhat shopworn. Heinze had approached Adair, too—circumspectly, of course—but had been rebuffed as well. George figured sooner or later Amalgamated would find a lever to use on the crusty old judge. Once they did, the vote would be three to two, Amalgamated, and the Apex law would become a bizarre piece of legal history and F. Augustus Heinze would own one forty-foot chunk of ground and everything directly underneath it. Hardly enough to continue mining on the scale Heinze enjoyed.

George had a good dinner in the dining room of the Capital Club and was looking forward to a few drinks and maybe a little sociable game of stud later in the evening. If the game didn't materialize, why, then, he'd just go visit his mistress for a few hours of recreation. His bodyguard would be happier with the poker game, of course, because then he could curl up outside the card room and snooze instead of waiting in an unheated cab outside George's mistress's small cottage half the night, but old George didn't give a tinker's damn what his bodyguard thought. The bodyguard was too unimportant to care about.

George Blankenship was a short, fat man who dressed conservatively. As he put it: "A judge has to look like a judge. Otherwise it makes folks uneasy."

His hair was white, his smile benign, his gold watch modest, and his gold toothpick—why, there wasn't anything gaudy about that, either. Sometimes he boasted the gold in that toothpick was gold he'd found himself on his own placer claim. That wasn't true, of course. Once he had his first J. P. job, he'd never dirtied his hands with manual labor, but it never did a man harm to be known as a workingman.

His modest belly bulged at his vest. His shoes were highly shined. Amalgamated had assigned him a bodyguard once the Minnie Healy matter started getting hot. The bodyguard was a Pinkerton named Jim. Jim was no great shakes with a six-gun, though he'd shot a few men. But he was a formidable brawler. Bent nose, heavy, thick legs, and the shoulders of an ape. He didn't like George Blankenship any better than George liked him, but he knew his job.

The Pinkertons paid seventy-five dollars a month, and it was soft work usually. A miner only made two dollars a day, and a cowboy was lucky to get forty a month and found.

Jim wasn't very comfortable in the Capital Club either. He felt out of place. Though he was wearing a neat suit like all the other members, his suit was cheap and it showed. Hell, even the servants in this joint dressed better than him, and they had a way of talking to him and bringing him his drinks that let him know, no mistake, that he didn't belong here—or any place else where gentlemen might be found.

In some ways George enjoyed having a bodyguard. Like his matched team of black Morgans, it was a sign of his stature. From time to time recently, George had been dreaming about the territorial governorship. He was in well with Amalgamated. He knew they wanted a governor with a little more dynamism. But George hoped sooner or later Amalgamated would realize that a dynamic man would pose a risk to them and they couldn't do better than faithful old George. Occasionally, George dreamed of driving up to the governor's mansion and alighting from his hansom on the arms of a beautiful woman. In his dreams, the woman was no one he'd ever seen, but she was quite beautiful and the horses that pulled the hansom were a matched pair of white Clydesdales instead of his black Morgans.

George Blankenship settled down in the cushions of the plush leather chair and belched. He was a happy man.

The other men in the room were as varied as you might expect. They all had money and power—most more than George—but some were ranchers, some politicians, one was the editor of the *Helena Record,* and two or three were railroad men—lobbyists for Jim Hill who wanted to bring his Northern Pacific Railroad through Montana and wanted to be paid damn well for doing it. The legislature had granted him a section of free government land on both sides of his tracks, and when he sold it off to homesteaders, it'd be good for everybody. The state, the railroad,

Jim Hill himself. Since most of the land was bone dry, it wouldn't be so good for the homesteaders, but you can't get the wool unless you shear a sheep.

The room was rather elegant, rather English, and completely Western. The wainscotting was the dark walnut of an Englishman's club on Saville Row, and the deep, cushioned, wingbacked armchairs would have been familiar to the gents who took their port at White's or Claridge's. The fire flickered in a shallow fireplace, and the standard portrait of a notable over the fireplace wouldn't have caused any surprise. Nor would the neat framed prints of Currier and Ives's sailing vessels, which interrupted the space between the boxed-in windows with their tasseled drapes and deep window seats.

But the picture over the fireplace was a portrait of Nelson Miles: the general who'd done more than any other to force Chief Joseph and Sitting Bull into surrender. And facing him, above the entryway, was a silver-mounted set of longhorns with a seven-foot span. A few other animal relics fit in where they could: a buffalo head stared glassily at the head of a huge silver-tip (*"Ursus horribilis"*) grizzly bear. The Rocky Mountain goat and bighorn sheep stayed in the hall because these animals never did have the full stature of the grizzly, the buffalo, or the longhorn. Someone's pick and prospecting pan were fastened beside the fireplace and, beside them, an identifying plaque that was too tarnished to read.

The club's servants wore livery: ruffled white shirt, dark evening dress, bow ties; but they were all old hands put out to pasture—cowboys who limped from one mustang fall too many—miners whose faces were pitted with the black granules of premature explosions. They bought drinks but they wouldn't light a man's cigar unless they knew and respected him. Montana was the frontier still, and many of the servants had come west before the men they served arrived.

Altogether too democratic, George thought, lighting his own cigar.

When Slocum and Heinze came in, they'd been on the trail two days and looked it. Slocum's razor had missed a few patches and Heinze hadn't even tried. His black jaw looked darker and more piratical than usual, and his expensive white linen shirt was soiled at the cuffs. Still, the first clubman who saw him broke into a welcoming grin and George did, too. Hell, he liked Heinze. Everybody did. A man had to admire somebody who'd buck Amalgamated, even if it didn't make sense. Somebody poured Heinze a stiff drink and Heinze handed it right on to Slocum before taking one for himself.

Without making a production out of it, Slocum was examining the faces of the men in that expensive club for any he knew in other times, under other names. When he saw no man he recognized, he relaxed. His hand, which hung somewhat carelessly near his Colt, relaxed too.

A couple of cattle ranchers came over and asked Heinze what was happening in Butte City. These men had nothing to gain, nothing to lose. When it came to the homesteader question they were fierce and implacable foes. They asked about the mine wars for the pleasure men take listening in on other men's quarrels.

Heinze laughed easily enough and launched into his tale. Slocum eased himself out of the circle and found a comfortable corner where he could lean with his back to the wall and learn what he could. He never was much of a man for gossip anyway.

Heinze was telling everybody about the day the miners came to lynch him and turned on the Amalgamated offices instead. He didn't mention that Slocum had saved his life. He spoke of himself with the kind of modesty that implies he was the only entirely human being present. Slocum didn't mind. He'd never wanted his name to be on every man's tongue anyway. Privately, Slocum was playing one of the gunfighter's games: "Who's Dangerous?" There were twenty men in that room, excluding the four dark-clad servants, and about half of them were fairly formidable. Without knowing their names, Slocum hadn't put either George or his bodyguard in the dangerous category. But most of the men in the Capital Club that day were old mossyhorns. Men who'd faced Indians, storms, blizzards, and rustlers to make their fortunes. These were men to be reckoned with. One of them, a tall, white-haired gent, strolled over to Slocum. The old gent had the kind of pale blue eyes that said he'd seen a few things and done some of them himself.

"McCormick's the handle," he introduced himself. "I've seen you somewhere before."

"Not that I recollect." Slocum's drawl was casual, but he was a wanted man and there wasn't anything casual about the thrill that ran down his spine and arms.

"Yes," the old-timer repeated, "you was in Yankton when they hanged Jack McCall. I saw you there."

Since Slocum hadn't done anything that day in Yankton except watch one man hang and shoot another one—nothing illegal—he said, "Oh, yeah, I was there."

"You was one of Hickok's friends," the old man added. "I remember. You and that Texas Jack. Whatever became of him?"

"Got shot."

The old man nodded. "He seemed like the type who would, sooner or later," he said. "But I never heard nothing bad about him," he added carefully. "If you was a friend of his."

It was Slocum's turn to nod, accepting what the old man had said as an apology, though he and Texas

Jack had never been that close and he felt no need to protect the dead man's reputation.

Seeing that Slocum wasn't feeling particularly talk-ative, the old gent joined a table of his cronies where he pointed out Slocum to a couple of other old-timers. "He was a friend of Hickok's," he said.

One of the old gents put on glasses and peered long enough to say, "He's cut from the same bolt of cloth, I reckon."

The old-timers agreed.

Heinze made his way through the club, shaking hands, exchanging stories, laughing, back-patting, gen-erally making his presence known. But when every-body who'd wanted to speak to him had, when his presence was no longer a novelty, when nobody was watching him anymore, he made a brief signal to Slocum and bore down on George Blankenship's chair like a homing torpedo.

"George," he said, smiling, "how's the shiftiest bas-tard in the territory?"

George smiled back. "Oh, hell," he said, "I ain't got that record. Not by a long shot. I get bought, but I stay bought."

Heinze stuck out his hand. "Sure. Never doubted it. Now, you keep your hands away from my pocket watch, hear?"

George snorted his laugh. He stayed deep in the chair and didn't rise to take Heinze's hand.

The bodyguard did stand up, though, and slid around to the side where he could keep an eye on Heinze. He'd heard about him. He'd been warned.

But he hadn't been warned about the tall, laconic stranger who stood just a few yards to his right, inspecting one of the prints on the wall. It was a print of the *Great Atlantic* under full sail. The *Great Atlan-tic* had seven masts and was the largest clipper ship ever built, and Currier and Ives had done it justice, showing it scudding before a wind, every sail unfurled.

"What are you doin' in Helena?" George asked. "You up here to join the bidding?"

"Bidding?"

"You gonna try to outbid Amalgamated and buy off Judge Adair?"

Heinze acted faintly surprised. "George, you're talking about an honest man. Never try to buy an honest man, he'll turn on you. Hell, you know the Apex Law's ridiculous and so do I. But if the Amalgamated keeps putting the pressure on Judge Adair, he's likely to vote with me out of plain spite."

George laughed. "Now, that's a strange attitude, coming from you. Ain't you the man who said he'd never met anybody couldn't be bought?"

"No. Maybe I can be bought—and I know you can be—but hell, George, there's plenty of men stupider than we are." There was something not so nice in Heinze's laugh.

"Well, what are you doing here, then?" George asked. After he asked his question, he took a good drink of whiskey and swirled it around in his glass— for all the world like if he didn't give much of a damn one way or another.

The bodyguard noticed something was wrong. Someone was threatening his boss—though nothing had been said openly or to his face. The bodyguard came a step or two closer, though he knew nobody'd try any rough stuff here. The flag of truce was always flying at the Capital Club. The members needed one spot where enemies could sit down and have a drink, if not with harmony and trust, at least without the threat of gunplay.

When the bodyguard took his step closer, Slocum rather casually moved with him, and for the first time, a prickle of alarm shot down the bodyguard's neck and his hands started to get slippery with sweat. He'd seen Slocum with Heinze but had dismissed their joint arrival as coincidence. Now he wasn't so sure. And since Slocum had the position on him, the bodyguard wished he were sure. He coughed loud enough to get George's attention, but George glared at him, irritated.

"You want something, Heinze?" George demanded.

"You." Heinze smiled a big smile at George, as if it was a little joke, just between the two of them.

And quick as that, George's eyes turned to his bodyguard. What he saw didn't reassure him. The man's eyebrows were puckered up with worry and he was jerking his head, pointing out the man on his blind side. "I got a man," George said. "Amalgamated hired him. I wouldn't know what to do if he was to turn on you."

Heinze was annoyed. "Oh, George," he said. "Shit. Look at it this way. If you want to buy a woman, where do you go? To a woman who can be bought. If you want to buy a bottle or a gun, you go to a man who sells whiskey or guns. Now, if you want to go to buy a judge, who the hell should you go to? George, you've been bought. You can be bought. And I'm in a buyin' mood."

George wished he wasn't so deep in the armchair. He wished his bodyguard didn't look so worried. He said, "We're voting on the Apex Law day after tomorrow. I'm voting for Amalgamated." He started to rub thumb and forefinger together in the ancient gesture of a man who's been paid, but he quit doing that when Heinze's sneer blistered him with contempt.

"I know that, George," Heinze said patiently. "And I just wanted to be sure you understood what I'll be payin' you. I'll pay you just five thousand dollars less than Amalgamated offered. Now that's pretty good, since they own fifty mines and I only own the one. And I'll pay you tomorrow."

George shook his head stubbornly. "Forget it," he said. "I won't be in here tomorrow."

Heinze shook his head sorrowfully, as though George had failed at his lessons. "George, I don't give a damn where you'll be. That don't matter to me, George. I just want your vote. And, by the way, congratulations."

"Huh? What?"

"You gonna pass out the cigars?"

"Cigars?"

"The way you keep repeating words after me, a man might think you weren't right in the head."

"What cigars?"

"Hell, George, I heard you was a grandfather. Ain't you proud enough to break out the havanas?"

And Heinze turned on his heel and marched away, ignoring the stricken look on George Blankenship's face, ignoring the hand George put over his suddenly racing heart. Slocum tipped his hat to George's bodyguard before he followed Heinze. "Always like to meet a man . . ." he said softly. He didn't say why, but the bodyguard didn't feel awful good about it.

Heinze made the street door before he hooted with laughter. "We got 'em, John," he exclaimed. "We got the bastards on the run!"

He wouldn't explain what he meant, but he kept repeating, "We got 'em!" and hollering out loud.

Helena, the territorial capital, had started life with the more humble name of Alder Gulch. It had been a boomtown, and Helena's Main Street still followed the twists and turns of the stream that had made a few men rich. Now the stream ran in sewers under the streets and the buildings that lined the sides of the gulch were a far cry from the log and mud hovels the early prospectors had used. When they dug the foundation for Helena's first two-story hotel they'd found enough gold in the basement hole to pay for the building. Slocum had grinned when he heard that. The man who'd owned the claim where the hotel now stood had died broke and hungry.

Life sure was funny sometimes.

Heinze was in a mood to tie one on. He had something working for him, and whatever it was, he was plenty confident. He found a good quiet bar, out by the Helena stockyard—a cowboy joint where none of his political opponents would happen across him. Heinze started working a bottle of Old Overholt.

The cowboy patrons viewed the well-dressed mine owner with some curiosity, but they kept their comments to themselves when they noticed the tall, mean-looking hombre who seemed to be his friend. The bartender stayed at one end of the bar with the cowboys, and Slocum and Heinze had the other end to themselves.

Slocum didn't want to get drunk. Unless he was by himself, at a campfire high in the wilderness, he never even got a little tipsy. He wasn't in the sort of business that easily forgave a man for getting drunk. Just sure as hell, some bozo would challenge him once he was in his cups.

Heinze had no such inhibitions. He was bound and determined to make a fool of himself before the night was out. Slocum suggested they get something to eat. "Sure, sure," Heinze said. But the hours rolled by while he talked about all the beautiful things he was going to buy. He'd seen plenty of statues and paintings in Europe, and he said he wanted them and was going to have a whole passel shipped over, soon as he had money in his pocket. He said he wanted three teams of matched thoroughbreds and a couple of hunters for weekends. He wanted a woman to wake him up, another woman to service him at noon, and still another to put him to bed at night. "A man is no account at all," he said, "if he can only afford one woman."

Slocum had to laugh.

But as the night wore on, and Heinze kept working at his bottle, his stories got vaguer and less interesting. He told Slocum in great detail how poor he'd been as a child. How his family had lived in on

New York's Lower East Side, in one room of a tenement. How his rare industry had obtained the scholarship that allowed him to attend university in Germany. How one day he was going to go back and buy that tenement and burn it to the ground.

"And what about you, John?" he demanded. "You never talk much about yourself."

"Not much to tell," Slocum said. But when he saw Heinze's eyebrows furrowing, he deflected him by saying, "Besides, with you it's hard to get a word in edgewise."

Heinze thought that was pretty funny, and his curiosity faded away.

About midnight, Heinze lost it altogether. His speech was slurred and what he was saying wasn't worth making clear anyway. Slocum said, "Heinze, let's go outside. There's something I want to show you."

Heinze peered for a moment while the words seeped into him.

"Oh, sure," he said. "Sure thing." He almost fell off the barstool but made the perilous descent okay. He dropped a double eagle on the bar for a tip. Slocum thought that was pretty crazy, but it was his money. What the hell.

The sky was dead clear. Not a cloud in sight. The moon was half full and hung huge and clear on the horizon.

"Hell, will you look at that?" Heinze muttered.

"Uh-huh. C'mon, mount up. It's time to call it a day."

Heinze's face got truculent. "Hell," he said. "I ain't finished drinkin' yet. Not by a long shot. You go to the hotel if you want, but tonight's my night to howl." He howled his last words, too.

Slocum nodded wearily. "Your funeral," he said. As he mounted his horse, he saw a couple of the cowboys peering out of the bar at the expensively dressed drunk who was stumbling toward them. *Well,*

he thought, *they probably won't kill him anyway.*
It wasn't any of his affair, but his hands on the reins
were rough enough so his mare squealed. She was
quite unused to such treatment.

The next morning, John Slocum was one of the first
customers of the pleasant dining room in the Cen-
tennial Hotel. The restaurant opened at six and the
waiters were still a little groggy, but they brought
Slocum his coffee before they asked for his order,
and Slocum sat by the window, drinking coffee and
watching the eastern sky change from gray to pink.
The restaurant was fairly busy with men—ranchers
and stockmen mostly—whose day started at dawn, because that's when the animals woke. A couple of them
held their coffee cups with the nervous hands of men
who'd had a little too much the night before, and one
of them was running the brim of his hat around in
his hands like someone who doesn't want to squeeze
his head into his Stetson, not just yet. Slocum thought
about Heinze for a moment; then, since that kind of
thinking was going to spoil his breakfast, he stopped
doing it.

He was almost finished with his steak and eggs
when the cab drew up in front of the hotel. Heinze
got out, though his legs weren't entirely under his
command, and paid the driver with some change in
his pocket. His dapper hat was gone, his shirt was
torn, his pockets—all except for one—were turned inside out, and his face looked as if somebody had
sanded it with sandpaper.

At least they left him his change, Slocum noted
to himself. The coffee was pretty good and he decided to have another cup before paying the bill.

It had gotten light, and the restaurant trade slowed
when the cowmen left. In fact, Slocum was quite
alone, with just his coffee cup in front of him, when
Heinze stormed into the restaurant. He'd found a
fresh shirt in his luggage and he was wearing a new

pair of pants. His hair was wet where he'd dashed some water on the unruly mess, but he hadn't bathed and the scratches and abrasions on his cheek glowed red against his sallow complexion. His eyes swept the room briefly. He marched over to Slocum's table. "You're fired," he announced.

Slocum took a sip of his coffee. He'd lingered too long and it was getting cold. Maybe he'd ask the waiter to bring him another one.

"Did you hear me, Slocum?" Heinze demanded.

"Uh-huh. Say, flag the waiter for me, will you?"

Angrily, Heinze summoned the waiter. "I said you were fired. I won't have any man working for me who . . ."

Slocum interrupted by asking the waiter for one more cup of coffee and the bill.

"Damnit! Listen to me!"

Slocum favored Heinze with a slow stare. "Friend, you look like something the cat dragged in. You smell like a horse with the runs. And I ain't bein' paid to listen to you. If you're all finished, why don't you raise some dust? I'll figure out what you owe me and we'll be square."

Heinze, still angry, pulled out the chair and sat down. Up close, his glowering face looked pretty bad: cuts, abrasions, and a two-inch slash that'd leave a small scar. He leaned over the table to capture Slocum's eyes. Slocum put down his coffee when he got a real deep whiff of him.

"We had a deal," he said.

"You was to stay alive. I was to keep you alive," Slocum agreed easily.

"Well, look at me. Will you take a look at me! There were four of 'em. They punched me down, and when I couldn't get up they kicked me with their boots. Then they took all the gold and folding money and my watch. One of them even took my hat. My goddamn hat! They didn't leave me anything except about three dollars in change. Where were you, Slocum? Where the hell were you!"

Slocum pushed the coffee toward Heinze. He was finished with it anyway. "Seems to me I kept my end of the bargain," he remarked pleasantly enough. "You ain't dead. I was right about that. Looked like a bunch of garden-variety jackrollers in that joint. Didn't look like any of 'em'd take any pleasure in killin' you."

Heinze's face fell. "You knew?"

" 'Course. Anybody with eyes could see them boys had themselves a big fat fish on the line."

"Well, why . . ." Heinze put his hand up to his head and felt it as if it were an egg with a possibly damaged shell. He winced.

"I ain't your wet nurse, friend. You got somebody comin' after you, I'll stop 'em. You want to go and jump off a cliff somewhere because you think you're a fucking eagle and you're just bound to fly, I ain't gonna do a damn thing about it. If I wanted to be a wet nurse, I'd get me some baby calves or some kids, maybe, of my own."

Heinze stopped exploring his head. It wasn't broken anyway. He stared at Slocum, but the low sun was shining directly in his eyes and he had to squint. The gunman's face swam in his vision. He grabbed the coffee, and by steadying one hand with the other, he managed to trickle some into his mouth. When the coffee fell into his stomach, he thought he was going to puke. When he could trust himself, he said, "I've got work for you to do."

"Thought I was fired."

"Well, forget it. Forget it." The second sip of coffee felt a little better going down. "I got a use for you tonight."

Slocum looked his question.

"Tonight, we get Judge George Blankenship to change his vote."

"I ain't gonna kill him on your say-so. I never was a hired gun and I'm a little too old to start."

Heinze made a face, but the movement of his facial muscles hurt him so he resumed his blankest expression. He felt around in his mouth with his tongue. Hell of a thing if he'd had a tooth loosened by some two-bit cowboy's boots. "George thinks he's got it whipped. Old George thinks that if he don't take too many chances everything'll turn out all right for him. George is a thief, pure and simple, and anywhere else in this United States, people'd stare at him and call him dirty names and he wouldn't be loafin' around in the fancy clubs. So you're gonna surprise old George."

"All right." Slocum didn't much care. He was wondering if he shouldn't cash in his chips and find another game, but he didn't feel quite ready.

"Damn," Heinze said. "We're gonna be rich."

"Seems to me you were talkin' about that last night. About how rich we were gonna be."

Heinze had the grace to wince. "I did, did I? Damn! You must think I'm all kinds of fool."

"No."

"No?" Heinze tried out a smile. It hurt.

"Most kinds. Not all kinds." And with that, John Slocum rose from the table and went outside. The early morning air was sweet, and he thought he'd take a walk down to the livery stable and see to the horses. When he passed the big front window of the dining room, Heinze was still there, his hands wrapped around his coffee cup and his head bowed as though it ached. It probably did.

The mountain pony had been rubbed down good; there was fresh oats in her pail and she had another bucket of fresh water. Slocum found the livery kid forking old straw out of the manger.

"I'm the man who owns the mountain horse," he said.

The kid set the manure fork aside to examine the

tall, soft-spoken stranger. *Gunman,* he thought. *Sure as hell.* But he said, "That's a beautiful horse. If you're lookin' to sell her, I could find a buyer by the time morning's out."

Slocum said, rather solemnly, "No, that horse suits me too well. I just meant to give you this." He handed the kid a silver cartwheel.

"What for?" The kid was staring at the money in his hand as if he hadn't seen any recently.

"For takin' as good care of her tonight as you did last night," Slocum said and turned on his heel. No matter what, Slocum took care of his guns and his horses. Nothing was too good for them. A good fast horse could mean his life, and he never knew when it would be needed. He didn't bother to check Heinze's horse. He wasn't no wet nurse and he wasn't no stable boy either.

Slocum spent a pleasant afternoon walking around, drinking a sociable beer now and again, picking up on the news. Man could never get too much information, and loafing around in the town square with the old-timers or drinking a sociable beer with some drifter was as good a way of killing time as any. Probably Heinze was sleeping it off, but Slocum didn't care too much, one way or another.

Slocum had an easy dinner with a faro dealer he'd known briefly in Deadwood, when Deadwood was the roughest town in Dakota Territory. The dealer said he remembered the old times. Slocum remembered that when the guns started smoking, the faro dealer was usually under a table somewhere. Since he didn't mention that, the dinner was fairly pleasant.

An urchin caught up with Slocum on the street with a note from Heinze. "Meet me at the Stockman. Eight o'clock. F.A.H." The urchin said Heinze had promised him a quarter. Slocum paid up.

It was a few minutes before eight and the Stockman was half a block down the street. Since he didn't know what he was getting into, Slocum unfastened his coat. Outside the Stockman, Heinze was waiting. He'd intercepted George Blankenship at the door. Heinze was all smiles and geniality. George's face was wary. His bodyguard leaned against the outside of the building with his hand resting on his gun butt, scanning the throng of people who paraded by.

It was a nice evening and it seemed like half the population of Helena was out for a stroll.

". . . got to do me this little favor," Heinze was saying. "George, you know you just have to uphold the Apex Law and lift that damn injunction. Powerful man like you, George—hell, you got to follow the dictates of your conscience."

George was getting pissed. Heinze was talking to him as if they already had a deal to betray the Amalgamated, and since that was the last thing on George's mind, since, in fact, he'd already borrowed against the money Amalgamated would pay him for his vote, Heinze's humor struck him as in extremely poor taste. Once a man's been bought, he's got to *look* bought. Otherwise nobody trusted him. And George was worried about being spotted with Heinze by some Amalgamated lobbyist—talking to Heinze like they were the best of pals. When his eyes touched Slocum, he made no particular connection because he wasn't looking for a man he'd met only once. He was looking for men who'd been paying him off for years.

Slocum handed Heinze the tersest of nods. Heinze threw his arm around him. "George," he said—and the smile never left his face—"this here's a good friend of mine and he's gonna peel you like an orange."

Now George's eyes remembered Slocum. Immediately his pudgy hand flicked and his bodyguard came closer for a near look-see.

The bodyguard had his hand on his gunbutt, ready for a draw.

"Yes, sir, George," Heinze was grinning like a fool. "Mr. Slocum here is gonna use you for a dust rag. Oh, he's a mean son of a bitch, and it's all I can do to restrain him. Hell, if I didn't keep a short rein on him, he'd be killing men every other day, and he doesn't like you, George, not one little bit."

"Hey," the bodyguard shouted, "what's going on here!"

He had his gun half drawn. He was no gunfighter and he wanted to have an edge. Slocum let him approach until he was just a few feet away. The situation stank. Old Heinzy had gotten them both in the shit again. But he knew for sure that he wasn't about to let this nervous-looking man get the drop on them. A ripple ran across his shoulder and Heinze's hand seemed to fall off of its own accord. Then Slocum blurred.

One minute the bodyguard was pretty much in control of the situation. He had his gun half drawn and could draw it more if he had to. No other weapons were in evidence, and, hell, Heinze and his man were practically embracing. When Slocum moved, the bodyguard tried to draw. The Colt slipped out of his holster but it was still pointing downward when Slocum's Colt jabbed him under the ribcage.

Slocum didn't want to kill the man, just stop him. So he unleashed his own Colt, shoved the gun barrel into the other man's gut, just below the sternum. The blow made the bodyguard's heart pause. The gun dropped from his deadened fingers and he folded over like a tired accordian. He even wheezed like one.

"Now see what I mean?" Heinze crowed. "Why don't you shoot him, John? Hell, he's just a Pink."

With his boot, Slocum kicked the bodyguard's gun into the gutter before he holstered his own. "Fuck you," he said to Heinze.

George's face color wasn't too good, and when he

spoke he sounded like a man being strangled. "What the hell? What the hell?"

Heinze explained, "It's simple, George. I ain't as big as the Amalgamated boys, so I got to be smarter and just about twice as mean. Now, I don't hold anything against you personally, you understand, but . . ."

The bodyguard had recovered some, though he still had one hand pressed to his diaphragm. He was red in the face, and when he spoke, his voice wheezed and that seemed to make him angrier. "Pretty slick with that gun, huh, cowboy? Glad you got that gun to hide behind, I'll bet. Just another fucking back-shooter. At least the rattler warns when he strikes, you dirty son of a bitch. You spavin-shanked, mean-eyed, hog-headed bastard."

John Slocum had had enough. He'd been set up to fight without a bit of say-so, and now this loudmouth was spitting poison at him. Slocum lost his temper.

"Hold this," he snapped, handing his Colt to Heinze. "If anybody interferes, you just try and shoot 'em, okay?" Then he peeled off his coat and draped it over the hitchrail.

And the bodyguard knocked him over it.

The bodyguard had fought bareknuckle in his youth, fighting men like Sharkey and Gentleman Jim, and though he'd never been much of a gunman, his hands were tough as scar tissue over stone and he could crack a man's ribs with one good blow. His first shot wasn't that good. He connected with Slocum's shoulder, numbing it, and the taller man looped right over the hitchrail onto his back.

Perhaps if the bodyguard had vaulted the rail he could have got to Slocum before he recovered, but he ran around it instead. He meant to kick his skull into mincemeat and end the fight quick. "In a short fight," as his trainer used to say, "only one man gets hurt. In a long fight, both of them do."

Slocum was on his feet again, one shoulder dead

numb where the fist had crushed a nerve against a bone, and the other hand dangling loosely at his side.

The bodyguard jabbed, but Slocum let it slip by his cheek. The bodyguard jabbed again, one, two, three quick jabs, and two of them landed on Slocum's chest. They didn't hurt too bad.

They were about evenly matched. The bodyguard weighed two hundred pounds to Slocum's one-eighty, but Slocum had a couple of inches of reach.

The bodyguard's face was a mask of crude scar tissue, and his ears had been pounded to two or three times their natural size. He was faster than he looked and he was getting through to Slocum, but not hurting much: love taps. The bodyguard was in the classic bareknuckle stance of the professional boxer. Slocum had his arms down and was circling him. Suddenly Slocum rushed, head lowered, and smashed into the man. The man went down and Slocum charged right over him. The bodyguard had lost his wind and had a knee scraped by the edge of Slocum's boots, but, hell, this was going to be a long fight, and as he rolled to get up, he was thinking that it'd be fun. He'd just wear down this rangy bastard and then beat him to death like he did with that kid in Wyoming two summers ago.

Slocum didn't fight fair. He kicked him. Like a man might kick a football. He'd aimed for the bodyguard's throat but overestimated, and his sharp-toed boot caught him in the jaw instead—and broke it. The man screamed and clasped his hands to his face. He was shoving at his jaw like maybe he could put it back in place, but it hung funny, and his mouth wouldn't close.

Poor bastard, Slocum thought, *I might as well put him out of his misery.* So Slocum kicked him again. This time the boot clipped the side of the bodyguard's head and he went down for good.

The bodyguard lay facedown in the dirt of the

street, but his back was still rising and falling, so he was still alive.

The crowd that always attends a fight hadn't had time to get together: It happened so fast that only a few onlookers were on the spot by the time the body-guard caught that second kick, and John Slocum was already dusting off his trousers. His eyes were bright green with fury and he didn't know which one to manhandle: George or Heinzy.

But Heinze had his arm around George's shoulder and was gently leading him away from the crowd. "You see, George, you're just not safe anymore. Amalgamated can't protect you against a man as mean as I am. I know it's hard, but there ain't anybody you can hire to keep me off you."

George turned then and faced Heinze, and though his face was pale, it was determined too. "So, then," he squeaked. He coughed and bent over to spit into the dust. He wiped his mouth with the back of his hand and began again. "So, then. I'll just hire two men next time. And if that doesn't work, I'll hire three. You can't touch me, Heinze. You can't touch me. If you kill me, I won't be able to vote the way you want." The crowd was gathering around the unconscious bodyguard. One or two were mock-punching, rehashing the fight. Nobody touched the man lying in the dust, though they talked about him. Nobody stared directly at Slocum either, who stood steaming mad on the sidewalk, though every man there glanced at him from time to time.

"George," Heinze said gently, "you're forgetting your grandson. Little John Doe at the convent of the Sacred Heart, in Twin Falls. Now, don't you think it'd be right to spread the good news among the good folks in Helena? Hey!" He shouted to the gathering crowd. "Hey! Come over here, men. Old George Blankenship's got an announcement to make!"

Under his voice he remarked, "And she sure is a

fine girl, George. Must have been a terrible burden for you to bear. Girl that pretty—growing up in your own house. Your own daughter, George. And those long, long winters."

A little ball of spit appeared at the corner of George's lips. His eyes rolled wildly in his head. Heinze began to fear that maybe he'd gone too far, and added, "Don't you worry, now, George. I don't want to hurt the girl any more than you do."

George turned a look on Heinze that would have shattered stone. The whites of his eyes were so big Heinze could barely guess the color of his irises. "I'll vote," he said. "I'll vote."

Now, it's true George Blankenship never did say just how he was going to vote, but Heinze figured he knew.

And the next day, in the austere courtroom of the Appeals Court of the Montana Territory, with all the other judges' eyes on him, George proved Heinze right. He said he found justice on the side of Heinze's arguments and upheld the Apex Law.

6

It was a lousy ride back to Butte. Slocum was furious at Heinze. Heinze had got him into a fight just to prove a point—a fight Slocum didn't care for, with a man he wasn't quarreling with. Worse, Heinze made Slocum feel like a hired gun, and in all his life, he'd never been out for hire. In short, F. Augustus Heinze had made John Slocum think poorly of himself and had done so lightly.

Heinze was happy as a pig in shit. He had the vote he'd wanted, the injunction was lifted, and the Minnie Healy could go back into production as soon as the news reached Butte City. He liked Slocum, sure, but, hell, no sense cryin' over spilt milk. Heinze had triumphed through shrewdness and courage and didn't understand why Slocum didn't see it that way. Heinze reminded himself that gunfighters were a dime a dozen. Most of the way to Wolf Creek, they rode in silence. Wolf Creek was a pretty little town: a couple of houses, a church, and the roadhouse. It was midway between Butte City and the capital. The roadhouse served good, simple grub, and its beds were mercifully free of lice. A man could have a good time in Wolf Creek when he was feeling good. That night, Heinze did, buying drinks for the other travelers until three drovers, two market hunters, and a marshal traveling from Great Falls were as drunk as he was. Heinze invited Slocum to sit in, but Slocum stayed outside while the partying was going on, smoking thoughtfully and watching the stars wheel overhead in their beautiful fixed orbits. The noise of revelry got lost before it got far beyond the front door, and Slocum didn't feel much like celebrating. He was wondering if maybe he should slow down some. Save up enough to buy a little horse ranch somewhere. Hell, he wasn't too old to start a new life, and he remembered one valley in the shadows of the Wind River range as lush and green and well watered as anywhere. Maybe he'd get hitched. After his Blackfoot wife had died, somehow he'd sort of dropped the idea of a wife and a family. Maybe he ought to pick that idea up again.

Slocum was kind of sick. Sick of himself and all the other grubby, mean-spirited men who walked two-legged when by rights they should have been crawling on their bellies like snakes. He was so sick of his fellow men that he shunned the clean, louse-free beds inside the Wolf Creek Roadhouse and bedded down in the stall with his horse. When he was feeling this way, it was good to sleep beside a trustworthy, simple beast who'd never done a bit of harm to anyone.

By the next morning, he was cheerful. Heinze wasn't. He'd had too much again last night and had talked too big, and when Slocum awakened him, none too gently, Heinze didn't want to do much besides die.

"Dawn," Slocum said. "Time to mount up."

Heinze was game. He managed to get out of bed, splash some water on his face, and get a couple of mouthfuls of the stuff down before he started upchucking.

Slocum rolled a smoke while Heinze struggled to swing the heavy MacClellan saddle over his horse's back and smoked it while Heinze tugged the cinch buckles tight. "Goddamn you," Heinze snapped. "Can't you see I need a hand?"

"Never hired on to be no hostler either," Slocum remarked mildly.

Heinze cursed him blue, but the tall, laconic rider didn't say another word. Finally Heinze was mounted.

Not mounted too well, mind you. His gear stuck out of his possibles bag like a laundry hamper, and his clothes weren't any too straight either. Slocum set off at an easy, fast lope toward Butte City. The mountain horse had a longer stride than Heinze's horse and was setting the pace. Heinze's horse had a nice canter but a bumpy trot. The mountain horse went best in between the two speeds, so Heinze had to keep switching gaits: up and down, from bumpy to smooth. When he puked again, his twisted stomach didn't bring up anything but bile. He fumbled through his saddlebags for a pint he knew he had there when they left Helena, and when he found it he sucked on it like a babe on the tit. It was like swallowing a lightning bolt, but it numbed his stomach and started him on the road to recovery. By the time they hit the top of the Continental Divide, with Butte City laid out beneath them, he was feeling pretty good again and remembering his triumph of yesterday. He didn't even feel so bad about John Slocum anymore. Hell, he had to admit that the rangy, black-haired man had pulled him out of a couple of bad scrapes, and he'd certainly done some damage to that bodyguard in Helena. If it hadn't been so quick, the way he dispatched old George's protector, George probably wouldn't have backed down. Yep, no question about it, he owed Slocum something. And F. Augustus Heinze always paid his debts. As they rode down the narrow winding road toward his own smelters, past the Tuolumne gallows frame on the right and the square black slagheaps on the left, Heinze was whistling.

Heinze swung north up the Hill to the Minnie Healy where a shaft of miners was already at work. The mineyard was filled with ore wagons and cursing teamsters jockeying for a spot at the tipple, and the yard was illuminated with big oil lanterns guttering on the posts. The ore skip was hustling up and down, bringing to the surface silver that had lain hidden since the beginning of time. Heinze took the congratulations of his superintendents graciously. Word had reached them last night via horse relay set up between Butte City and Helena for just that purpose. Heinze was his most charming and even paid some attention to his superintendent when the man warned him of strange goings-on at the Black Rock and odd threats made by Amalgamated Miners.

The court had lifted the injunction on the Amalgamated properties, too, and all their mines were back in business. The whole damn Hill was busy, bustling, and if a man had to walk, he ran; if he rode, he rode at a gallop. It was infectious and Heinze felt it was all because of him.

He dismounted rather gaily in front of his house and was banging at the door. Since Slocum had nearly lost his head in front of that very same door, he cast a wary look around before following.

Even Heinze's old servant Murph was wreathed in smiles. "Welcome back, sir. We all know what great things you done in the capital. Sure, and the men are happy to be workin' again, and if anyone asks me I tell 'em it's Mr. Heinze you owe this to. It's Mr. Heinze who did it."

Without invitation, Slocum went into the front room and drew the curtains before uncorking the brandy bottle. It was good brandy, but he didn't notice that. It cut the dust.

When Clare came into the room, she was hanging on Heinze's arm and she was cooing at him. From time to time she'd ruffle his hair and giggle. Her face was lit up with excitement. Her gown was so low cut, it seemed to present her breasts as offerings to any man strong enough to take them. Heinze poured himself a drink, sat down at his dining table, and pulled Clare down onto his lap. He was laughing, too, and she laughed as he slipped his hand into her bodice to cup her breast. But business first. Without removing his roaming hand, Heinze eyed Slocum steadily. His laughter stopped. Heinze stopped feeling Clare and said softly to her, "Why don't you wait outside, honey. Just for a minute."

She pouted, but she adjusted her dress and went.

"She's quite a handful, that one," Heinze said with a man-to-man smile.

Unconsciously, Heinze wiped his hand on his coat as if her breast had got it dirty. "Slocum, I owe you an apology."

Slocum said nothing.

Heinze waved away the past. He smiled at his own foolishness. "I mean it. I owe you an apology. And," he admitted, "there aren't many men who can say they've got an apology from me."

Slocum thought the number might be in the hundreds, but let it ride.

"Look," Heinze cajoled, "I'll pay what I owe you until now. And a thousand-dollar bonus. But I'd rather you stay. I'm sorry I set you up for that fight, and I know I been a little bit, well, damn fool lately, but I can promise you it won't happen again."

"So?" Slocum took a drink of brandy. He tasted it this time. Somewhere in the house a clock was chiming. Eight o'clock.

"I'm going back to New York. Me and Clare, and you, if you will. I'm going to meet with old J.P., the man himself, and tell him that I'm keeping the Minnie Healy open come hell or high water. I'm gonna meet the man on his own ground and back him down."

John Slocum was thinking about George Armstrong Custer. Custer was a braggart, too, but unlike Heinze, he was humorless.

"And I want you there. You ever been to New York? Hell, I already asked you that, didn't I?"

"I don't think I'm cut out for this kind of work."

Heinze pointed his finger at him. "Well, there's one kind of work you are cut out for. If Amalgamated makes another move against me, they'll hit the Minnie Healy. It'll be dynamite or a fire. They've done that before to a couple small operators who got in their way. I'm gonna need a captain at the mine. Someone who knows how to fight."

Slocum was wondering what the Bitteroot was like now that spring was really settled in. He thought it was probably real nice. He was remembering the freshness of the Chinese girl. Surprising, because he didn't ever expect to see her again. "I'll think on it."

"Ten thousand." The offer was so high that the sound of his own words made Heinze blush. But once he'd said the words he had to back them up. He couldn't waffle on any offer he made to this man. "Help me beat Amalgamated. Help me fight them off, and I'll pay you ten thousand in gold for doing it."

When Earp was Marshal in Tombstone, they paid him two hundred dollars a month. Ten thousand dollars would buy a hell of a horse ranch. Maybe that ranch in the Wind River Country Slocum had been dreaming about. "I'll think about it," Slocum repeated.

Well, give Heinze this much credit: He knew it would be the wrong time to press. He raised his glass in a toast and said, "Whatever you decide, I thank you. And if you're with me, we leave for the railhead tomorrow morning at eight. We'll use horse relays."

Slocum got off his backside and squared his hat on his head. Without another word he went to the front door and pulled it aside. This time he waited until his eyes had scanned the cobblestone courtyard before he stepped out. Behind him, he heard Clare's high-pitched giggle. He sighed. Sometimes life was awful damn confusing. He decided to go down to Irish World and get laid.

Heinze had requested the Union Pacific to have a special train waiting at a siding at Promontory Point with a special car for its wealthy and distinguished passengers. First time Slocum saw it, it looked like a mirage. The three had been riding four days and nights and they all looked like death warmed over and coated with the white alkali dust that seemed to be the special treat for travelers across the Utah deserts this time of year. His hands were parched, and when he ran his tongue around in his mouth it collected grit. And besides, Slocum's neck hurt from watching their backtrail.

Ever since he'd decided to take the trip with Heinze, he'd become suddenly, unaccountably nervous. *Like some damn haunt is standing on my grave*—that's the way he put it. Several times, as they rode hard through the desert, he'd thought he'd seen something. Once, he thought he heard hoofbeats, but it never came to anything. He saw nothing when he lay back in ambush to see who or what was following them. Finally he put it down to nerves.

He was riding through Utah, and the Mormons had a bounty on him still, unless they thought he was dead. Maybe that was what was making him so damn jittery.

Heinze rode fast and hard, though he wasn't really much of a rider. His thighs were raw. He limped at the rest stops and rubbed his buttocks. But he never complained. Maybe he didn't see any sense in complaining about what couldn't be avoided.

Clare, on the contrary, was a fine horsewoman. She rode each of the relay mounts as if she'd known it all her life and kept to a steady, ground-eating trot. They were making a hundred twenty-five miles a day, which is considerable on horseback in rough country, and she didn't complain once. Not to Slocum at any rate.

Still, nobody was sorry to see the train waiting at the siding. Nothing much else: a water tower; the double line of tracks stretching east and west; a curl of steam from the big 2-4-2 locomotive. In his telegram Heinze had ordered that the engine be ready to go at a moment's notice, and so it was.

A man—a Ute Indian, by the look of him—was waiting in the shade of the water towers for the exhausted horses. While they dismounted and unfastened their saddlebags, he waited by the horse's heads saying something soothing in his language. When they mounted the steps of the private car, he dug his heels in and rode back the way they'd come. The sun and alkali dust conspired to make him vanish.

The private car was dark enamel blue with gold trim that outlined the windows and formed a curious monogram at the rear. The paint was dust-streaked, but there was nothing travel-worn about the man who greeted F. Augustus Heinze when he mounted onto the rear platform. The man was tall and distinguished-looking. The hint of gray at his temples and his dark formal suit seemed to indicate that he was the car's rightful inhabitant. With a hint of deference—but no more than a hint—he greeted the weary party. "Good afternoon, Mister Heinze. I am Currier."

Heinze stuck out his hand, and the man pretended not to see it until Heinze realized his mistake and withdrew it. "Very well, Currier. Signal the engineer. We'll be leaving at once."

"Very good, sir." Discreetly, he stood aside while the three westerners entered the car. "The cook has a light luncheon ready, and a fresh bath has been drawn. May I suggest that you'd like to clean up before you dine?"

"You can suggest anything you want," Heinze said absently. He was inspecting the interior of the car. The car was paneled with rare wood, set off by brass fittings. The carpets on the floor—surely they were Oriental. And the furnishings weren't the heavy leather and horsehair of any railroad car Slocum had seen. The chairs were so graceful and so burnished they had to be antiques. The table was laid for three, with linen, crystal, and silver. Slocum picked up a heavy sterling knife and asked, "What's this monogram, friend? I ain't ever seen it before, but I don't believe it's Pullman's."

Currier permitted himself the faintest smile. "J.P. M., sir, Mr. Morgan's monogram. Now, if the lady would like to wash up after her journey . . ." His hand gestured toward the front of the car.

Slocum draped his saddle bags over a Queen Anne chair. Augustus Heinze, who was lifting a bottle from the well-stocked sideboard stopped as if he'd been shot. "Morgan? This is Morgan's car?"

This time Currier's smile was quite genuine. "Oh, yes, sir. One of them. He thought you'd be so much more comfortable traveling in a fully appointed car."

"How the hell did he . . .?"

Heinze didn't finish his question, but Slocum knew Heinze hadn't told Morgan he was coming to New York. Heinze's face set hard as concrete. He was wishing he could turn down the offer, but after a moment's reflection, Heinze forced a pained smile. "That's very, uh, handsome of Morgan. Perhaps one day I can return the favor."

"Yes, sir." Currier was enjoying his guest's discomfiture. "No doubt you can."

When Heinze pulled the stopper out of the decanter, the butler hurriedly produced a snifter, but Heinze was already rinsing his mouth out with the brandy. He spat into a convenient spitoon and rubbed his mouth crudely. "Dusty out there," he said to the butler, who was still holding the glass outstretched.

The man blinked and set the glass on the sideboard.

With the slightest jerk, the car was moving, moving east.

The car was so softly sprung, there wasn't much sense of motion, even when the train got up speed.

In the locomotive the engineer and two brawny, soot-streaked firemen forced the big 2-4-2's engine faster and faster.

This was J. P. Morgan's private train, and on his specific orders, it had two speeds: full speed and stop. The 2-4-2, fresh from the Baldwin works, was the newest steam locomotive in America and one of the most powerful. When she was rolling with a light train like this one, and the firebox was glowing red, the big wheels clipped along at better than eighty miles per hour. And since they had the green light from here to Pennsylvania Station, there was no worry about other trains. Even the transcontinental passenger trains were held in sidings while Morgan's train roared by. The passengers on those stalled trains stood on the smoker's platform and wondered if the special train that had delayed them belonged to a general or a governor— whether it carried a president or a visiting king.

John Slocum rested his bare feet on a fine old Chippendale chair and drew the smoke of a havana into his lungs. Morgan had laid out fresh outfits for all three of his guests, but though the clothes were the finest materials and cut, though Slocum's garb was almost as travel weary as he was, he didn't want to put on another man's uniform before he'd signed on. He was lounging in a dressing gown while Morgan's man tried to sponge his battered clothing and boots into some semblance of order. The man had his work cut out for him.

Neither Heinze nor Clare shared his reluctance. Eagerly, Clare pulled through a trunk full of the newest fashions, everything her size. As she held up one gown after another, she exclaimed, "God, Augustus, isn't this beautiful? Why just last month I saw an outfit like this in *Ladies Companion*."

Heinze selected a simple dark suit from six other simple dark suits. The suit bore an unfortunate resemblance to the suit that Morgan's man Currier wore, but the resemblance was slight and was, perhaps, unintentional. As night fell, they crossed the River Platte, the car swaying as they hurtled across the bridge that had taken so many lives—white and Indian alike. Idly, Slocum peered out the windows and watched as the sun set behind them on the low, rounded foothills.

Heinze, stomach full, dinner on the way, and decanter at his elbow, was expansive. He gestured with his cigar, indicating the rare antiques, the painting hanging over the wall, which Currier told him was a Titian. A little bosomy for Heinze's taste, maybe, but pretty fancy. He'd asked Currier where he could get one like it and the butler had smiled one of his smiles and said, "Perhaps Mr. Morgan has an extra one, sir. They're rather rare."

"Well, I ain't exactly a pauper, you know," Heinze said.

"No, sir." But the butler never lost that smile.

"What do you think of it, John?" Heinze asked.

"At least it's furnished," Slocum replied.

The back of the car was lounge and dining room. The front of the car included Pullman-type bedrooms, pantry, and kitchen. From time to time when the butler came out of the kitchen, a delicious smell leaked into the back of the car.

"Ain't this the life, John?" Heinze asked.

Slocum grunted. To tell the truth, he would have been a whole lot happier beside a campfire in the Rockies with a pot of trail coffee and a can of beans, but he didn't figure Heinze would understand that.

The butler thought the tall man made a funny picture sprawled out beside the window in a too-large dressing gown, his Colt on the table beside him. When Currier took the green-eyed man's clothes, the man had carefully separated his holstered weapon before he let the clothes out of his sight.

With some distaste the butler handed Slocum his

folded pile of clothes. Once Slocum had his own clothes on again, he felt a good deal more comfortable. The butler handed him his battered plainsman's Stetson as if it were a bag of dead fish.

"Thanks, bud," Slocum said, and dug into his pocket for a quarter.

The butler stared at the money in his hand, horrified. "Oh no, sir," he said. "We can't . . . Mr. Morgan . . . we work for Mr. Morgan, sir."

"Not when you're cleanin' my duds," Slocum said. And the look in his eye made the butler take the money, though he surely didn't want to.

The locomotive and private car roared across the great plains all night, passing through Omaha, Rock Island, and Decatur, whistle hooting at the night and sparks flying from the big black stack.

Heinze got pretty drunk, and when he took Clare into their bedroom, her cries were audible though, naturally, Currier never showed by the lift of an eyelash that he heard a thing.

At dawn they stopped in Cincinnati for more coal and water. Slocum had refused a bed and sat up all night in the lounge. When Currier had shown signs of weariness, Slocum told him to get to bed himself. He was quite comfortable, thanks, just leave a pot of coffee. And John Slocum sat all night, watchful, smoking those long, fine havana cigars.

In the early morning light—the light of pale shadows—Slocum walked beside the train, hands clasped behind his back. The train stopped outside the Cincinnati yards though Slocum could see the tall arch of the new Cincinnati Station. They changed crews, the exhausted engineer and fireman stumbling as they climbed down from the high cab. Slocum asked the engineer, "You always travel wide open?"

The man spat onto the roadbed. "Always. We're gonna lose one of Morgan's trains one of these days."

"Maybe," his black fireman said, "but he pays double time."

Slocum nodded and resumed his careful circle of the train. He didn't know why he was examining the train as if it was some kind of elaborate snare, but all his senses were very slightly alarmed.

As soon as the tender water tank was filled, the fireman jumped into the cab of the locomotive, which had never lost its head of steam, and with a fine spray of water and a shriek of the steam whistle, the J. P. Morgan express was rolling again.

Slocum stood on the back platform and watched Cincinnati recede behind him.

The butler served breakfast as the train roared through the tall canyons west of Pittsburgh. Slocum had ham and eggs, but Clare chose eggs Benedict and Heinze had a bowl of caviar washed down with champagne.

It was going to be a lovely day, and the sight of the squalid black slums outside Pittsburgh didn't ruin Slocum's appetite.

As the train thundered across Pennsylvania, Slocum dropped his hat over his eyes and slept for a couple of hours. Many years ago he had learned the soldier's trick of going for days with only occasional two-hour catnaps.

While John Slocum napped, Clare tried on one new gown after another, tossing her discards carelessly on the floor, while a bored F. Augustus Heinze read through newspapers they'd taken on in Cincinnati.

Alert telegraphers flashed notice of the train's passage, and as they rolled through the lush New Jersey farm country, the milk trains were sidetracked for their rapid passage.

The ferry had waited the better part of an hour for the train at the Hoboken terminal. The deck passengers ogled the train that panted aboard, wondering who the visiting royalty was.

Slocum woke easily when the train stopped against the bumpers that marked the end of the transcontinental tracks. Already some engineers were talking about putting a tunnel under the Hudson, but skeptics claimed it was just a pipe dream.

Slocum got off the train and stood on the gently rocking ferry floor as the huge ferry made its careful majestic way across the Hudson toward the skyline of New York.

Sloops, barges, and steamers plied the busy blue Hudson. Fishing boats had nets dropped in one of the greatest fish spawning grounds on the Atlantic Coast. The sky over New York City was gray with smoke.

Heinze joined Slocum at the rail and watched as the big ferry slanted toward the ferry slip, its big sidewheel paddles clawing at the water. Heinze was feeling great. "There it is," he gestured. "Isn't that something."

"Uh." Slocum was noncommittal.

Before the passengers were allowed to disembark, the train rolled off and in a few minutes the 2-4-2 and its single car slipped into Pennsylvania Station.

The station was bedlam. Thirty trains were clustered under the hundred-foot roof, belching smoke and steam, taking on passengers or letting them off. The terminal's ceiling rose above them, like some vaulted cathedral.

The three westerners hurried across the enormous marble floor, under the frescoes. One fresco depicted a buffalo hunt. Slocum glanced at it long enough to note that he had never seen buffalo hunters that looked like that, nor buffalo either.

Their luggage traveled on a little cart, and the butler, Currier, walked beside them.

The first cab in the rank wore the same familiar blue-and-gold monogram. Heinze paused. "You know," he said to Slocum, "I think we might check into a hotel before we go see Morgan."

Slocum stood quiet. He was learning, not talking.

Twenty cabs lined up behind Morgan's. Heinze stepped to the second hansom in line, ignoring the butler's distress. "Can you take us to the Plaza Hotel?" he asked.

The man stared straight ahead. "Sir," he said. "This cab can only take you to J. P. Morgan's."

Heinze's puzzled face grew angry. "What the hell?"

Currier said, "Mr. Morgan thought it would be better this way, sir," he said. "New York can be quite dangerous to strangers."

When Heinze turned to the third cab in the rank, he got the same answer. When he offered the fourth driver ten dollars to take him to the Plaza, the man apologized, "Sir, it would be worth my job to take you." He gestured at the row of cabs behind him. "We have orders to take you and your associate to Mr. Morgan's home directly. Your, uh, lady, is to go to the Plaza Hotel, where rooms are waiting for her."

Heinze turned his rueful countenance to Slocum. "Well, Slocum," he said, "like they say—when rape is inevitable, you might as well lie back and enjoy it."

Clare was pretty unhappy. She'd wanted very much to meet the great J. P. Morgan and had even dressed especially for the occasion. "Who the hell does he think he is?" she wanted to know. But Heinze whispered briefly in her ear, and when she boarded the cab, her face was wreathed in smiles.

Slocum was curious. When the two gentlemen were rattling along in their cab, he asked Heinze what he'd said.

"I promised her a diamond," Heinze replied shortly.

"Oh."

When Heinze climbed down in front of J. P. Morgan's mansion, he said, "Looks like a damn tomb."

"Or a fortress," Slocum said. And it was true. Slocum had never seen a house so able to withstand a protracted siege by armed men. High spike fence to break up the charges and windows as narrow as rifle slits in the impervious white granite walls.

The gate swung open easily when Slocum tugged at it. In response to Heinze's banging on the great brass knocker, one of Morgan's servants let them in. Though Heinze was full of questions, the servant said not a word as he led them down the cool halls, past the antique suits of armor. The light was quiet and almost blue. It pointed out the slim veins in the white marble, like veins in the arm of an ancient aristocratic woman.

Morgan's office wasn't any warmer than the hall. There were rows of books inside locked bookcases, a plain raw wood desk behind which the great man sat, and two flimsy wooden chairs for his visitors.

Morgan's eyes were locked on the two of them from the moment the servant ushered them in.

Morgan was in his early fifties, a stocky, powerful man. His suit was elegant, almost flamboyant, and was the only splash of color in the otherwise barren, chilly office. No fire flickered in the cold fireplace. The clock over the mantel had stopped. Morgan had the broad face of a peasant, and his hands were stubby. His eyes were the palest blue Slocum had ever seen, so pale that it was hard to tell where the iris and white met. His stubby hands gestured, "Take a seat." Heinze checked Slocum before he refused. Morgan's eyes were registering them. When he'd examined Heinze for a long minute, he turned his attention to Slocum and gave him the same slow inspection.

"I trust you had a pleasant journey." His voice was soft, low, and carefully neutral.

"Yeah," Heinze said. "Augustus Heinze, at your service."

"I know you, sir." Heinze, who'd come forward to shake Morgan's hand, stopped, check-reined.

Slocum took out a cigar and a lucifer. He popped the lucifer on the underside of Morgan's desk. Since he couldn't see any ashtray, he deposited the burned match on the floor. The cigar tasted pretty good.

"And you are John Slocum," Morgan stated. Slocum smoked his cigar. Morgan was trying to put the Indian sign on him and Heinze, but two could play at that game. He blew a smoke ring.

"Why have you come here, Heinze?" Morgan asked in that same quiet expressionless voice.

Heinze grinned. "I came to tell you I got you by the balls," he said. And aping Slocum he fired up a cigar. "I came to tell you that the Apex Law's been upheld in the Territorial Court and that I'm gonna take every pocket of ore out of the Butte Hill."

"Unless?"

Heinze was momentarily confused. He'd expected more defiance from the king of the merchant bankers —a man powerful enough to unseat most of the crowned heads of Europe.

"No 'unless,'" Heinze snapped. "We can come to some agreement if you like so we can both get rich. Or we can fight about it and I'll still get rich." A furious puff on his cigar. "No difference to me," he added airily.

Morgan's hands rested on top of the great desk, and Slocum understood one of the man's sources of power: He was a listener, not a talker.

"I hope the clothing fit," Morgan said, ignoring Heinze's proposal. "Mr. Slocum—you didn't find them to your satisfaction?"

"I think it would be hard for you to pick out clothes that fit me just right," Slocum said carefully.

"Perhaps. Perhaps it would." Morgan's eyes flashed briefly. "Will you sell the Minnie Healy, sir?"

"Hell, no!" Heinze puffed clouds of smoke from his cigar.

Morgan stayed still as a statue. "Mr. Heinze, you are a rather ingenious young man. The Apex Law— the Minnie Healy—that was quite a stroke."

"Yeah. It was, wasn't it?" Despite himself Heinze was pleased—even a little flattered. Slocum was wondering where he'd seen immobility like Morgan's before. The image of a Gila monster suggested itself.

"Heinzy," Morgan began. "It is 'Heinzy' your friends call you? The diminutive? Well, no matter. Every year I meet a number of ingenious young men. I do not seek them out. Rather, they force themselves upon my attention. My interests are so wide that any young man out to acquire wealth, sooner or later finds himself in competition with me, or my colleagues, Frick, Astor, or Rockefeller. We see them all."

Heinze was a pretty good-sized fish. He didn't like being treated like a job applicant. "I'm not looking for handouts, Morgan," he snapped.

"Quite so. Quite so. The ingenious young man never does. Correct me if I've misjudged you, sir. You have come to propose we share wealth that, until your Minnie Healy, was mine alone. You think that would be just. Since you are an ingenious young man, you have also come to crow."

Heinze was taken aback. "There's plenty for everybody," he said.

Morgan's eyebrows raised a fraction. "Not correct," he said.

Slocum walked over to the window and drew the curtain. The window was covered with bars. "Homey place you got here," he said.

Slow as a lizard, Morgan's head turned to Slocum. "Mr. Slocum. I meet many men every year, but not, I confess, men of your type."

Slocum was still looking out the window. It was raining, and the water splattered the sidewalks and sent the pedestrians hurrying to cover. "What type is that?"

Morgan didn't answer him directly. "You were an officer with the Confederate Army."

A little chill down Slocum's back. Not many men

knew that, and it wasn't a thing he jabbered about himself. "Captain," he admitted.

Morgan was dead still. "So you are Mr. Heinze's captain now?" he asked.

Slocum nodded his head.

"Would you be interested in more congenial employment?" Morgan asked.

"Nope."

Morgan accepted the refusal without a blink. "Mr. Slocum, it's rather easy for one man to learn about another. "If"—Morgan shrugged—"he has resources. It's simple to determine the state of a man's finances: his creditors, debtors, marriage status. Even"—here he looked at Heinze—"his sexual preferences."

"The Pinks," Slocum suggested.

A shadow of a smile crossed Morgan's face. "And others," he said. "The curious man will always find answers. Don't you think so?"

Heinze didn't like the direction the talk had taken. Hell, it almost seemed like the great J. P. Morgan was more interested in a cheap gunfighter than in the Minnie Healy's owner.

Heinze snapped, "What the hell does this have to do with my proposition?"

"Hush, sir. You'll have your turn," he said, as if he were reprimanding a schoolboy. "I have inquired about John Slocum," he noted. "In 1865 you were discharged from the 114th Mississippi Rifles. When you returned home to your family farm, you found others in possession. There was an altercation in which two men were slain. Though posters were drawn and a modest reward was offered, you were never caught. In fact, you seem to have vanished. Under your own name."

Slocum had used so many different names in his travels, he couldn't remember them all. He'd never wanted to be notorious. For a man on the outlaw trail a little fame was very dangerous.

"Now," Morgan continued, "sometimes a man of your description appeared in the West, committed a felony, and vanished again. Such a man, named Mac-Guire, held up the Nations Bank in Ardmore, Oklahoma. Another man, one 'Willis,' is wanted for stage robbery in New Mexico. The Mexican government is looking for someone with the improbable name of Gabe Dawson. He made off with a gold shipment from the Sonora mines. Makes quite an interesting pattern, don't you think?"

Slocum was feeling the power of this man—power that could ferret out all the aspects of his life and examine them as if under a microscope. "Sure," he said briefly. "Some might find it interesting."

Now Morgan's smile was quite broad, even welcoming. His teeth were small and neat and regular. "I am offering you employment, sir."

"I already turned you down."

"Ah, loyalty. How refreshing. Mr. Slocum, suppose I were to furnish the appropriate authorities with the information I possess. Now, if I were to give over the files I've had compiled on your, uh, activities, I suspect Mr. Heinze would lose his captain. Though I'm sure Mr. Heinze is very ingenious, I think he does need a good captain. It would be to my advantage, don't you think."

Slocum grinned at him, a fierce reckless grin. "You got a lot of money."

"Yes."

"And you own a few senators and governors and judges and maybe the President of the United States."

"Yes."

"You have a hell of a good time, don't you?"

"I do."

"You bulletproof?"

"What?"

"I just asked you if you were bulletproof."

Morgan shrugged. "I can hire a thousand guards.

I can . . ." He said no more because Slocum's hand fluttered, like the flutter of a hummingbird's wing, and suddenly J. P. Morgan's upper lip hurt. Slocum's Colt had smashed into Morgan's lip, just under his nose. Slocum held the cold circle of steel against Morgan's face, pressing pretty hard. "Call them," Slocum suggested softly. "Call your guards."

When J. P. Morgan opened his mouth, he stuttered, "You'd ha–ha–hang."

Slocum's grin was the grin of a man who'd find the hangman funny. " 'Deed I would," he agreed, without removing the revolver.

"Hey," Heinze said. "That's enough. The joke's not funny anymore."

"Ain't no joke, is it Morgan?"

The man's voice was even once more. "It isn't," he said.

When Slocum uncocked his pistol and holstered it, Morgan couldn't stop himself from rubbing his deadened upper lip. "Why don't you call your guards, Morgan," Slocum said in a weary flat voice. "Why don't you turn over all your suspicions to the law?"

"Because you'd kill me," Morgan said, quite calmly.

Slocum agreed. He also said that he was glad to be a type of man Morgan didn't meet too often. If Morgan called out the dogs, John Slocum would make it his entire and total business to kill J. P. Morgan. He said he'd had a little practice at that sort of thing and could probably do it. "If I was to die killin' you, I'd be honored," Slocum said.

Morgan knew men. He knew Slocum would do just what he said. "Yes," he said. "I will not act against you."

Once more Slocum nodded. He touched his hat to take his leave, not in respect for Morgan's wealth, but in respect for Morgan's word.

Morgan protested, "But I have rooms upstairs for you and Mr. Heinze."

"I'll bet you do. It's a little close in here. I'll meet you tomorrow, Heinze."

As John Slocum walked out of the room, Morgan called that they would all have lunch at the India Club, tomorrow at noon.

"I'll let you know," Slocum said.

The cold rain felt good on Slocum's face, and he didn't give a damn that water collected on his hat brim and dripped down his back. Soon his shirt was soaked through. Somehow it made him feel clean. He remembered the night he left Heinze to the tender mercy of the cowboys in Helena. This time he'd left Heinze with a much nastier customer.

People noticed the tall, rangy westerner as he made his way down Madison Avenue, because he was so tall and because he didn't seem to give a damn how wet he got.

Slocum walked south until he found a little bar off Gramercy Park. The bar was called Pete's, and he asked for a glass of rum. He rubbed his hands dry and drank his rum in peace, then took to the weather again.

He found a small hotel facing the park and took a room for one night under the name Ellis.

The next morning he woke early, had breakfast in the hotel, and after asking directions at the desk, started to walk downtown. The elevated trains rattled overhead and the horse-drawn trolleys made the streets hazardous, but he enjoyed his walk, rubbernecking like any other tourist. He passed the new headquarters of the Atlantic Cable Company, which had just completed its undersea connection with Europe. Further along he stopped to admire the lobby of F. W. Woolworth's elaborate "Temple of Commerce." New York City was busy, prosperous, and growing—in the wake of the financial panics that had finished U. S. Grant's administration.

The India Club was situated on a small square

dominated by the tall, triangular headquarters of the Cocoa Exchange. Once he'd located the place, Slocum strolled over to the East River docks. He had a little time to kill, so he sniffed the humid air and watched the stevedores hustling cargo ashore from the clipper ships and the stodgy steamships.

Until Slocum mentioned J. P. Morgan's name, the doorman of the India Club didn't want to let him in.

Slocum expected to find Morgan in a private dining room, but, no, he had a corner table in the main dining room. He and his two guests. Both Clare and Heinze were more interested in the financier than in each other. Clare was showing herself to best advantage, and Heinze was being witty as hell. The table was separated from the rest of the vaguely nautical dining room by a velvet rope, which the captain lifted for Slocum.

Morgan was the genial host. "Good afternoon, sir," he said. "I trust you slept well."

"Yeah."

With his own hands, Morgan poured his glass of champagne. "Monopole, fifty-nine. An exceptional year, don't you think?" he waited for Slocum's opinion. Heinze sipped the champagne judiciously, though he hadn't been asked.

"Tell you what, Morgan," Slocum said, "I'm like the first cowman ever saw a sheep. I know they're all different, but they all look like a bunch of wooly bastards to me."

"It's quite good," Heinze said decisively.

Morgan ordered lunch for all of them. Fresh shrimp, lobster, and clams on the half shell. And more champagne, of course. Always more champagne.

While they ate, other diners paused at the rope to exchange nods with J. P. Morgan. But seemingly none dared to pass the simple velvet rope, and Morgan didn't say much more than hello to any of them.

With his fork, Morgan pointed out a lovely tawny-haired girl who was dining with an older man. Her father.

"You want her?" Morgan asked Heinze. "I understand you go for that sort of thing. I'm assured she is a virgin."

Heinze examined the girl like a man buying a horse. "She's a fancy looker all right."

Morgan ate a little more lobster. "Her father will be ruined if I don't intercede. Do you want her? No obligation, of course—since we're going to share the wealth, we ought to really share it, don't you think so, Mr. Slocum?"

Slocum ate lunch. "The fish is pretty good," he said. "They got pretty good fish in San Francisco, too."

Morgan's eyes were amused, "Tell me, Mr. Slocum. What are your impressions of the world of finance?"

Slocum asked, naively, "Oh, you mean with the fancy eating place and the champagne and being able to buy the girl and all?"

"Of course."

Slocum shrugged. "I've known a lot of pimps. Some of them were okay. Most of them were scum."

"Jesus, Slocum," Heinze snapped. "Watch your fucking mouth."

Slocum put down his fork and raised his eyes to Heinze. Briefly, Slocum smiled. "You two make a deal?" he asked.

"Mr. Morgan and I are going to let bygones be bygones," Heinze said in a voice that meant: *Who are you to be asking?* "I'll operate the Minnie Healy and he'll operate the Amalgamated."

"Then I expect you won't be needing my services anymore?" Slocum didn't care too much, one way or another.

"Why, no," Heinze said quickly. "Hell, John, I wasn't born yesterday. Let's say I keep you on for a while—until I'm satisfied that things are going smoothly."

"Very sagacious," Morgan agreed. "Very sagacious indeed. Have some more of this lobster. No? How about some pastries then?"

Slocum ate quickly and deliberately. It was good food. It was fuel.

"Mr. Slocum"—Morgan kept after him for some damn reason—"yesterday I said I meet a good many men with ingenuity. I said I wasn't too impressed with them. But Mr. Heinze—he's rather a different case, don't you think?"

The damn fool, Heinze, was glowing from the praise, and it was hard for Slocum to keep from groaning.

"He's a pisser all right."

One of the hovering waiters brought a pastry cart to their table. Clare and Heinze oohed and aahed. Slocum and Morgan had coffee. "I have to watch my weight," Morgan said. "But surely you, Mr. Slocum, you can have something—a torte perhaps, an eclair?"

Slocum shook his head no.

"Mr. Heinze has scope," Morgan decided. "And scope with ingenuity is a rare combination."

Slocum drank his coffee and got up. "Good grub," he said.

Morgan was surprised. "Why, Mr. Slocum, where are you going?"

"I came here to eat," John Slocum said. "I've ate."

7

New York City was the biggest city in the world, but to John Slocum it was Indian country. On the crowded, busy streets he felt the same inexplicable tingling of nerve ends he'd felt when he was the only white man between the Missouri and Fort Bozeman —the only white man in Sioux country.

After lunch with Heinze and Morgan, he'd returned to his hotel, only to check out twenty minutes later. He caught a cab, switched to the elevated, and watched for the watcher's eyes he felt on him. At the last minute he changed trains. He waited on the high windy platforms until every other soul had boarded. But nothing eased his worried spirit. Someone had his eye on John Slocum, and this wasn't his natural place —he didn't know the right responses here. Finally, he checked into a fleabag on Elizabeth Street. Most of the hotel guests were workmen, and the rooms were wire enclosed cubicles; but for the moment, Slocum felt that he'd shaken his tail.

He waited in the lobby, his Colt concealed by the newspaper he kept in his lap. Once or twice he thought he had his man. A burly, swarthy workingman caught his attention when he asked the price of a room and then marched right out again. Once a furtive face peeked into the lobby from the back, but it was just a Chinaman collecting hotel laundry.

After an hour or so watching the entrance, Slocum figured he'd lost his shadows for good. He checked out of the fleabag and began a long walk around town. This was the heart of the Jewish settlement, and the street merchants who noted his hard, angular face and peculiar eyes thought of the Cossacks they'd fled in the ghettos of Russia and Poland. Slocum carried his saddlebags slung over his shoulder as he ambled through the polyglot crowd, enjoying the vendors' harangues and the impassioned bargaining over a bolt of cloth or a tin pot. He let his impressions run into one another without a pause. Slocum didn't feel any particular need to understand the astonishingly variegated life he saw all around him. He was satisfied just to take it in.

He thought about Heinze and wondered how long it would take Morgan to pick him clean. John Slocum had seen his share of thieves and grifters, but he'd never met a man as slick as Morgan. *He'd cut your throat between the soup and salad,* he thought.

Clare was sulking when the bellman knocked softly on the door of her suite. After the lunch with Morgan, Heinze had given her the brushoff. "Some business to discuss," he'd said. But his eyes never left the auburn-haired virgin even while he spoke to her. "Yeah," she'd said, "monkey business." Heinze laughed.

The bellman told her a gentleman was waiting downstairs and she flew into a panic. *Heinzy has changed his mind,* she thought, *and my hair's a mess.* Her hair was tousled and her face was ugly from crying. Hurriedly, she made up her face. She rushed for her hairbrushes. And half an hour later Clare sauntered into the lobby like a princess of the blood.

Her face fell. "Oh," she said when she found Slocum in the hotel bar, "I thought . . ."

"That Heinzy was comin' back to you?" Slocum grinned his most infuriating grin. "Have a drink."

"Some white wine, please," she said in her little girl's voice.

When the barman brought her wine, Slocum tapped his glass to hers and said, "To crime."

"That's not very funny." Her mouth was in a pout.

Slocum shrugged. "Heinze still hanging on Morgan's coattails?" he asked.

"They have more business to discuss," she said loyally.

Slocum liked the look of this girl. He liked her gray eyes, her milk-white complexion. He didn't care much for her personality, but he'd met worse.

"Morgan'll eat him raw."

"Augustus can take care of himself."

"Yeah. But he don't want to. He wants to be loved, and I don't think old J.P. ever made that mistake. You want to have dinner with me?"

Clare had spent five hours in her suite feeling sorry for herself. She hadn't a thought in her head unconnected to Heinze and what Heinze might be doing. So she said, "I was going to take in a concert. The Berlin is playing at Carnegie Hall. They are introducing Wagner to America."

"Uh-huh. All right. But first let's get some eats."

So Slocum left his saddlebags with the hotel clerk for safekeeping and accompanied the graceful, aristocratic lady into the dining room. Slocum asked Clare a few questions to get her started and then didn't say very much more. Once Clare was talking about her favorite topic, she could talk for hours. The hotel food was mediocre, but they drank two bottles of champagne and didn't notice the food.

Clare had been born in St. Louis—her father was part owner of one of the steamboat companies that were the lifeblood of the plains in the early days. A prosperous burgher, he'd raised his only daughter to take her natural place in the scheme of things. Early on, she'd been removed from the public schools. Clare attended schools for ladies, schools that emphasized deportment instead of McGuffy's Reader, and though

none of the eager young things could add a simple
column of figures, they could assess a man's wealth
with the accuracy of an accountant. Clare knew how to
dress and how to be charming. And, according to her,
F. Augustus Heinze had taken her maidenhood. She
didn't say "maidenhead" because that word was a little
too graphic for a woman of refined sensibility.

"And now," she said sadly, "he has found another
prize to pluck."

"The girl at the India Club?"

"Did you hear that damn Morgan?" she said
fiercely. "He was offering that girl to Augustus on a
platter!"

"Uh-huh."

"Well," she turned her head to show off her best
profile, "I think it's disgusting. It's lewd and immoral."

Slocum didn't think anybody who'd rattled the
springs with her lover and a whore had much call to
get uppity, but he didn't say anything. Clare needed
plenty of illusions. She covered his rough hand with
her delicate one. "Mr. Slocum . . ." Her tongue pushed
out between her lips like a promise. "I do so wish to
see the concert. When we return to Butte City, all the
other belles will die from envy."

Slocum had a slight fondness for spirituals, campfire
songs, and the bawdy songs soldiers sang to pass the
time on a long march. He'd been to a concert once in
Denver, and it put him to sleep. But, what the hell,
maybe there was something in it. Besides the girl, of
course.

When the waiter presented the check, it was high:
just shy of twenty dollars, and Slocum had it charged
to Clare's room. After all, she was Heinze's girl; let
him pick up the tab. He added a generous tip before
signing with a flourish, "F. Augustus Heinzy."

It had started to rain again, and they waited in the
hotel lobby while the doorman flagged a cab. Though
nobody in the lobby showed any particular interest in

the pair, Slocum felt his neck hackles rise and knew that whoever had been on his trail before had picked him up again.

The closed hansom was damp and cold, and even the heavy lap robe didn't do much to dispel the chill. The gas lights lined Broadway north to the barren space that was in process of becoming Frederick Olmstead's park.

A crowd of well-dressed New Yorkers was waiting outside Carnegie Hall, hoping for last-minute tickets. Morgan had donated his private box to Clare—else they wouldn't have had a prayer of getting in. The sign over the ticket booth read: Sold Out.

Clare kept her face pressed to the isinglass windows, looking for celebrities, hoping to spot some of the Four Hundred she'd read about in the magazines.

Out of habit Slocum kept his face inside where a random shot would have a little trouble finding him.

His nervousness made him angry. He'd faced danger a hundred times before and never faltered. Why was he so worried now? It was the unknowing. Once he found out the shape of the danger, he'd meet it head on. But until the danger declared itself, he felt helpless as a target in a shooting gallery.

Clare skipped down lightly from the cab at the ticket office, waving her precious pass. A few well-dressed patrons grumbled when she swept right by them. Some meant to grumble at Slocum when he followed, but held their tongues. There was something explosive about the plain-dressed, rangy man that no sensible person would care to ignite.

Carnegie Hall was less impressive outside than Slocum had imagined: just a plain high brick building and a short Italianate collonade where people could wait out of the weather. Clare handed Morgan's pass to the usher. Open sesame. The usher beamed and called another to watch his post while he escorted them personally to their box. The stairs were wide and covered with a soft red carpet that felt like prairie turf under Slocum's boots.

Slocum examined the door to the box after the usher left. He locked up. The death of Abraham Lincoln went through his mind, but with his Colt on the seat beside him he could dismiss the thought. Lincoln hadn't been a gunfighter.

The box was newly painted and newly upholstered, the plaster nymphs at the railing had been recently touched up, and the space smelled of J. P. Morgan's cigars. It was a little too personal a place for Slocum's taste and reminded him too much of Morgan's heavy-handed power.

He thought the Berlin Symphonic looked silly when it came out on the stage: The forty men in identical tuxedos looked like toys. Clare didn't pay the orchestra any mind; she was too busy examining the occupants of the other boxes and receiving their examinations in turn. Slocum sat rather far back from the edge of the box. From there he could pick off anyone in the audience—and he didn't think he was immune to anybody with the same idea. His eyes flickered constantly over the faces in the nearest boxes, matching men with his memories, but didn't see anything more unusual than one old gentleman who had his hand deep in the gown of the giggling girl who shared his box.

The house lights dimmed and the orchestra tore into the first strains of the overture from *Tannhäuser*. John Slocum was no music lover, but this loud, soaring stuff captivated him. The horns reeked of bloodshed, war, and valor, and though he thought it was a little bit cornball, his body stirred with the grand heroics of it all.

He free-floated. From time to time, usually when some instrument fluffed a note, he checked the faces of the other spectators, seeking his danger; but he spotted nothing. Nothing at all.

At intermission, Clare wanted to go downstairs to

mingle and Slocum wanted to stay where he was. She did. He did. She left without much grace. "Well, honestly, John. Don't you know how a gentleman's supposed to behave?"

"Nope."

The second act was more of the same, and this time, Slocum's spirit didn't soar with the music but remained earthbound and cynical.

Music like this would lead men into horrible battles before it was forgotten. Slocum got restless and insisted they leave early. He figured that the after-concert confusion would be a golden opportunity for a knife-man. They strolled down the wide staircase alone, Slocum eying the ushers who stood like so many sentries outside the rich men's doors.

Clare was quite gay. She was babbling about the names and faces she'd seen. Jay Gould, Frick, and one of the Mellons had attended the concert, and she wondered what they thought of her and Slocum in Morgan's box without the great man present. "I'll bet they're just dying to meet me," she enthused. "I'll bet their eyes just fell out of their head."

Slocum grunted.

Slocum accompanied her to the door of her suite, just as though he had every right in the world. After inserting the key in the lock, she turned around to shake the tall man's hand. He bent over and kissed her, his mouth pressed hard against hers, his hands crushing the delicate fabric at her waist. It quite took her breath away. She opened her mouth to protest, but he'd unlocked her door, and now she was in the ante-chamber to the suite and shaking her head, no, no, no.

"John," she whispered, "we mustn't."

He laughed. With something like cruelty in his eyes, he kissed her again and she felt her knees trembling. With one hand she tried to push him away, but there was little conviction in her shove.

He took her hand and led her into the brightly lit

parlor of the suite. Then, deliberately, he unfastened her bodice and shoved it aside. She blushed when he drew back to let his eyes caress her full breasts, which were harder-tipped than she might have wished.

Then she bolted right into the bedroom and slammed the door behind her. She didn't lock it, and Slocum took time to take off his boots and shirt before he pushed the door open.

Clare lay in the ruins of her gown, pink as a seashell in the middle of the bed. She had her hand across her eyes. She kept it there while he peeled off his pants.

"I don't think we should," she said, when she felt the weight of his body on the bed.

The smell that rose from her was heated and ripe.

She said, "John, no," as he spread her knees apart. She kept her hand over her eyes.

He pulled her hand away and looked deep into her eyes as his cock settled into her inch by inch.

8

A heavy banging woke Slocum from a deep, deep sleep. At the first bang on the door, his hand snaked across the bed and found the butt of his Colt. On the second bang, his eyes opened. "Message for Mr. Slocum," a muffled voice cried. "Urgent message, sir."

Outside, the sky was still black. Slocum turned up the bedside lantern and sat up, Colt in hand, trying to get his bearings. His watch on the bed table read 3:15. Hell, he'd only been asleep a couple hours. The banging resumed. "Urgent message, sir."

The girl beside him stirred slightly but did not wake. Without disturbing her, Slocum slipped naked out of bed and padded noiselessly to the door. "Slip it under the door," he said, his hand drawing back the hammer of his Colt to half-cock.

A creamy yellow envelope with a familiar monogram embossed in the corner appeared. Slocum heard the messenger say, "Good night, sir. Sorry to disturb you." Slocum listened until the man's footfalls disappeared down the hall.

He tore the envelope and pulled out a folded sheet of notepaper that bore the same monogram.

"Slocum," it read. "Something big's come up. I need your gun to back me up. Meet me at Number 4 Minetta Alley at 4 A.M. F. A. Heinze."

Slocum swore aloud and dropped the message. Luckily Clare was sleeping deeply and wasn't likely to wake. His cock rose to salute her memory, though she'd milked him dry not two hours ago.

He splashed a little water on his face and examined

his rough features in the mirror. He could use a shave, but it would have to wait. He dressed neatly and economically, without a wasted move. He'd have to wear yesterday's clothes; but then he wasn't going to a fashion show. He emptied his Colt and rolled the cylinders, checking alignment. He snapped the hammer on an empty cartridge case he kept for just that purpose. The sear was fine; a little rough maybe, but it'd do. Inside his saddlebags, he found an Arkansas toothpick. A long stiletto with a blued twelve-inch blade. The knife wasn't any use at all for skinning a buffalo, but it'd put a man's lights out sooner than you could say good night. He strapped the sheath to his wrist so the handle was just inside his jacket sleeve. He shook his arms to see if the knife was right and, satisfied, scooped up his Stetson. His coat was a short buffalo hide coat, and he figured it'd keep him warm. He didn't expect it to save his life. Slocum thought of his two Remington .41 double derringers but decided he was carrying enough iron to handle the situation.

Before he left the suite he kissed the girl who lay so quietly under the blankets. She muttered something in her sleep, something about Heinzy. *True love,* Slocum thought, and grinned.

Slocum didn't hurry down the stairs, and he paused before the entrance to each floor. If someone had been listening for his approach, he would have been thrown slightly off timing by Slocum's pause. That might have made a difference. Nobody was waiting, but Slocum could smell something faint in the air, like the smell of a bear cave: teeth, bones, and half-rotted flesh.

Nobody was in the spacious lobby at that hour except for the desk clerk and a solitary old bellhop. The bellhop came over real quick when Slocum beckoned him. "I'm Slocum," the tall rider said. "Who gave you the message?"

"It was a cabby, sir. He said it was urgent."

"Which cabby?"

The bellman looked confused, so Slocum said, "Okay," and gave him a four-bit piece. The generosity prompted the bellman to rush into the fog to collar a cab before Slocum could restrain him. He didn't want the first cab to stop in front of the Plaza Hotel tonight. He'd asked the second one, though surely there was no reason for his suspicion.

The cabby knew the address and didn't object when Slocum came up on the box to ride shotgun. The driver said, "Don't get too many fares riding up here, sir. Oh, sometimes, when the weather's fine, you get a sport who wants to take the air, but usually when it's foggy like tonight, the gentlemen like to stay inside."

Slocum handed him a dollar. "I ain't no gentleman," he explained. The fact was, he wanted every bit of vision he could get and behind those isinglass curtains he'd be blind as a bat.

The fog hung low and brown over the streets. It didn't swirl like the San Francisco fog; it just hung there like a cloud on a mountain peak. But a man couldn't see much. The horses seemed to be wading in fog rather than walking, and the clop of their hooves was muffled.

Slocum couldn't guess how the hell the driver knew where he was going. You could only see one side of the street at a time, and the lines of gaslights were futile glows in the darkness and fog.

Slocum pulled the lap robe over him, but his eyes never stopped roving. Too many damn fine spots for an ambush. That's what he didn't like about New York. You couldn't relax; a killer could be hiding anywhere.

Slocum caught another whiff of the feral smell he'd smelled in the hotel. Instead of scaring him, it sent a very faint smile to his face. Slocum liked this. It was the waiting that was hard. The killing was pretty easy.

As the cab proceeded down Fifth Avenue, past the

mansions and churches, Slocum was doing the gunfighter's mental exercise. He emptied his mind of
compassion for his fellows and of fear for himself. He
told himself that he was just a dead man walking, that
he should have been killed years ago, and that it
wouldn't make the slightest difference if he was dead.
That was the gunfighter's edge. When the pistols
roared and muzzle flashes lit up the night, the gunfighter didn't give a damn whether he lived or died.
Because he was as good as dead, he had neither fear
nor hesitation. Unlike an ordinary man who found
himself in a fight, a gunfighter's nerves never interrupted the passage between perception and reaction.

If a kid had set off a firecracker beside the cab,
Slocum would have killed him and it would have been
a few seconds before Slocum knew what he had done.

Slocum relaxed. He no longer felt the clammy
dampness on his cheeks. His hands weren't cold. He
didn't bother to grip the butt of his revolver. He could
find it quick enough when the time came. He didn't
wonder what Heinze wanted. Maybe Morgan had
turned on Heinze too early. Maybe something else.
Slocum's nerves were untuned to the sophistications of
the business that had brought them so far. But he was
attuned to danger.

The driver beside him was scared. He didn't like
having anybody on the seat with him, and if he'd had
to choose a companion, this dangerous-looking man
would have been low on the list. Slocum was whistling
some tune, and the driver strained to make it out.
Slocum was whistling "Tenting Tonight on the Old
Campground" in a mournful key, though if anyone
had asked him, he wouldn't have known what tune
he was whistling or why.

The cab passed through the high white arch of
Washington Square and into the warren of old narrow
streets south of it.

Maybe the horses were picking up the same smells

that had disturbed Slocum, because they threw their heads back and the driver had to whipsaw them with his reins. When the driver pulled onto the narrow street that funneled into Minnetta Alley, he said, "It's up there, just a couple hundred feet," as if he were trying to reassure himself. The driver felt something cold dropped into his hand, and when he turned to his passenger, the man had vanished into the mist. The driver opened his fist and saw a five-dollar gold piece. Quickly, he clucked to the horses and hurried them back through the fog. Hell, this was enough business for one night. He was going back to the stables where he and his cronies could drink away the rest of the dismal night.

Slocum slipped down the street, smooth as grease. The buildings beside him were very old. One-family dwellings during Revolutionary times, they now housed a variety of small businesses. All were dark.

The fog seemed heavier here, and the back of Slocum's buffalo coat was slick as otter skin. Slocum kept his hand tucked inside his coat on the butt of his pistol. He passed a couple of grocery stores, then the narrow opening to Minetta Alley. The alley served carriage houses when the tiny shops had been private homes and, from the smell, there was at least one stable down this way.

Slocum didn't move faster than the fog swirled and eddied around his body. He moved the way a black-snake moves through the walls of a house, seeking prey to mesmerize with a flickering tongue and crazy eyes.

He moved so slowly, he scarcely seemed to move at all, and when he edged around the corner into the darker alley, his body flowed around the bend. His eyes were wide open, his pupils big to catch the light. Inside the alley, he drew his Colt. He kept it at his side, his thumb on the short hammer.

His boots were noiseless on the slick stone alleyway.

Close to the wall, he cast no silhouette in the lighter rectangle of the street opening behind him. His ears strained but heard nothing but the lonesome moan of a foghorn on the Hudson.

The alley was L-shaped. Slocum darted across the street before the turn of the L so he would remain invisible to any watcher deeper in the lane.

Number four had no windows on the street floor and only one shabby door. The number was nailed into the brick next to the door with a square nail and the number had been twisted askew years and years ago.

For the first time Slocum was glad of the fog. No gunman could get a clean shot in this mist. Not a killing shot anyway. When Slocum opened the door, he pressed himself into the damp brick beside the black hole of the doorway. Ben Thompson had died on a stairwell just like this one. Men at the top and bottom cut him into rags before he could do very much with the scattergun he always carried.

Inside, Slocum felt like a bull sniffing out the last chute in a slaughterhouse. He didn't like what lay ahead but couldn't turn around now. His Colt preceded him now, extended slightly, butt in close to his hip. As he crept up the steep, worn stairs, he stuck close to the wall. If anything moved on the staircase above him, it would die. Slocum would make his explanations later.

The fog lay below him now, and he was moving into a new atmosphere. The air was hotter. Slocum smelled the bright, hard smell of metal and burned oil. The smell of deep madness or fear. Maybe he was smelling himself.

His boots didn't make a single sound up the long staircase, but the single door at the top of the stairs squeaked when he pushed it open. He half expected a gunflash to blossom in that dark room. He half expected to die right there. But his Colt would still fire, and he was leaning forward so the shock of bullets wouldn't disturb his sure and certain revenge.

The room was very slightly lighter than the staircase. A couple of windows were open to the night, and gas streetlights cast the faintest light into the room, enough for Slocum to guess its size: big, maybe forty feet on a side, occupying the whole second story of the building. It was one shade brighter than pitch black. Slocum could see the pale windows but couldn't tell whether the room was furnished or not.

He paused at the door until all the echoes of the single squeak had diminished into nothing and then waited five minutes more. Someone was inside the room waiting for him, Slocum could smell him, but without the sound of breathing or a heartbeat, Slocum couldn't move.

Nothing. No sound. No movement. Even the air was dead still, and if it touched another man it gave no sign.

When a man is set for you, he has all the obvious advantages, but a few disadvantages too. He'll expect you to come one way or another. He'll have spent time guessing your plans. He'll cover one approach; one tactic or maybe two. The assassin is vulnerable to the unexpected.

Slocum closed his eyes, slipfired the Colt, and dove through the door. Maybe the glare would blind his enemy. Maybe a nervous finger would touch off a shot and locate him. Then, number two and number three in Slocum's gun could cut him down. It might have worked, too. Ninety-nine men out of a hundred would have responded to fire with fire of their own, and if Slocum worked fast, he could tag the other man before he tagged him.

But it didn't work, and Slocum nearly died. Because his enemy didn't have a gun, he had a knife.

As soon as Slocum fired and came diving into the door, his enemy went after him, the knife held like a nail to fasten Slocum to the floor. But the enemy didn't count on Slocum's half-roll, and when Slocum turned, the knife skidded against the buffalo coat. It slashed the hide and ripped the lining between the coat and Slocum's shirt. It never caught flesh.

Slocum brought the Colt up, hammer cocked. It was a hard shot. He tried to bring the gun across his body to fire at a man above and behind him. Something like a club smashed across his wrist, and all the nerves in his hand went dead and the Colt flew from his hand like a ball he'd hurled. Later, Slocum decided the man had kicked his wrist, but now he thought the man had a club. John Slocum's Colt had crashed into the wall across the room somewhere and his enemy was above him. A man could get killed that way.

He flipped over once, twice, three times, and the scurrying sound meant his enemy was working to stay on top of him until that knife could slash again.

Slocum spun so his feet were facing his enemy and, in the same motion, his legs came back, coiled against his chest, and he let fly. The blow felt good to him. He caught his enemy full and the man made his first sound—the involuntary grunt of air driven out of him. Slocum's bootheels tore a chunk out of his chest and spun him half around but didn't finish the fight. Not by a ways.

Slocum bounced to his feet, knees bent and left hand out in the knife fighter's attitude. His numb right hand was useless, but the Arkansas toothpick was in his left, ready for belly ripping, constantly moving like a serpent's tongue. Except for that one short "Ooof," his enemy had made no sound, and no mistake either. Suddenly, Slocum backed up, real quick, indifferent to the noise of his scuttling feet. The windows lay against one wall, opaque in the blackness. Slocum wanted a wall at his back and his enemy against those windows. His enemy figured his intention, and Slocum caught just a glimpse of his shape before the man dropped down below the window line, but it was enough.

There isn't any science in a knife fight in a black room, only madness. The human body can take a lot of knifework before it dies, and the critical hit zones are impossible to find. Generally, you locate your enemy with slashes, and while you're cutting on him, he's cutting on you. Generally, the winner is the man with the most blood to lose.

But Slocum got lucky. When he sprang at that shape and crashed into the other man's body, Slocum's knife found the other's forearm. It was the knife arm, and Slocum's razor sharp Arkansas toothpick stabbed right into the bone.

The man roared and threw both his arms up, and Slocum flew off him like a featherweight. But Slocum's enemy had lost one arm, and his knife. Slocum landed pretty good on the balls of his feet, and his toothpick was ready to strike again.

The man broke. Slocum glimpsed a man's shape in the doorway hole and then he was gone. He hit every fifth step on the way down. A fool might have thrown the Arkansas toothpick after him, but Slocum had already pressed his luck as far as he could. Below, the street door slammed open. Slocum dropped down in the corner of the room, his legs shaking. After five minutes, he fired a lucifer to find his Colt. The room was big and empty. His enemy's knife was a cheap, heavy butcher knife—the kind of knife a butcher uses to chop through gristle and separate bone from bone.

9

The Minnie Healy shaft stations were nowhere as regular as the stops on an elevator. Near the surface the tunnels were thick in the veins of gold. But there were no tunnels on the four, five, or six hundred because test borings had only found country rock. The seven hundred tapped a silver vein and snaked after it in relentless pursuit. Where the vein widened, the tunnel widened too. Where it branched, the miners opened up a stope: a big cavelike room where they could scrape up every ounce of the precious ore.

The Minnie Healy was a highball operation. Three shifts of men on the workface and a double crew of timbermen, propping up the tunnel behind them. The miners were all working on bonus, and they rammed the tunnel through—sometimes as much as fifty feet a day.

Often as not, Amalgamated engineers at the Black Rock had the same drill cores as the Minnie Healy crew and knew, just as well, where the richest veins lay. Almost all of them lay directly under the Black Rock property, but Heinze, with his damn Apex Law, was sucking the riches from under their feet.

Naturally, the Black Rock superintendent drove his own tunnels after the silver, on the seven, eleven, and thirteen hundred where the deepest veins of high grade silver waited.

Already, twice, Minnie Healy miners burst into the Black Rock workings, chasing a vein that had already been mined out from the other end. They sealed the bulkheads immediately, thankful they hadn't met a tunnel filled with Amalgamated miners.

Often, the Minnie Healy crew would hear the sound of blasting ahead of them, and feel the fine dust that shook down as the Amalgamated pushed ahead, just as fast as the Minnie Healy crews.

One night, during the graveyard shift, they collided. The graveyard crews, despite higher bonuses, were always a little short-handed. Nobody likes to be getting up when everybody else is going to bed, not even the greedy.

Four men on the Minnie Healy eleven hundred. The vein was thick as a man's wrist and running native silver, and they'd followed this vein like a great silver cable. The tunnel they dug was no larger than the space a man needed to work and load the ore cars. The four-man crew was headed by a burly Finn by the name of Kievela. He was the one who tamped in the three sticks of forty percent and touched off the fuse before the crew ran back down the tunnel into a safety cage the timbermen had constructed for just that purpose. And it was Kievela who led the way back down the tunnel, the air acrid with smoke, and the rock dust glistening in the light like heavy dust motes.

The floor of the tunnel was littered with chunks of rock that had fallen from the ceiling with the blast, and as the crew moved back to the face they pried at the ceiling with long steel bars, dislodging the slabs of loose rock above them. It was a slow, careful business. Every miner knows what a man looks like when a couple of tons mash him into a bad joke.

The blast had exploded in the relatively thin rock that separated the Minnie Healy and the Black Rock. The blast broke up the face in the Minnie Healy tunnel and, like a hand clapping the skin of a drum, shook the Black Rock crew off their feet and punctured a couple of men's eardrums. The noise wasn't too bad, just a heavy thump.

Magnusen, the foreman of the Black Rock crew, caught the wooden butt of a pick in his teeth and spat angrily, spitting broken tooth and blood. His powderman was lying against the tunnel wall, mouth open and hands pressed against his head where a trickle of blood ran under his fingertips.

The air was full of dust on this side of the wall. And the rock was shattered as if someone had cracked it with a great hammer.

"Come on, you muckers, let's dig," Magnusen hollered. And half a dozen men threw themselves at the wall, ignoring the vein of silver, not even bothering to load the cars. They just pulled the rock out, hacked out, pried it loose, and the muckers shoveled it into a broken heap behind them.

The Minnie Healy men operated at a more leisurely pace and weren't thinking of what might happen on the other side of what was—to them— only another routine blast.

But then they heard the faint *clink, clink* of the Black Rock crew's picks. Kievela moved into the center of the tunnel, his ears cocked. Obviously they'd tunneled into the Black Rock and, what's more, another crew was facing them. Oh, shit.

Kievela didn't know whether to build a quick bulkhead to seal off the tunnel or lead his men and their ore cars back into the shaft station. They'd run out of silver here, that was sure.

Kievela was no quick thinker, and it honestly never occurred to him that the blast might have some effect on the men working the Black Rock. He was quite astonished when a rock bounced out of the wall, hands cleared away the edges of the hole, and a big, bloody face stuck itself through the hole between the two mines. "I'm gonna split your fucking head for this," Magnusen shouted, spewing blood from his wrecked mouth.

Kievela took half a step back as the wall dissolved before him. He wished he was back at the shaft station. His men had put down their tools. All were staring at the workface.

One of Kievela's miners snarled, "Fucking Amalgamated," and the Black Rock men were suddenly transformed from miners like themselves into strangers. Kievela took a grip on the rock hammer he carried to clean out the drill holes. One miner scooped up a three-foot length of scrap 2X4. Another held his shovel at his lip like a jousting lance.

"You're on Minnie Healy property," Kievela shouted.

Magnusen's outraged face appeared again at the hole, now enlarged enough for his entire trunk, and snarled, "We'll fucking see about that! Bunch of goddamn thieves, that's all you bastards are!"

Kievela spun to snap an order at his ponyboy. "Get back to the shafthead. Send every mucker you find here. I don't know how many of those bastards . . ."

The boy was already scampering down the tunnel for help. Magnusen was wriggling through the narrow hole. Without pressing very hard, the miner with the shovel-lance put the wooden butt against his neck, delicate as a fencer executing the stop-thrust.

"You son of a bitch," Magnusen hollered, more angry than hurt.

Kievela hefted the rock hammer experimentally in his hand. One swipe from that short, heavy hammer and this man wouldn't be cursing anybody anymore. Kievela liked a man to keep a decent tongue in his head. Magnusen withdrew again, but the hole enlarged steadily as his crew shoveled the rock behind them. One of the Minnie Healy crew picked up a fistsize rock and pegged it through the hole. Followed by another. Yells. The sound of a man hobbling around.

Magnusen himself drove through the hole, and this time the miner with the shovel failed to intercept him. But when Magnusen came to his feet, the miner swung the shovel, blade-end-to, and whacked him flat on the chest. Magnusen let out a howl and jumped on the man, sending the shovel clattering. He bowled the other man to the ground and started bashing his head against the rock floor. The man's eyes were half glazed when Kievela started tugging at Magnusen's hands from behind, but Magnusen was mad enough to kill, and he didn't let go until Kievela smacked him in the head with the flat of the rock hammer. Then Magnusen put one bewildered hand to his head and turned, dazed as a steer. "Who did that?" he asked. Because Kievela didn't want to kill him with the hammer, he retreated, and his crew moved back with him and gave up hurling their rocks through the hole.

Maybe Kievela had some idea of getting help. Maybe he was just thinking that he was getting miner's pay, not warrior's pay. But Magnusen seemed terrible to him, more terrible than a man ought to be. Kievela broke. He yelled, "Let's get out of here," and ran back toward the shaft station and reinforcements. And his men ran with him, all but the shovel bearer, who was still pretty much dazed. Magnusen was sitting on his legs anyway as he yelled his threats to the retreating Minnie Healy crew. "You bastards. You yellow-bellied bastards. Come back and fight."

When the Black Rock crew heard this, they came through the hole, too, and as soon as they got Magnusen to his feet, they started off down the tunnel like a riot.

One of them, still deaf from the explosion, was

angry enough to pick up Kievela's rock hammer and crack the dazed shovel man in the head. He meant it to render the man unconscious, but he wanted to hurt the man, too, like he'd been hurt, so he hit him too hard and fractured the man's skull. The man's eyes went white and rolled back, and his head hit the rock floor again, without a wince. The blow didn't kill him, but he'd never be right again.

Unfortunately for the Minnie Healy crew, most of the graveyard shift was working the thirteen hundred, and the mancage and skip were down there too. On their run toward the shaft, Kievela collected a couple of tunnel men, but the pony boy was still at the edge of the shaft pulling at the bell rope that called the cages up. "I can't get anyone to answer," he shouted to Kievela.

The Black Rock crew was more numerous than Kievela's, and twenty men were charging toward them, with Magnusen in the lead, blood pouring out of his mouth.

They were so close on Kievela's heels that he didn't have time to set up a defense even if he'd known how to. He did turn to face the attacking mob. Him, four men, and a boy.

One of Kievela's men swung a pick into the wall of flesh in front of him. He gutted a miner named Babcock, who opened his mouth and grabbed for the pick, which seemed to be stuck in his stomach. Babcock sat down and cried.

The rest of the Black Rock men swarmed over the Minnie Healy crew. The hardest job was getting in an unimpeded punch. Nobody took a swing at the boy. He was a noncombatant and shrank into a small space beside the timbers, making himself as small as possible. "Get him," Magnusen shouted at the swarm of men who were beating Kievela. "He's the bastard that started it."

And the men hit Kievela until anger was satisfied. They were very angry men, and when Magnusen's boot nudged him over the edge of the shaft, Kievela didn't feel a thing. Nor did he feel anything when he crashed down on the ore skip two hundred feet below —which was the first real notice the rest of the Minnie Healy men had that anything was wrong.

The top frame of the skip broke what few unbroken bones remained in Kievela's body, and he hung over the frame like a doll with most of its stuffing knocked out.

Above, on the eleven hundred, once Kievela's body sailed into space, the Black Rock crew backed off, a little horrified. Magnusen said, "That'll serve the bastard," but nobody echoed the sentiment. The cowering boy had his eyes covered and he was weeping, though he was all of thirteen years old and too big to cry.

The remains of Kievela's crew were lying on the rock floor where they'd fallen. The miner with the pick in his guts had pulled it out. He held the hole with both hands so he wouldn't fall all over the filthy floor of the shaft station.

After some indecision, Magnusen ordered his crew to withdraw. He'd heard the mancage doors close below and knew it'd be full of angry Minnie Healy miners coming for his hide. He also knew there were manways—narrow vertical tunnels that climbed between the levels—and he expected Minnie Healy miners were rushing toward him even now. *Just like rats,* he thought.

Like a military captain, he followed his men's retreat, keeping on the heels of his miners and chivvying them faster. They reached the workface ten minutes before the first of the Minnie Healy men.

Some reason of delicacy made Magnusen insist on blowing the tunnel closed on the Black Rock side.

Maybe he thought he was morally right on Black Rock property. He told his powderman to get six sticks in the roof and bring it down. He had to shout his instructions because the powderman had been one of those partly deafened by the initial explosion.

The powderman was a craftsman and didn't care to set charges in cracks when there was a perfectly good rock drill nearby, but he understood the urgency. He crimped the fuses into place and clamped fuses in the sticks he'd pressed into deep cracks in the tunnel ceiling and in the sidewalls. At the end of the quick fuse he fastened the slow fuse and asked Magnusen if he should drop the ceiling on the Minnie Healy men when they came poking into the Black Rock workings.

But Magnusen was suffering a revulsion from his anger. He wanted to be safe from pursuit, but he balked at dropping the ceiling on other miners. He'd been underground for twenty years, and deliberately blowing a roof in on other miners seemed unspeakably obscene.

The powderman, who had a technical interest, was slightly disappointed but set the fuse for two minutes. Time enough to get clear without drawing the Minnie Healy crew.

The Minnie Healy miners heard the story from the terrified boy in the shaft station and started down the tunnel. Nobody had empty hands. Before they got to the workface, the familiar earth tremor and roar of dynamite let them guess that the pursuit would be futile. They were right. At the workface they found only a mass of fallen rock and one miner who gazed at the men and smiled a curious, crazy smile full of innocence and trust.

Amalgamated's man on the spot heard the news about the underground battle and telegrammed Morgan.

He received this reply:

To: Superintendent, Amalgamated Copper
      Company
      Butte City, Montana
      Take necessary steps to impede Minnie
      Healy Operations.

                              (signed)
                              Morgan

That same morning other telegrams arrived asking Heinze's bankers to cut off his credit, urging Heinze's suppliers to sell him no more tools, rope, or dynamite. Some of Heinze's creditors swore, some vowed they'd never knuckle under to a rich Eastern bastard, but all of them finally complied.

Heinze had been back in Butte City for two days. They hadn't raced from the rail terminus north, they rode easy and slow. After New York City, its towers and more towering wealth, the West seemed small potatoes to F. Augustus Heinze. And besides, Slocum hadn't shared his enthusiasm for the city. He'd claimed Morgan had tried to have him killed and produced a ripped buffalo coat as evidence. Heinze looked at the coat and his first thought was: *How tawdry.* His second thought wasn't any more generous: He suspected Slocum of slashing the coat himself.

And though often he'd said Clare was as free as he was, Heinze didn't like her with John Slocum. Heinze hadn't any complaint. He'd had the banker's virgin in the city, and though she hadn't been much fun—she'd cried the whole time he'd fucked her—he had fucked her, and if he wanted her again, by God he would have had her again. And sure, Clare could sleep with whomever she liked but Heinze didn't like lying under his blankets, listening to his ex-girl and his employee giggling in the night—and the liquid rhythmic *slap, slap* of their frequent matings.

Heinze hated it, but couldn't think what to do. Morgan didn't like Slocum, he'd said as much himself, and even suggested Heinze get rid of the gunman. But for some reason, Heinze balked. "No, no, J.P.," Heinze laughed. "I ain't givin' up all my cards."

As soon as Heinze got back to Butte, he told Clare he was selling the house and moving into rooms at the Silver Bow Club, the millionaires' club, just down the street from the courthouse. He didn't say, but didn't deny, that she'd have to find someplace else.

Her indifference to being thrown out on her ear didn't please him, although, by rights, he ought not to have cared. She'd said, vaguely, "I suppose I can find somewhere." And he knew she meant Slocum. And the Silver Bow Club after New York, seemed a pale imitation of Morgan's club, its stained-glass windows imitative, its servants too raucous, and its brandy inferior.

Heinze knew he'd never be full partner with a man who controlled much of the wealth in the United States, but he wouldn't settle for the title "Junior Partner" either. Morgan had hinted at some kind of restricted partnership. "Perhaps, Augustus," he'd said in that fatherly way of his, "my mining interests should all be handled by one man." Heinze had no difficulty guessing who that man might be.

Slocum had vanished. Privately, Heinze thought Slocum was hiding from the assassins who'd attacked him in New York, and Heinze found that amusing. He'd never run away from ghosts in his life, and this fancy gunfighter was buried so deep that nobody could find him.

For three days he stayed with Clare in a back room at Irish World. Sometimes, another girl joined them. Sometimes Blondetta herself loosened her stays and crawled into the big rumpled bed. "R.H.I.P.," she'd say.

Heinze was topside when the fight broke out underground, and he was there when the cage brought dead miners to the surface. His men were furious. His superintendent was ready to start issuing weapons.

A whey-faced F. Augustus Heinze rode downtown to the Amalgamated's new offices and stormed upstairs to see Marcus Kelly.

"Kelly," he said, "if you don't restrain your men, I'll wire Morgan and have him shut down the Black Rock."

And Kelly had agreed with him that it was a mistake. Hell, Kelly practically groveled. But he was laughing, too, at the funny way things turned out and saying he'd never dreamed Heinze and Morgan were partners.

So Heinze had gone away satisfied, but uneasy. That night he sent his man Murph to track Slocum down and bring him to the Silver Bow Club. Heinze felt naked without him.

And that night, Pinkertons in the employ of Amalgamated bored into the Minnie Healy tunnel on the thirteen hundred. They came in between the workface and the shaft station, so nobody saw the quiet men slip into the tunnel. They didn't plan for anybody to get hurt, but an unfortunate ponyboy was killed when the tunnel roof exploded on the thirteen-hundred-foot level of the Minnie Healy mine.

The next morning, Heinze stood on the shaft platform surrounded by the miners on his morning shift. These men came in all shapes and sizes. All of them were mad.

They wore miners' uniforms and each had a lunchbox tucked under one arm and a brand-new Winchester, just fresh from the grease, tucked under the other. Some of them held the guns like they were picks or shovels. A few held the weapons as if they knew what to do with them.

Slocum stood some distance away. Like the rest, he wore miners' coveralls and hard hat with carbide lamp. Unlike the others, he carried nothing in his hands but a ten-gauge double-barreled shotgun loosely under his arm, and a loaded cartridge belt hung from his hips. He carried no other tool of any kind.

Heinze was so damn angry he had to swallow twice before he could speak. "Men, the 'gentlemen' of the Amalgamated Copper Company have cut off most of my credit and made me buy supplies like these—he touched the nearest man's rifle—"at the very highest prices and at the back door. Simultaneously they are closing the Minnie Healy tunnels and killing honest miners who only want to make a decent day's wage for their families." (The night before, Heinze had made an appearance at the murdered ponyboy's wake. The miners were in a mood to follow him anywhere.)

"So," he said, "I'm broke. When you boys go down the hole today, I don't know how I'm going to pay you. They've got us, boys. By God, they've got us by the balls."

Kievela's brother was a shift boss on the thirteen hundred. "Pay us in silver," he yelled. And the men took up the cry. Heinze sensed that the tide was on the flood, and with a cheer he yelled to the shaftman, "Brave men. We'll lick 'em yet. Cut the rope." And the mancage dropped.

Slocum smiled at Heinze, thoughtfully. Heinze stuck out his hand. After just the slightest delay, Slocum took it. "No hard feelings about Clare," Heinze said, earnestly.

Slocum grinned. "Not anymore, there ain't."

Heinze's eyes flashed and his face went red, but he held his tongue until he could speak in his normal tone of voice. "I'm hirin'" Heinze said. "I want you to lead those men."

"I thought you was broke," Slocum said.

Heinze waved his hand. "More or less," he said airily.

"Uh-huh. Well, I guess I'll go to work, Heinze,"

Slocum said. "For you the price just doubled. And when I come for my money, you better have it."

Heinze's eyes got hard. "I'll have it."

Slocum went down the hole alone—the miners were already scattered at their work, their Winchesters stacked in neat piles nearby.

John Slocum prowled. He didn't know much about fighting underground. He'd read a few books about war, but none of them spoke of fighting at the thirteen-hundred-foot level against an opponent who approached by digging and blasting. He had to know the terrain. He could guess that his enemies would be the Pinkertons, and he'd seen the Minnie Healy forces (and groaned). Couldn't be helped. Before noon, John Slocum had walked most of the working tunnels and a few of the abandoned tunnels and stopes. He said howdy to the miners he met but let his eyes tell them he was passing through, on private business of his own.

No trouble from the Black Rock yet. Slocum was under no delusions that could last.

Then he rode back to the surface, looking for the mine engineer. Soon the two of them were poring over mine maps and charts.

"When your core drill goes into the Black Rock workings, you know it, don't you?"

"Oh, sure. We've done that a dozen times. We just pull her back and try somewhere else."

"Can you get a map of the Black Rock?"

"Hell, no. They ain't gonna want us to know where they're workin' "

"But you've got that core drill," Slocum said.

The grin spread over the mine engineer's face.

The next morning, Amalgamated stopped all mining operations at the Black Rock. They had plenty of mines filling their coffers and didn't want ordinary miners involved in a bloody war.

The men who lined up for the first shift were Pinkertons, more accustomed to tracking outlaws and infiltrating workers' organizations than to mining. Some were pretty nervous. Two turned tail as soon as they could get on a surface-bound cage. But most followed the tunnels and listened to what Marcus Kelly had to say. Kelly had a lot of underground experience and wanted to lead this battle himself.

The Pinkertons were dressed like miners, but each carried a Winchester as well as the Colts each man had inside his coveralls. They couldn't dig as well as experienced miners, but when the shooting started, they'd be in their element. That's how Marcus Kelly saw it.

Kelly didn't know where he could intersect the Minnie Healy tunnels, but like Slocum, he had some pretty good guesses. So he set his Pinkertons to digging, and they soon complained of blistered hands and aching backs. "C'mon," Kelly yelled, "you bastards are moving like snails."

Heinze couldn't afford the luxury of a shutdown, so his miners worked the ore pockets as quickly as they could. Carelessly, too. The Minnie Healy was strictly a high-grade operation. What Heinze's miners left in their stopes would have satisfied many a mine operator for years.

And while Heinze's miner dug, John Slocum prowled the tunnels, shotgun slung carelessly under his arm. By now he'd asked the miners everything they knew about the location of the Black Rock tunnels and had a drill boring toward the Black Rock and a two-man crew responsible only to him.

Think of two moles digging toward each other: the blind seeking the blind.

The Pinkertons broke through on the eight hundred in a tunnel that had been abandoned just four months ago. By Heinze's orders, the timbermen had pulled two thirds of the timber sets for use in more active tunnels, and the roof of this particular tunnel was poorly supported. Marcus Kelly flashed his carbide lamp into the dark tunnel and noticed the absence of timber and the missing narrow gauge rails.

Nobody in his right mind strayed through the old tunnels. All miners with exploratory tendencies had been killed years ago. The rock above the tunnel was constantly shifting and creaking, and the roof might come down at any minute. Kelly sniffed but couldn't smell any gas in the tunnel, and it seemed to be dry. He walked a couple of hundred yards down the tunnel, though none of his Pinkerton gunmen would follow him. As one of them said, "We ain't gettin' paid to die."

Kelly hoped to locate a Minnie Healy crew working further down the tunnel, but no such luck. *Well,* he thought, *an abandoned working is better than none, and maybe he could scare the Minnie Healy miners a little.* So he sent one of the Pinks back to the Black Rock powder room to get a case of sixty percent. Marcus Kelly laid the dynamite—a long string along the length of the tunnel—and touched it off himself.

The explosion was three or four times bigger than necessary. It blew the roof down, of course. It also shook the roof on the seven hundred, which was well timbered, and collapsed part of the eight-hundred-foot shaft station.

And it scared the hell out of the Minnie Healy crew. Heinze's miners were drawing four dollars a day, which was twice what they could have gotten at Amalgamated. But that wasn't enough money to have a roof dropped on you. Every shift was a few men short now, no matter how earnestly Heinze recruited. Even when Heinze raised the daily salary to five dollars, men made up their grubstake and quit as soon as they could. Heinze was always short-handed.

Most of the miners who stayed did so because Slocum was underground with them. Somehow, the sight of the laconic gunman with the blunt shotgun hanging from his shoulder reassured them. Slocum had moved permanently underground. He didn't know when or where the Black Rock crews would break into the Minnie Healy, and he had to be on the spot. So he brought his bedroll down to the fifteen-hundred shaft station, and curled up in the corner when he wanted to sleep. Every day, Heinze sent him down food and water. Heinze always had the food delivered in a neat wicker hamper. Included was a wineglass and a small bottle of chilled Monopole. Slocum would hunker over in the mud, picking at the elegant picnic basket with his filthy hands.

The Minnie Healy got a break when one of the wall crew heard the sounds of shovels digging toward an abandoned stope on the thirteen hundred. A timberman rushed to the shaft station and rang the bell three times, then another three, then another three, the signal they'd agreed on. Then he carefully gave the thirteen-hundred signal to let Slocum know where to come.

Five minutes later, Slocum's cage dropped into the shaft station. The timberman motioned for him to follow, and the two set off down the tunnel on a dead run. The walls were tight and Slocum ran hunched over, but that didn't slow him any.

When they reached the stope, the sounds of shovels clinking against rock were much louder. The Black Rock men were just a few minutes from breaking through. Slocum checked the stope briefly, though he'd been in here a couple of times before. The roof of the stope soared eighty feet over his head, but the stope itself was only about forty feet wide. The floor was covered with huge chunks of slab rock, some of them weighing five or ten tons, and Slocum figured they'd make good cover. He told the miner to bring him five sticks of dynamite with caps. He wouldn't need a bigger charge, and more might collapse the whole damn tunnel. When the dynamite arrived, he wrapped it and set it on a high ledge above the spot where the digging sounds were loudest. Then he eased behind a good-sized slab of rock and told the timberman to make tracks. Once the sound of the man's footfalls had faded, he snapped off his carbide light and waited.

In the dark he listened to the sounds of the digging. He could hear men talking now. He also heard the constant drip of water off the tunnel roof and, now and again, the odd rustle of mine rats.

As he sat there, in a blackness so dark he couldn't see his hands, he started thinking of his family's farm in Georgia. It was green in the spring with the dogwoods blooming first, followed by the redbuds and the startling white mountain laurel that surrounded the old stone spring house. He wondered who had the land now. After his fight with the carpetbaggers, he burned the house and both big barns. He suspected the Slocum land had been attached to one of the adjacent places. Three hundred acres of fine bottomland. He wondered who was using it now. He wondered if the dogwoods were blooming and, if so, who noticed them. It made him a little homesick. He'd never see the place again, he knew that.

With a clatter, a prybar shoved a chunk of rock to the floor. Now there was a crack in the wall between the two tunnels, and through it appeared the occasional gleam of a miner's carbide lamp.

"I'm through," somebody whispered. "Joe, go and get Kelly. We'll open up, but he ought to be here."

Now the gleam of carbide lamps was steadier as the men clawed the opening out. The irregular hole grew until it was three feet square. Slocum watched the faces of the two men widening the hole with bars. They clawed the rock down behind them. Their lamps flickered over the rubble-filled stope, and Slocum pulled his head down behind the slab so they wouldn't spot him. When the two Pinkerton gunmen paused, he could hear their heavy breathing. Neither of them was in shape for this kind of work.

"You want to wait?" one whispered.

"Naw, let's give the place the once-over. It'll save time when Kelly shows up."

Slocum waited for the two men to crawl through the hole. He waited for them to get a good grip on their Winchesters. Slocum had never killed a man from ambush and wasn't about to start.

He stood, head, shoulders, and ten-gauge above the slab of rock.

"I guess that's far enough," he said mildly.

Both Pinkertons went for their iron. Strictly reflex. Slocum's ten-gauge roared twice before the Winchesters could be brought into play. They shouldn't have moved a muscle, but fighting was why they were here.

The right-hand barrel shut off one man's carbide lamp and destroyed the face beneath it as well. The Winchester flew out of the dead man's hands as the shotgun blast scrambled his brains and opened them to the air.

Slocum's left-hand barrel caught the other man high in the chest. The shotgun was loaded with double-ought buck. Each pellet was the size of a .22 slug, and half a dozen of them struck the man in a pattern that spread the width of his chest. Two drilled through his heart. One collapsed his left lung and three others ruined his right lung, too. It didn't matter. He fired once and the bullet ricocheted around the rock room like a crazy bee, but he was dead.

His carbide lamp gleamed from the floor like the eye of a giant one-eyed rat. Slocum drew his Colt and put a bullet into the Pinkerton's skull. He thought the man was dead, but he didn't want to take the slightest chance of burying him alive. Slocum backed out of the stope as flashing lights and shouts signaled the arrival of Black Rock reinforcements.

Slocum didn't want to get into an exchange of lead

with the Black Rock men. He waited until the first man poked his head cautiously through the hole before he fired at the dynamite caps a few feet above him.

The blast knocked Slocum off his feet and slammed him against the tunnel wall. God knows what it did to the Pinkertons. The face of the stope lifted briefly into the air and then settled, closing the hole and burying four of the Pinkertons who had gotten too close to the opening. When their mates dug them out, one of them was still alive but had been buried too long, and his right arm was no wider than a halibut steak. They cut it off a couple of weeks later.

Marcus Kelly's body wasn't injured in the explosion, just his pride. He stared at the heap of busted rock that covered the route into the Minnie Healy. "Heinze," he swore, "I'll get you for this. I'll fucking get you for this."

Then he bent to the work of digging his men out. To give Kelly credit, he worked harder than any of the Pinkertons digging, and when they found the survivor, Marcus Kelly tied the tourniquet above his shattered elbow with his own hands.

A dozen Minnie Healy miners ran down the tunnel toward Slocum. They'd exchanged their mining tools for the less familiar Winchesters, and they were ready for trouble. Slocum was glad to see them, though they were too late to do him any good. They made him feel less alone.

When Heinze sent down his congratulations and a note suggesting Slocum come up one shift and for a bath and a woman (did he mean Clare?), Slocum said no thanks. He scribbled a brief reply on the back of the note: "The war ain't over yet, bub. I'll stay. J.S." Then he cornered one of the shift bosses. He told the man he wanted a few modified ore cars on each working level for the miners' use. The shift boss heard him out and thought Slocum's idea was a pretty good one, and he'd set a blacksmith at work on the modifications as soon as he went topside.

The blacksmith removed the high iron sides of the cars but left the front and back. He bored two small holes—just the diameter of a rifle barrel—in the iron. It was a primitive armored vehicle. A miner could push it, protected by the double steel plate, while another rode and fired through the holes.

The work took the better part of a day, and as soon as the modified cars were ready, they were dropped down to the work crews on the skip.

As events turned out, Slocum's cars got a test run within twenty-four hours.

The Pinkertons broke through into an old manway that connected the eleven and twelve hundred levels. Nobody was working the eleven hundred since the first fight, but a small crew was following a telluride vein on the twelve hundred.

Lately they'd been posting a rifle guard on the ore cars so the ponyboy wouldn't be alone as he traveled between the workface and the shaft. The mules were quiet on a mud floor, and perhaps that's why they saw the Pinkerton before he spotted them. The Pinkerton was taking a piss when the bullet blasted by his ear. The Pinkerton let out a howl, pissed all over his leg, and drew and fired at the approaching ore train. The Pinkerton was a handy man with a Colt, and his Colt spat one, two, three, four, five, before he'd really identified his target. Two mules went down, shot in the chest. They were thrashing in their harness, tangling the lines of the mules behind them. One bullet whined by the rifle guard's ear and scared the hell out of him. He ran back toward the workface. The ponyboy let go of his useless reins and hotfooted it after. The Pinkerton was cursing his wet pants leg and loading his Colt as two more Pinks slipped into the tunnel. They all fired at the retreating miners but missed. The tunnel took a gradual turn ahead, and this turn saved the Minnie Healy men.

The three Pinkertons followed slowly. The tangle of mules was pretty nasty. One of the dying animals was lashing with his hooves, and a man had to be pretty quick to get by without a busted leg, or worse. The stink of dead mule and blood was strong and offensive.

All three Pinkertons advanced with drawn guns. "Maybe we should wait until we get a few more troops," one suggested in a whisper.

"Naw. They're up here ahead of us. Let's just ease along this tunnel and sting 'em a little."

Behind them, at the shafthead, two miners heard the brief exchange of gunfire and signaled for Slocum. When the gunman stepped off the cage, a few minutes later, he looked like something from the far side of Hell. He hadn't shaved or washed in a week. His sleep had been snatched in short naps whenever he could spare the time. His coveralls were caked with mud. Only the scrupulously clean ten gauge proclaimed him for what he was.

"Gunfire down the tunnel. About five minutes ago."

Slocum nodded. The miners on the twelve hundred had one of his armored ore cars. He hoped they'd have the good sense to use it.

When the fleeing miners rushed to the workface, their fear and confusion were infectious. One man suggested they abandon their weapons and let the Pinkertons do what they would—blow the tunnel, smash the tools, whatever. A cooler head reminded them that the Pinkertons would probably just kill them, too. That was their courage. The courage of desperation.

It was an open secret in Butte City that Amalgamated had a hundred-dollar bounty on each Minnie Healy miner—a thousand for Slocum. Heinze didn't carry a price. If anybody wondered about that, they never wondered aloud.

The Minnie Healy miners were frightened, too frightened to wait at the blank end of the tunnel like lambs at the slaughter.

The shift boss ordered one man to disconnect the steam hose from the rock drill. He ordered another to lie flat in the ore car with two loaded Winchesters. He organized the rest of his men into a squad behind the armored car and took the heavy canvas steam hose himself. The steam roared through the hose at a temperature of 250 degrees. *Hot enough,* he thought.

The ore car grumbled on the track. The miners behind rattled stones no matter how carefully they meant to walk, and the three Pinkertons had plenty of time to get set. One slipped into a hollow in the tunnel wall. The other two were slender enough to get behind the twelve-by-twelve timbers. It was a good ambush except they couldn't stick their heads out. The Pinks waited until the rumble of the ore car was very near before they came out shooting. They killed the shift boss with the first blast from their Winchesters. Their bullets clanged into the armored ore car and dented it but didn't make any impression on the concealed marksman. He wasn't much of a shot, but the Pinkertons were only twenty feet away and he was protected. He poured it on. Later he figured he'd fired fourteen rounds down that tunnel. He hit with three of them. He broke one Pinkerton's knee. He gutshot another. He hit the man he'd gutshot again. This time he tore off the man's ear, though this Pinkerton was in too much pain to be much of a threat to anyone.

While he was firing, another miner crawled alongside the ore car and pulled the steam hose from the shift boss' dead hands. He didn't think he was being brave, although he was. He was simply angry at the Pinkertons who'd killed his friend.

He released the petcock at the end of the hose, and

the tunnel ahead of him filled with live steam. A dense rush of superheated water sought out the remaining Pinkerton in his rock hollow and flayed the skin from his body. The man screamed. Though he dropped his gun, the steam stayed on him because the man behind the hose couldn't hear anything above the noise of rushing steam.

It got unbearably hot for a moment. The man died.

Afterward, when one of the miners described it, he said, "And when Clancy shut down the hose, we came up on the Pink and his clothes were all steamin' and the skin was peeled off his poor dead face like a chicken that's been in the pot too long."

Slocum arrived too late for anything but congratulations. Most of the praise went to the gunner in the ore car and the man who'd used the steam hose. The former was crowing like a banty rooster. The latter was cradling the dead shift boss's head in his hands. He was weeping, and the tears cut rivulets in his dirty face. Slocum looked at the four dead men and wondered how much longer this could go on. Both Amalgamated and Heinze buried victims of this war as "mine injuries," but sooner or later there'd be lawmen poking around down here. Besides, Slocum had had just about enough. Pausing long enough to order a bulkhead over the hole the Pinks had made, he returned to the fifteen hundred. Alone on the station platform, he sat wearily on his pile of bedding. It was moldering here in the damp. He didn't care. He shut off his carbide lamp. He'd spent so much time in blackness he was getting used to it. He found the blackness comforting. He'd been underground so long he avoided talking to the other miners, even when he could. They only came into the mine for one shift. He lived here. When he fired up a quirly, the match flare was painful in his eyes. When he closed his eyes, it was more comfortable. In his mind's eye, he saw the dead Pinkerton, his face flayed to the bone by the steam. Suddenly the taste of his cigarette made him gag and he went over to the shaft and puked into space.

Reeling on the edge of a pit whose sump was a thousand feet below him, sick of his own smell and sick at heart, John Slocum said, "This has gone far enough." He popped his carbide striker and once the low flame was burning, he tugged at the bell rope to summon the cage.

John Slocum rose into the light after ten days underground without heeding the tiny square of daylight, the shaft opening, far above him. When the cage cleared the shaft platform, he heeded the light. It blinded him. He pressed both hands to his face and stumbled from the cage, trying to dim the light through cracks in his fingers. The shaftman took his arm and Slocum let himself be led to a pile of timbers, where he sat.

It was an ordinary, bright spring day. The distant peaks of the Rockies still glistened with last winter's snow, and the sky overhead was the pale, pale blue of five thousand feet above sea level. Slocum saw none of it. His pupils had gone from large to tiny so quickly his eyes hurt. As he sat there, bit by bit, he widened the cracks between his fingers until, finally, he could stare down at his own shadow.

The shaftman was asking, "You all right? Jesus, Mac, you look like hell."

Slocum said, "Thanks, friend. I'm just fine."

When he stood up he weaved, and the shaftman's arm caught his elbow until he was steady again. John Slocum shook his head. He'd been a little close to madness down there. *John Slocum's grave,* he thought.

He borrowed the mine superintendent's horse and rode down Anaconda Road. People stared. He was six feet tall, wearing a miner's helmet and the filthiest miner's coveralls they'd ever seen. When he reined up in front of the Silver Bow Club, the flunky who tied up the gent's horses took a dim view of his attire. Slocum's face was caked with mud—the same white mud that hung heavily on his coveralls, broken at the joints. His hair was glued together with mud. His carbide lamp still burned.

Only his cartridge belt gleamed. And the shotgun he had slung on his right shoulder. The flunky forced a smile and said, "Afternoon, sir," and Slocum asked him for the time.

"Why, it's five o'clock, sir. I expect we'll be hearing the bells of Saint Patrick's any minute now." The sweet sound of the bells followed close on the man's words. Slocum took a deep breath of air and coughed when he inhaled some of the grit in his nostrils. "Jesus," he said.

The bells tolled the hour of matins, sweet and soft. A few late robins hopped around in the window boxes of the club, trying to unearth the odd earthworm.

He marched right up the front stairs of the club and, without ringing, went right in.

A man was assigned to guard the portals of the Silver Bow Club against intruders—which Slocum was. But the doorman decided he didn't want to bar the way to an armed maniac this fine spring day. "Looking for someone, sir?" he asked, hoping Slocum wasn't —or that the man he was looking for would be somewhere else.

"Where's Heinzy?" Slocum growled.

The doorman started to explain that Mr. Heinze wasn't a guest just now, but the involuntary flicker of the eye toward the smoking room told Slocum what he wanted to know.

As he marched into the cool opulence of the smoking room, his boots left greasy clots of mine mud on the fine Turkestan carpet. Slocum didn't notice, but the doorman did. In an attempt to salvage some of his duty, the doorman followed Slocum to the door of the smoking room and announced in a high-pitched voice. "Gentleman to see Mr. Heinze." Heinze was startled out of his chair and Slocum spotted him.

"Good Christ almighty!" Heinze said.

"Afternoon, Heinzy." Slocum removed his miner's helmet and tossed it into an empty chair where it deposited its load of mud.

"You look like . . . you look like you need a drink," Heinze said, keeping his eyes on Slocum as he reached for the heavy decanter behind him.

"I do."

Heinze slopped some brandy into a glass and handed it to Slocum. "What . . . what . . ."

Slocum downed the brandy in a single swallow.

"You want to talk here?" Slocum demanded. "Must be twenty pairs of ears in here, love to know your business."

Heinze whirled around to face the old-timers of the Silver Bow Club. There wasn't one head uncocked. Every eye was on the two of them.

"Sure, sure." Heinze reached out for Slocum's elbow but released it when he touched the mud. He closed the smoking room door behind him and motioned for the doorman to cease hovering. The doorman departed reluctantly. He would have given twenty dollars in gold to overhear this conversation.

"You want to keep working the Minnie Healy, right?" Slocum asked.

"Well, sure, sure I do. And I meant to tell you what a fine job you've been doing. I hope you've been getting the lunches I send down. I've been back in the kitchen here myself. 'Don't you put too much salt and pepper on that chicken, Joe. Mr. Slocum likes his chicken *au naturel.*'" Heinze laughed. Slocum didn't.

"You want to lick Morgan?"

"Of course I do." Heinze's face was puzzled. He wasn't catching Slocum's drift.

"Then you got to go on the offensive," Slocum said. "You got to hurt him back."

Slocum told Heinze what he planned to do. Heinze worried. Slocum asked how many miners had died in the Minnie Healy since the outbreak of hostilities. Heinze told him. Slocum said it was too many.

A gleam of interest appeared in Heinze's eyes—as if some train of thought had been running in his mind and just now come into the station. Heinze was thinking of what money can buy.

So Heinze told Slocum he'd go along with the plan. Heinze offered Slocum a room at the Club. He said he'd have new clothes sent around immediately.

When John Slocum got into the tub of hot water on the second floor of the Silver Bow Club, he had to change the water three times to get himself clean.

TELEGRAM

To: J. P. Morgan
      Chairman
      Amalgamated Copper Company
      New York, N.Y.

      The Black Rock shaft is only one of your shafts connected to the Minnie Healy workings.
                                          John Slocum

What Slocum said in his telegram was perfectly true. The Minnie Healy was connected on the south to the Elm Orlu, on the north to the Granite Mountain and Badger, and on the west to the Speculator shaft.

The shaft is the core of any deep mine. All men and materials pass through it. Water lines, steam lines, and pump lines drop from the surface along the sides of the shaft. It houses and encloses the ore skips and mancages. Though often levels are connected within the mine by manways and sometimes by hoistways as well, the main artery of a deep mine is the shaft.

Heinze decided to travel to Helena. He thought he could do some fence mending with the legislators. He also thought the climate would be healthier.

Slocum slept for twenty hours. When he woke, he dressed in his new clothes and went down to the club dining room for dinner. He ate an enormous dinner, drank two glasses of fine champagne cognac, and had the meal put on Heinze's bill. Then he took a cigar in the smoking room alone. He didn't speak to any of the other members in the club, not even to those friendly souls bursting with curiosity about this man and about what was happening underground at the Minnie Healy.

Then Slocum retired upstairs, where he slept for another eight hours.

He woke, as he'd intended, at four A.M., a good hour and a half before sunrise. He had no particular reason for selecting such an early hour. Once word got around about today's doings, he wouldn't be safe in Butte City, proof or no proof. Slocum's habitual desire to keep his business private made him select an hour when few men were abroad on the street.

He dressed carefully. Though the Club's valets had done their best with his mine coveralls, he was through with the simple sack suit. If he was going to die today, he'd die in his own clothes. The hardhat and lamp—he'd need those. That's all.

Morgan had plenty of time to warn the Amalgamated men in Butte City. Slocum hoped Amalgamated had pulled all its men out of the Black Rock. Maybe they'd put on extra guards.

That was okay. How many times do you have to rattle before you strike?

The lobby of the club was deserted, and the doorman slept in a chair beside the door. Slocum unfastened the heavy bolts without waking him and slipped out into the night.

The boy at the livery stable was asleep, too, but

he woke up to take Slocum's money and fetch his mountain horse. The horse seemed glad to see him. Too much inaction can make a horse restless and peevish. The mountain horse was too well-mannered to show it, but Slocum knew he'd have to let it run once he left town. If he left town.

The stars were out. The white-washed band of the Milky Way swooped across the night. Slocum speculated. Maybe on some planet attached to one of those myriad suns some warrior sat by a campfire waiting for the sunrise and a battle.

John Slocum was never alone. Too many warriors had died and they all knew each other in their blood.

The horse clip-clopped up the Anaconda Road. The Amalgamated mines were humming, the ore wagons rolling hard down the dusty road toward the smelters that'd turn the silver ore into ingots.

The miner at the Minnie Healy gate was carrying a rifle. When he saw Slocum, he leaned his rifle against the gate and tipped his hat. Slocum tried to remember the man from those dark nights he'd spent underground with the moles. He couldn't place him: Powderman on the twelve hundred? Timberman on the fourteen hundred? Shaftman? Slocum touched his own Stetson in return. He had the hardhat tied behind his saddle. He hoped tonight was the last time he'd need it.

The mine superintendent greeted Slocum at the shafthead. Slocum slung his shotgun over his saddlehorn. He unfastened his holstered Colt and put the gun away in his saddlebags. Tonight would be knifework. Slocum said, "Bring the shift out of the hole. And I want you to send somebody—a ponyboy, anybody—over to the Black Rock and tell 'em there's a fire in their shaft."

A mine fire is the most feared of all mine disasters. If there were any miners down the Black Rock, the rumor of fire would send them packing.

Pretty soon the mancage was hustling up and down the Minnie Healy bringing bewildered crews topside. Since it was a hurry-up job, men rode the empty ore skips, too, hanging like flies on the steel metal sides. "That's it, then," the superintendent said when the mancage came up empty. "There's nobody down the hole."

Slocum took one last look around. The wind was blowing the smelter fumes off the hill, and for once the air smelled sweet. He took a deep breath of the air before he strapped the Arkansas toothpick to his wrist. The knife wasn't concealed. The sheath was belted over his shirt on his forearm.

The mine superintendent couldn't take his eyes off the knife. He shook his head as though shaking off a bad dream. He said, "Better you than me, brother. Good luck."

John Slocum smiled faintly.

The cage dropped him down to the twelve hundred and stopped. It'd stay here in case he returned.

The mine smelled particularly foul to Slocum, though the fans were working. He'd been out of the mine for thirty-six hours. The workings of the Minnie Healy were strange to him. The muck beside the tracks already covered his boots above the instep, and he knew this set of clothes would only see one night's wear.

He stopped once before he reached the bulkhead that closed off access to the Black Rock workings. John Slocum lifted the heavy bar that guarded the powder room—set deep in an abandoned stope where an accidental explosion wouldn't destroy the whole mine.

He selected his dynamite carefully from the freshest cases. Dynamite is just sawdust soaked in nitroglycerine, and when sticks lie around long enough, the nitro seeps to the bottom, forming a heavy yellow stain that is as unstable as a prude in a whorehouse. Slocum tested and unwrapped five minutes of slow fuse and opened a new box of caps. The caps were fulminate of mercury and, unlike the dynamite, could be set off by fire, an electrical shock, or a sharp blow. Twenty sticks of capped dynamite make a bundle the size of a five-gallon keg. It isn't heavy, but it's awkward, and Slocum thought he might need to use both hands before he used the dynamite. He stuffed the dynamite into an old sack, knotted the sack, and slung it easily over his shoulder.

A couple of prybars waited for him beside the wooden bulkhead over the hole the three unfortunate Pinkertons had made just two days ago. Two days? Was it that recent?

Slocum pried the heavy boards off the bulkhead and stacked them neatly against the wall. If he had to come back through here in a hurry, he could.

Since the Minnie Healy tunnels drained into the Black Rock, Slocum had to drop five feet to the Black Rock floor. His light flashed over the timbering. It wasn't much. Amalgamated had always skimped on timber, and in the deserted tunnels they were even worse. Slocum saw a single timber set forty feet ahead, and rock scraps lay on the floor of the deserted tunnel like some giant had shaken it.

It was hard walking. Slocum had a sense that the tunnel was poised to collapse, waiting for the slightest commotion to provide an excuse. So he walked gingerly, his lamp focused on his feet. Hell, he didn't even want to kick a rock down the tunnel.

At least the tunnel was dry. And it dropped slightly toward the Black Rock twelve-hundred-foot main.

Slocum walked softly enough to hear somebody coming or even just the breathing of a man who stood and waited, but he didn't expect to run into anyone until he was in the main.

Slocum was quite at home in the mine now. He felt as if he'd been born and raised twelve hundred feet under the surface of the earth.

When Slocum reached the main, he paused just inside the cross tunnel and listened. The mine smelled mustier than the Minnie Healy. The Amalgamated didn't believe in too much comfort for its miners and economized on fans.

Faintly, Slocum heard the hoot of a steam whistle: *hoot-hoot-hoot*. Then a silence and repeat. The fire signal. Probably most of the Black Rock crew was heading for the surface, scared out of their wits. The fire didn't have to reach you in a mine fire. The gases and smoke would kill just as sure.

With no more effort at concealment, Slocum hurried down the main toward the shaft. The tunnel, with its lamps burning every hundred yards or so, seemed to him like a brightly lit avenue. The tunnel was a good deal wider than the Minnie Healy's. Amalgamated had all the time in the world to draw its ore. It didn't have to skimp on tunnel size.

When Slocum was a few hundred yards from the Black Rock shaft, he could hear the cages and skips, hurrying men to the surface. He also heard the shouts of alarm.

The twelve-hundred-foot shaft station at the Black Rock was a permanent installation, with poured concrete floor, a turnaround for the ore cars, and a neat device that tipped the ore car into the skip. A pipe delivered surface water for the miners to drink, and there was even a small board shanty where the stationmaster held court. Slocum slipped up on the shack, but it was abandoned. Its open windows glowed yellow in the big room.

Slocum unknotted his sack and fastened the five-minute fuse to one of the caps. Sympathetic detonation would set off the rest of the caps.

Topside, the Black Rock yard was bedlam. Marcus Kelly was yelling at his superintendent while the Pinkertons made a nervous circle around the two men. "Where the hell did you hear about a fire?" he yelled.

"It was one of the ponyboys, I don't remember which one."

"We're not hauling any damn ore out of the Black Rock. Where the hell did the ponyboy come from?" He slammed the heel of his hand against the superintendent's chest. The mine whistle hooted its shrill song from the gallowsframe. "And shut that fucking thing off!"

With the whistle stilled, some of Kelly's rage departed too. As Slocum had expected, Morgan had responded to his warning by telegramming Kelly to watch for an attack on the Black Rock.

And then the light dawned. Kelly grabbed his rifle and headed toward the mancage. With an impatient hand he urged the Pinkertons to come with him.

Two or three slunk to the back of the crowd. After some nervous looks at their fellows, three men headed for the cage.

And the bell signal rang. Twelve times. Someone was on the twelve hundred.

"Goddamnit!" Kelly hollered. "It's Slocum." And what had been a rush became a stampede. He and his three men got into the cage, Kelly shouted, "Cut the rope," and the cage dropped down the hole at thirty-two feet per second.

The stationman's shack was lit on the twelve hundred but nothing else. The bell rope hung beside the cage swaying gently, as if the hand that had tugged it had just this minute let go. "Fan out," Kelly snapped. "He's got to be down here somewhere."

One Pinkerton, Colt at the ready, slipped around to the back of the shafthouse. For a moment nobody noticed his absence. Everyone else had his own corner to search, and the back of that shack was out of sight and nobody was eager to notice that the man who'd gone back there hadn't come out.

"Harry?" A Pinkerton shouted. "You got anything back there? Hell," he snaped. "If he's in trouble . . You there, Mr. Kelly. Come around the other side."

Cautiously the two men came around both sides of the building and found Harry lying broken on the bland concrete floor.

John Slocum eased himself up on the roof and dropped down onto the other side. The Pinkerton saw him rushing soundlessly at him but was too frightened to scream before the Arkansas toothpick drove up under his ribcage and pierced the lobe of his heart. Then he didn't say anything more, though he gurgled.

That left Kelly and one other. Slocum looked at the man he'd just killed and smelled him, ranker than the musty odors in the mine. Kelly and his partner were around the back of the wooden shack trying to revive Harry.

Slocum was tired of killing. He bent, lit the fuse, and tossed the sputtering length into the shaft. The Amalgamated men didn't see who threw the bundle, but they recognized the hissing trail and knew what it was. Marcus Kelly dropped his rifle and ran for the cage. He yanked at the bell rope.

Slocum stood in the middle of the big room watching the two men as they frantically signaled for the cage to lift. If either one had turned, they could have killed him easily, but they were too terrified.

Slocum ran back down the main tunnel. He ran easily, like a long-distance runner, making good time but watching his feet. He wouldn't want to sprain an ankle. Not with that dynamite hissing away at the bottom of the Black Rock Shaft. There was enough explosive power in that bundle to blow the whole damn mine down, and the blast would travel up the shaft and through the tunnels like a tornado, carrying everything before it.

He ran somewhat more slowly through the deserted tunnel but still kept up a pretty good pace. Like as not, the blast would drop this tunnel flat, and he didn't want to be in the Black Rock when it happened.

He almost made it, too. He was just outside the Minnie Healy bulkhead when the blast arrived. He heard it as it reached him—a distant, heavy crump, like a building falling on itself.

And then the blast hurled him into the Minnie Healy. It plucked John Slocum off his feet and tossed him right through the hole in the wooden bulkhead and against the wall opposite. He went black for a moment and slid down the wall, gagging for breath, sucking for wind. Dimly he heard the roar as the Black Rock tunnel collapsed and pebbles shot through the hole like they were trying to escape. The floor under Slocum quivered. He didn't look up at the ceiling, he didn't want to see it coming if it fell.

After a very long time, the noises and creaks stopped and his breathing steadied, except for a slight stab in his chest when he took a deep breath.

Carefully he touched his chest and winced. Yep. Cracked rib. Maybe two. But his breathing didn't sound wet, so he hadn't punctured a lung. Something to be thankful for. He felt his kneecaps before he bent his legs. Slocum already had one bad knee, and getting tossed into a rock wall wouldn't improve it any. The knife sheath was still strapped to his arm, but the knife was gone. Slocum unstrapped the sheath and dropped it. He never cared for that knife anyway.

At least he could walk. It was a painful, long trip down the tunnel to the Minnie Healy shaft, but once he was on the cage and had tugged the signal rope, only five seconds passed before the winch tightened and the cage rose. *Must have had his hand on the throttle,* Slocum thought.

Heinze was waiting at the shafthead when the cage surfaced, and he took a quick step toward it. "Christ," he said, looking at the battered bloody man in the cage. "Oh, Christ."

Carefully, Slocum stepped onto the shaft platform. It wouldn't do to stumble. Not now.

Somewhat distantly he noticed that Heinze had a scrap of paper in his hand. Heinze seemed to be pretty excited. Slocum couldn't see anyone else in the Minnie Healy yard. Probably they were all over at the Black Rock. Miners always forgot their differences when there was a mine disaster.

Heinze wasn't talking about the Black Rock explosion. He was talking about a telegram.

With shaky hands, Slocum fished a havana out of his coat. When he took a puff, he coughed and the coughing hurt, so he dropped the cigar and stubbed it out.

Heinze was saying, "We won. Don't you understand? We won." John Slocum was looking at his mountain horse. If he was lucky he could ride twenty miles from Butte City before he had to lie down. He looked at the mountains. They looked pretty wintry, but maybe he could camp on a lower slope until he healed up. "I know we won," Slocum said.

"You don't understand, man," Heinze spoke slowly, as if talking to someone not quite right in the head. "Morgan's buying me out. He'll give me three million for the Minnie Healy. He says he wants me in New York. He wants to talk about a partnership. Don't you understand?"

John Slocum understood.

EPILOGUE

"The pilot fish should never insult the shark." Slocum was thinking about Heinze and Morgan.

It was a beautiful day in late summer. Slocum and a slender brunette sat at an outdoor restaurant on the wharf in San Francisco watching the fishing boats as they unloaded into the waiting fish vendors' carts. Slocum was drinking brandy. The girl, who knew him as James Murchison, was drinking red wine. Slocum stretched in the seat and sniffed at the pungent, salty, fishy air. It didn't hurt when he stretched. His ribs had healed months ago.

The girl commented on an argument between two colorful wharfside characters: a stocky Italian and a mustachioed Greek. Slocum was less interested than she. He didn't find quarrels picturesque.

He folded the *San Francisco Chronicle* back to the business section and read the article again. The report was straight from the *New York Sun*. "Heinze Bankrupt" was the headline. The article went on to say that the West's newest *Wunderkind*—sometimes rumored to be J. P. Morgan's confidant—had been busted out in a stock swindle. Heinze was expecting a trial but didn't fear the outcome. "I'm an honest man," he said. "History will justify me."

Slocum grinned at that.

He hadn't had too many laughs during the last six months. His ribs had hurt him longer than he'd expected, and it had been painful to ride. He'd changed his name twice, and now he carried sleeve derringers at all times and generally hid a second Colt in a shoulder holster in addition to the Colt he kept stuck inside his belt.

The Pinkertons were after him in full cry. They'd tracked him south and he'd had to kill two in the Palace Hotel before he gave them the slip. Now, as Murchison, with five thousand in gold deposited at Wells Fargo, he thought he'd take it easy for a year or so. Until J. P. Morgan gave up on him, anyway.

But he stayed cautious. He had two horses (with trail gear) in two different liveries in the city and had given standing orders that they should be ready to go at a moment's notice.

He noticed the tiny mole at the corner of the slender girl's nose. After they finished their drinks, they'd stroll over to Golden Gate Park. A firemen's band was scheduled to play some of the new Sousa music that afternoon. Afterward, they'd probably go back to the girl's apartment and make love. It sounded like a fine program to John Slocum.

A couple of John Alden schooners rushed by the ways, rich man's boats; they were said to be the fastest thing under sail. The wealthy young people on deck were drinking from stemmed glasses and staring at the dockside crowd with disdain.

Though there were plenty of Chinese in San Francisco, most of them stayed within the boundaries of Chinatown, so it was unusual when the two Chinamen came into the café and bulled their way toward Slocum. And these were fairly unusual Chinamen. People said, "What the hell," and "Would you look at those Chinks." They spoke under their voices because of the big Chinaman.

He was a giant. The other one was more usual— maybe dressed a little fancier than most Chinese, but by himself he'd be no occasion to comment.

"Hello, Io," John Slocum said.

Chang Tung inclined his head. "Mr., uh, Murchison, I believe. You are a hard man to find."

Slocum smiled a smile with no warmth or humor in it. "I try to be," he said.

"Won't you introduce me . . ." the girl began.

"No," Slocum said. He kept his eyes on Io, who was regarding him like he was fresh meat. "You're a long way from Butte City," Slocum observed. "Last time I saw you you were gonna be the boss Chink of all the West. You make it?"

There was no humor in Chang's smile either. "No," he said. "My family is disgraced. My reputation is ruined. I am unable to form the marital alliance I had counted on."

Slocum raised his eyebrows but didn't comment. The derringers felt reassuring tucked into his sleeves. He could get them working in a half-second, and each one carried two .41 caliber slugs.

"Io has business with you," Tung said icily. "You have disgraced and ruined us."

"How's that?"

"My niece, Mr. Slocum. You dishonored her."

Slocum was puzzled. "I brought her to you. Just like I was hired to do."

"She was no longer a virgin!" Tung hissed. "She was ruined for marriage."

"Oh," Slocum said. "Damaged goods, huh? Well, some people believe a lot of foolishness. But I ain't gonna change their minds." He paused. "So it was Io threw that damn iron thing at me . . ."

"The iron star." Chang smiled and meant it. "It is one of Io's favorite toys."

"And in New York. It was Io with the knife in that room. Hell, I always thought that was Morgan's doing."

The giant watched him impassively. Slocum scratched his head. "So now this big son of a bitch has a bone to pick with me, is that it?"

Chang Tung bowed formally. "I am a man of honor. You are a man of honor. Io feels his honor has been stained by his failures to kill you. It is the only way to settle the matter."

Io grunted his assent. Slocum noticed the size of the giant's arms. He'd seen muscles like that before, but usually he'd seen them in the shoulders of a range bull.

"Let me get this straight. You tried to kill me twice, once with the iron star, once with a knife. Now you want to do it with your bare hands?"

Io smiled for the first time. He didn't have too many teeth.

And John Slocum laughed. He laughed at the beautiful day and the absurdity of warriors. He laughed at honor and the virginity men valued so high. He laughed at himself, the biggest damn fool of them all.

Then he shot the two Chinamen to death. One. Two.